Bill James

ETON CROP

W9-BMA-441

W. W. Norton & Company
New York   London

First published 1999 by Macmillan Publishers Ltd.

Copyright © 1999 by Bill James

First American edition 1999

First published as a Norton paperback 2000

Manufacturing by Courier Companies, Inc.

Library of Congress Cataloging-in-Publication Data

James, Bill, 1929–
    Eton crop / Bill James. — 1st American ed.
    p. cm.
    "A Foul Play Press book."
    ISBN 0-393-04761-X
    1. Title.
    PR6070.U23 E86 1999
    823'.914—dc21

                                                    99-36544
                                                        CIP

ISBN 0-393-32098-7 pbk.

W. W. Norton & Company, Inc., 500 Fifth Avenue, New York, N.Y. 10110
www.wwnorton.com

W. W. Norton & Company, Ltd., 10 Coptic Street, London WC1A 1PU

1 2 3 4 5 6 7 8 9 0

1

Iles said: 'Harpur's going to tell you about a lad called Raymond Street.'

'I've heard of Street,' she said. 'His death.'

Iles stayed silent a moment. Then he said: 'I dare say. Everyone has. But I want Harpur to run through it with you. A Detective Chief Superintendent has resonance.'

'Why don't *you* run through it, Mr Iles?' she asked. 'An Assistant Chief has even more.'

'I don't talk about Ray Street,' Iles replied.

'So you order others to talk about him.'

With a cheery lilt, Iles said: 'One thing you'll find, Naomi, is I don't react to insurbordination, even from a woman officer in your rank. Do I give a shit for hierarchy?' The lilt faltered slightly and his voice edged towards a gull scream. 'What did hierarchy ever do for me? I'm stuck here as Assistant to a . . . to a . . .' The volume fell from scream to tortured whisper. 'Well, leave that. Ask Harpur if I give a shit for hierarchy. Do I give a shit for hierarchy, Harpur?'

Iles liked replies to his questions, especially when to do with his essence. Harpur said: 'The crucial point, Naomi, is never to use so much stuff when you're with them that you get clouded. You'll have to use *some*, for credibility. But under control. It's hellishly difficult – the balance.'

'That what happened to Raymond Street?' she asked. 'He

1

started using too much? Forgot where he was? Forgot who he was supposed to be? Wham.'

'The stress can be big,' Harpur replied.

Iles said: 'As a matter of fact, I *do* talk about Ray. I talk about him to the Chief. Whenever Mr Lane wants to put someone into a drugs gang undercover I remind him of what happened to Detective Constable Street. Harpur can confirm this, can't you, Col?'

Harpur said: 'Infiltration of this sort, the key is to take it very slowly, Naomi. Always an eye on the exit.'

Iles said: 'So, you'll ask why are we putting you into a gang if I fight the proposal every time the Chief makes it.'

Naomi said: 'So, why are you putting me into a gang if you fight the proposal every time the Chief makes it?'

'You don't have to go,' Iles replied. 'This work's only for volunteers.'

Harpur said: 'You come out at the least sign of suspicion from them. Ditch everything – money, clothes, the commodity, no matter how much. We'll give you a full eject drill.'

Iles said: 'If their behaviour changes towards you one day – more friendly, less friendly – get out at once. Especially *more* friendly.'

'Did Street hang on?' she asked.

'Street was a great detective,' Iles replied. 'Beyond Harpur's range.'

'Beyond *yours*, sir?' Naomi asked the ACC.

'Yes, he hung on too long,' Harpur said.

'The general view is you subsequently killed the people

who killed Street, Mr Iles,' Naomi remarked. 'Unproveably, of course. You're an ACC, for heaven's sake, know how to shape things. When I say "general view", naturally I refer to a confidential general view within our game.'

Iles looked suddenly enraged. The skin of his face seemed to coarsen and his chin grew witchlike and militant. None of it would spring from what Naomi had said: in fact, to be accused of avenging Street and getting away with it through professional flair was sure to delight him. No, this degree of anger in the ACC could only be caused by discovery or rediscovery of some blemish in his appearance. He had been stroking his neck appreciatively while the three of them talked and his fingers eventually came upon his adam's apple. This part of his body always infuriated the ACC. He had once told Harpur it was unforgivable in a Creative Force to produce the muted loveliness of his slender neck and then deform it with 'this farcical adjunct'.

Naomi misread the cause of change in him. 'I'm sorry, sir,' she said. 'Tactless.'

She was sitting legs uncrossed opposite the ACC in Harpur's room, and Iles stared intelligently into the tidy V of her jeans. 'Oh, those alleged executions of villains. Women insist on enhancing me by gorgeous myth, Naomi,' he replied. 'I don't begrudge. It brings them a little tremor and moisture, I've learned.' He half stood in his chair so he could check in the mirror that this neck thing was really outrageously there, and as foully un-Iles-like as it felt. He gazed briefly, then resumed his seat. 'But, yes, courts *are* a problem. Their little fussinesses and fairnesses get in the way of . . . of what's right . . . of what has to be done. And then there's the Chief, tragically weakened by rectitude. I grieve for him, the prim saint.'

'Naomi, I've been undercover myself,' Harpur said. 'And—'

'It's true,' Iles said. 'All right, you'll ask how the hell – because Col's face, his body, the haircut, his tirelessly envious eyes all proclaim cop. But somehow he did manage it, I swear. A less grubby character background and he'd have picked up the Queen's Police Medal.'

Harpur said: 'Naomi, once you're installed, besides pacing yourself, doing everything slowly, so slowly, the other essential is to drop more or less everything of your previous life. That means, mainly, you never go to where you're living now. And don't come anywhere near this building either. Not even if you're quitting your role at a rush and think you need help.'

'Harpur will let you know some rescue points. To be memorized. We'll have a posse there, or the means to one fast. We've improved after Ray Street. I wouldn't mind if you ran to my house. It's called *Idylls* in Rougement Place.'

'I don't think so, sir,' Harpur said.

Iles turned abruptly away from Naomi's trousers and gave one of those smiles at Harpur, an Iles smile, not mellow or wry or fully human: 'But I'm sure it would be all right for her to run to *your* dim place in that dog-turd road, wouldn't it, you crate of lech, Col? You've been lining this one up for an age, haven't you? What's your student bird going to make of that, then – Naomi panting at your door around three a.m., whispering your name, requiring succour? Yes, succour.' He exercised his lips.

'*Idylls*?' she asked.

'It's a big meaty poem from another time,' Harpur said. 'Mr Iles told me the full title is *Idylls of the King*, but he loathes advertising.'

'Drop all my previous life?' she said. 'Does that mean—?'

'Ideally it would entail cutting adrift from your boyfrien— from your partner, for the whole period of undercover,' Harpur replied. 'But, realistically, we—'

'We've done some profile work on him,' Iles said.

'You've fucking what?' Naomi yelled. 'He's a private citizen, without any—'

'We know what's reasonable, what's possible,' Harpur said.

'Did Street have a love life?' she asked.

'Your chum seems a sensible enough sort,' Iles said.

'Some meetings with him should be all right,' Harpur said. 'Not at your own place, naturally.'

'Harpur will fix spots.'

'Will he be in bed with us?' Naomi asked.

'This is a lad named Donald McWater, yes?' Iles replied. 'I never used to go much on the Scotch – those hellish noses raw from the cold – but this *Trainspotting* fellow seems to get a nicer angle on them. Your friend, twenty-six, a supermarket undermanager? I went and had a look at him at work. It's important to get the rounded picture. Harpur will arrange meetings for the two of you in Donald's holiday times or even his days off. We've got a proposal about that relating to the next few weeks, as a matter of fact. I say Donald is sensible enough, but is he sensible enough to know he should be sensible enough not to ask why the switch in lifestyle, and not to come poking about, looking for you? That's potentially awkward.'

'Naomi will tell him she's on the Special Branch course and can't leave the college for long at a spell, sir.'

'We'll owe you promotion at the end, Anstruther,' Iles said. 'Done the exams – all that jibberish?' He gave his longish, quiffed grey hair a flick back with one finger. Iles had abandoned the *en brosse* style he favoured for a while after a season of Jean Gabin films.

Naomi asked: 'Would Street have been promoted if . . . ? What I mean is, Mr Iles, you said he was a great detective.'

'I regard the slaughter of the two people who killed him as an act of God or of someone in that ballpark,' Iles replied.

Harpur said, 'I'm your contact, Naomi. Your only contact. We'll have our private communications system. You'll get a new name, of course. We'll open a bank account in this identity for you and keep it stocked. This is extra money to your pay. Don't go to your own bank, ever. They have tipsters working in banks, and you don't want your face linked with the monthly police cheque. You carry no documents of any kind in the name of Naomi Anstruther, especially not a warrant card. Make sure none of your clothes have identity labels.'

'So, *did* Street have a love life?' Naomi replied. 'This was something else that messed him up?'

'Hotels, travel for you and McWater, we'll pay the lot,' Iles replied.

'We'd like you to go out of circulation now,' Harpur said. 'Take an immediate holiday somewhere for a fortnight. Can he go with you? Abroad, whatever you like. And then come back eventually to an address I'll give you down the Valencia district. After your break, you get a concentrated course at Hilston Manor in detailed undercover skills, not just the outline we've discussed now. That's another advance since Street. You'll meet some expert people. Psychologists, the lot.'

Iles said, 'Col's such an expert himself, as I mentioned.'

'Hilston will want to see us together at some stage,' Harpur replied.

'You'll be in good hands, Naomi.'

'Don't get obsessed by the shadow of Ray Street,' Harpur said. 'Just be temperate, whatever it is – crack, coke, horse. Make a modest show. Remember, some pushers don't use any product at all. Your cover doesn't require you to be forever high.'

'Street was?' she asked.

Iles said: 'Do you know how to be temperate, Naomi? You came right off, yes? I gather you used a bit before you joined the service. How did you fool the buggers at selection? But that's good – shows nice duplicity. We need that. Can you go back and keep limits? Can you sniff small?'

'I've been practising,' she replied.

'Harpur bought you the stuff?'

'Nice little trips, but I stayed compos,' she replied.

'Col, put it on your expenses as "lost wagers in greyhound corruption case",' Iles said. 'Now, are you going to tell her the full tale about Street?'

'No, I don't think so, sir,' Harpur replied.

2

Mansel Shale pointed to his heart and said: 'What I got, Alfred, is this feeling they'll try to put someone in on us undercover, their dirty term. One thing I learned long ago is listen to these brilliant hints I get from deep inside, what is known as the subconscious. Well, I suppose you heard of it.'

'With respect, Mansel,' Ivis said, 'the Assistant Chief has been opposed to any sort of undercover work in the drugs trade since that Raymond Street business. Mr Iles was very upset.'

'He's a fucking assistant, the *Assistant* Chief,' Shale replied.

'Oh, certainly, even Iles, but Manse—'

'Mr Mark Lane, he's the full Chief. Mr Lane plays it quiet at the top, but that's where he is, Alfie, on top. He's the one for what's known as the overview. I know how Mr Lane feels, overviewing. This is the spot you got to make big decisions from, and Mr Lane believes in undercover, he's famous for it.'

'Well, nobody would deny, Manse, that, when it comes to overview, you—'

'Have a sniff around, see if someone's coming in, Alfred. Get one of our people to. We got any voices coming from inside HQ these days?'

'Things are thin, Manse, since Sergeant WP Jantice . . . well, since he died that tragic way, a while ago now.'

'Fucking Jantice.'

'I dare say, Manse, but—'

'You know the signs when they're selecting for under-cover, Alfred. This is someone young, lad or girl, maybe someone who had a habit or at least a liking pre the service, and this officer is suddenly out of circulation, like some sudden course or special leave to look after a sick aunty in the Shetlands. This is the preparation stage, supposed to make everybody believe the officer was never really there at all. Then Hilston Manor. They got their funny little drills.'

'I hope we're always alert to the possibility of infiltration, Manse,' Ivis said. 'My own impression, though, for what it's worth, is that—'

Shale gave him a nice portion of teaching voice. 'Mr Lane looks out upon his bit of the world and he's unhappy at what he sees, Alf. He decides he got to do something, not just saunter along with the situation like it is, or otherwise known as the *status quo*. And what he decides to do is put someone aboard our operation, or Panicking's. Same thing. We're confed now. So what the fuck Iles don't like it? Lane's Chief.'

'With respect, Manse, I wonder if, because of your own unquestioned leadership flair, you credit the Chief with more influence in their team than he actually has.'

'Get a fucking inquiry going, Alf,' Shale replied. 'See if Harpur is talking a bit to some special youngster who looks built for spying – not the usual animal cop face but delicate, sly. Didn't WP Jantice mention somebody lined up like that just pre death? See if anyone's dropped out of sight all of a sudden.' Shale did not mind having a discuss for a while with Alfie but eventually or sooner you had to terminate. The thing about Alf was he could be a gem in many ways, and that big meaty face could have happened to anyone, think of Sir Edward Heath. But don't ask for no fucking vision. They were in Alfie's place now drinking gin and pep, what used to be a genuine lighthouse that he was converting into some sort of home, the sort someone like Alfie and his wife would want. If you climbed up to where the light used to be you got plenty of views, obviously, but views were not vision.

'That DC Raymond Street situation – so unkempt that was, plus a rotten aftermath,' Shale said. 'I wouldn't want nothing like that in our enterprise, Alfred. We locate whoever's coming and neutralize him-stroke-her as we're surely entitled. But with neatness, with decent finality. I got an idea Jantice said it was a girl Harpur had his eye on for this mission. But it didn't work out then. Maybe now it's being brought out of the cupboard.'

'Girl? Yes, probably Harpur *would* want to use a girl,' Ivis said. 'It's a close relationship, if he's her Controller, Manse.'

'That bastard still dick-driven at his age? This is a father of two and going on, what, thirty-eight, forty, yet still giving it its head? Self-control, a marvellous virtue, Alf, but don't expect none from police.'

They were sitting in the room where the foghorn machinery used to be. There was a long window and Shale could gaze out at the grey sea and some damn grubby rocks that this lighthouse and the foghorn used to warn of. Probably they had some other way of doing that now, more electronic. He hated how those rocks looked so permanent. They were the kind that would never get ground down into a decent sandy beach, like other rocks had in previous times. When Shale was old or even dead those rocks would still be there the way they were now, fat and brown, shoving up through the waves regardless. It always made him nervy to sit in this room. If you did not stare out at the sea and those fucking rocks you had to notice the deadbeat furniture and sick bits of trench-war carpet.

'It upsets me, Alf, this attitude of Mr Lane,' Shale said.

'I know, I know. Given that we would wish to offer friendship, it's ungrateful of him. Prying – I'm sorry, but it's the only word.'

'Oh, ungrateful, yes, prying, and maybe worse. Maybe aggressive, Alf.'

'Yes, that's possible.'

'Mind, I don't say a thing against him for being Catholic. People can have their fancies.'

'Typically understanding of you to say so,' Ivis replied.

'And yet what Catholics have is the sin of despair. You heard of that? I was told about this by one of the girls I had living in for a while. She was a Catholic. Catholic girls will live in but they got to regret it later. It might've been Carmel. Or Lowri. There's Welsh Catholics. Despair is the worst sin of them all, Alfie, because it means you give up trying. And this is what Mr Lane is afraid will happen to him. Why he wants to put someone undercover.'

Ivis chuckled admiringly and lifted his mug of gin and pep in a kind of toast. He took a mean little Alfie-type sip. Then he said: 'You can look at a situation, Manse, and see the deeper aspects. Sometimes philosophical and sometimes even religious. Theology's among your fortes.'

'When Mr Lane gazes over this manor you might think he would see a beautiful peaceful situation now we got this arrangement, Panicking Ralph and me, the two businesses run in a handsome, civilized way, no fucking blood on the streets for months. Think what it used to be like, Alfie.'

'Absolutely, Manse. Chaos. Lord knows how many groups fighting for the trade. Jungle.'

Sometimes Ivis would slime away behind his teeth agreeing like this and sometimes he would niggle. Shale did not know which he hated most, the 'Yes, Mansel' side, or the 'But have you thought, Mansel?' side. He kept Alfred on the staff, though. Well, in a way he was what could be called *Chief* of Staff. Probably, if you counted up all aspects, he was a plus. He had a nice style with the pushers, strong but never purple, except when unavoidable, of course. And education. If you could believe him, Alfie went on in school for quite a distance and definitely had some of his own flairs, such as history of the Royal Navy and bones of the human body. He almost understood accounts, and Shale let him handle several low-level books. Alfie could not really be blamed for the sort of kids he had, doing archery and other kinks. Children was a gamble for everyone. Alf knew guns, but it was a long time since anything like that was required, except ducks and pheasants that he had proper leggings for.

'Yes, a while ago I looked at that disgusting chaos in the business scene you mentioned, Alf, and I decided it was not right. The idea come to me – alliance with Panicking. A decent confederation which would produce wholesome peace, in the interests of all-round trading and general safety.'

'And you delivered, Manse.'

'What I mean about Mr Lane being Mick.'

Ivis nodded, but Shale could see from his hanging teeth that he did not understand.

'The despair item,' Shale said. 'Mr Lane observes this grand tranquillity in our trade and *part* of him is bound to like it. Yet he cannot accept it, Alf. They're taught that, Catholics – never accept. Never accept what is not kosher with the cardinals and so on.' Shale's voice went low with sadness. 'When you get right down to it, Mr Lane sees our treaty – the one between me and Panicking to run the drugs scene – yes, Mr Lane sees this as bad. Maybe worse. Well, I got to say it, I'm afraid he regards me and Panicking as evil, Alfred.'

'Oh, Manse, I can't believe Mr Lane fails to realize that if you two hadn't agreed to—'

'As evil, Alf.'

'Peace on the streets is evil?'

'Ah, that's how *you'd* see it, how *I* would see it. Not Mr Lane. My business is viewed as vile by him, and so is Panicking's. To accept this vileness would be that terrible sin of despair. He thinks it's like saying to himself, I cannot fight this confederation so I better put up with it. Despair, Alf. For them, the unforgivable sin. This is what Carmel called it. Or the other one, Lowri. So, he orders attack. He says, "Go undercover." In a way you got to admire him. This is guts, this is Mick integrity.'

'You're generous, as ever, Manse. Others might say that if Mr Lane—'

'But Iles, he'd see the wisdom of the current sensible alliance between me and Panicking Ralph Ember. Iles and probably Harpur.'

'Mr Iles is definitely a pragmatist,' Ivis replied.

Shale was about to take a drink from his mug of gin and pep, but paused, the mug not quite at his lips. 'Oh, I never heard that, Alf. Yes, he'll fuck anything, especially very young, but not boys, not to my knowledge.'

'Mr Iles knows that if you and Panicking hadn't hatched this lovely powerful concord, Mansel, the London people would be in and taking over here. Or Manchester. Even Yardies.'

'The London people *are* here, set up,' Shale replied. He drank. 'Mr Lincoln W. Lincoln, and associates.'

'I know it. But Panicking and you together, you're big enough, strong enough, to hold them down, Manse.'

'What the alliance is all about.'

'And again I say, you've delivered. They're next to nowhere in the trade.'

'They do a tiny bit at the very edge. That's where they'll stay. Will they?' Shale wanted to change his seat or pace about, so he did not have to watch the unhelpful eternal rocks. But he hated walking on Alfie's carpets. He always felt he could detect a creepy greasiness that went up through the soles of his shoes, climbed his legs and wrapped around his balls like effluent. Shale said: 'Mr Lane got this block about handing over certain aspects of law and order to the trafficking firms – to me and Panicking Ralphy. Lane is police, and he thinks this has to be police work only. What the benefits are don't signify to Mr Lane.'

'Ends and means.'

'What's that about?'

'Well, what you said, Manse. Mr Lane won't allow the end, although a good one, to justify—'

'But I wonder about Iles,' Shale replied.

'A pragma—Mr Iles would see the sense.'

'He've got rough aspects to him, no question, the mouth and shagging, plus filthy pride, but what he've also got is vision, Alf.'

'That's the word for Mr Iles, vision.'

'I don't say Mr Lane haven't got his own kind of vision, also. But that's a different vision, and it's fucking inconsiderate, Alfred.' Ivis's children would be home from school shortly and Shale did not want to be here then. Pretty soon one of them should be old enough to get sent off a good distance to a boarding school well up north and this would be a start, although two would be left. Shale always thought when he saw Alfie's kids that they were the kind of kids who would live in a lighthouse, their faces a bit of a jumble and one of them with a slant walk. Shale stood. He put his empty Brer Rabbit mug down on a side table that had seen some life. 'In this situation we can help Mr Iles, Alfred. He's been told to put an officer into one of the firms, most likely a girl, so he has to do it. Orders. But if we can locate this officer and see to him-stroke-probably-her with decent finality, this is going to assist Mr Iles long-term in policy arguments with Mr Lane. Iles would be able to say to the Chief, *Sir, this is two officers slaughtered when undercover.* Of course, they won't find this officer's body who's coming in now, not the way they found Street. But they'll see what it means, the neat disappearance, won't they, Alf? Then, Iles says to the Chief, *This policy cannot work, sir. This policy will get you in rough with the Press and Home Office, losing officers one after the other, especially if one's a girl.* The public would not like that, a girl, even if it *is* equal pay. Iles would say, this policy must be abandoned, Mr Lane, and peace restored via a careful and happy arrangement.'

Shale had ridden to Ivis's place on his old-style Humber bicycle and they went outside to it. Now and then, Shale liked leaving the Jaguar at home and coming through back lanes by bike to Alfie's place. Ivis said: 'This is a lovely piece of strategic thinking, Manse, a sweet reading of the situation, and typical. If I may be permitted one reservation, though. Have you thought—?'

'You're scared of a retaliation from Iles – if this snoop officer had to be slaughtered?'

The wind blew spray up over the cliff and struck Shale and Ivis on the face. Alfie laughed like he owned it, like it was a mischievous dog. He thought this flying water made the place more genuine. Didn't he realize the sea was getting over the cliffs that were supposed to keep the fucker in its place? Alfie was not one to think ahead. He could not imagine a time when them cliffs were worn away and nothing left anywhere but sea and rocks, like right back to the beginning of life in the world. Shale was bent fixing his cycle clips. He wiped his face and stared up at Ivis.

Alfie said: 'I wouldn't put it as *scared*, Manse. But perhaps I *do* envisage problems. I mean what happened to those people who were supposed to have done Raymond Street, though acquitted. That was savagery.'

Shale prepared to mount. 'My feeling is Mr Iles would see this action against an undercover officer as quite a good bit different from Street. This would be a *constructive* matter, well handled, and designed to shape general policy in a positive way.'

'Yes, I do follow that, Manse, but Iles is—'

Shale gave him a very friendly interview-over wave as he pedalled away. One of the main things about leadership was how to use your time.

3

Now and then people called on Harpur at home in the middle
of the night. They came unannounced and did not usually
ring the front bell but knocked on the kitchen door that led
into the back garden or tapped a rear window, especially
that. Harpur kept open house, but in a quiet sort of way.

Most of these dark-hours visitors to 126 Arthur Street
were informants with some knowledge to offer, or in need
of very swift help, such as an air ticket and a rejigged identity.
Informants did not trust the telephone, and none of them
would want to be spotted going into Harpur's house or even
near it. What informants feared more than anything was
information, about themselves. And hence the subtler
approaches to Harpur. He sympathized. Informants lived
with plenty of shame and endless peril. They were entitled
to their secrecy, the way Field Marshals hankered for renown.
Despite this caution, he would lose a grass occasionally –
dead, like Keith Vine, or forever wheelchaired and forever on
soft foods, like Honest Foul-Barnaby, or aliased and hiding
abroad like . . . like four or five. Five. For a while, the night
visits might fall off. Harpur would feel neglected, would feel
disabled. So far, the calls had always picked up again,
though, thank God. A detective was nothing without gifted
private voices. Always he considered them worth getting out
of bed for, even when Denise was with him in the bed,

almost the best antidote he knew to feeling neglected or disabled.

Tonight, for instance. She heard the tapping first: young fresh ears, young fresh everything. 'Oh, God, Col,' she said. 'Keithy's ghost?'

They were lying on their backs, her right hand in friendly fashion on his crotch and his left hand in friendly fashion on hers. They had been discussing fidelity. She was in favour of this, for Harpur. At her age, and as a university undergraduate, Denise felt she should have a certain liberty, because it was in the nature of students to collect new experiences and have their eyes opened.

'Eyes? Fuck that,' Harpur had said.

'Along those lines.' She also thought that being in his late thirties and uncharming Harpur would score only with sleep-around older women and might bring back crabs.

'But *you* want to be a sleep-around woman,' Harpur had replied.

'Yet discriminating and not older.'

'Mr Iles had crabs. Perhaps has.'

'Well, there you are then.'

'What do you mean, there I am then?'

'There you are then.'

Harpur said: 'I told you that so you'd stay away from him. He's very keen on opening young girls' eyes and so on. Iles *does* have charm, but charm plus crabs, possibly.'

She heard the tapping then and went silent. Taking her friendly hand from him, she had held up a finger above the bedclothes, asking for silence. He listened and heard the tapping, too. She muttered her dark joke about Vine.

'This is at the front door,' Harpur said, 'and someone using their knuckles.' Vine had always come to the rear downstairs window and rapped it with a coin. This was not even the same species as Keithy.

'But you said these people never risk coming to the front,' she replied.

'Right,' he said.

'What do you mean, right?'

'Right,' he said. They both kept their voices down. His address was in the telephone book, 'Colin Harpur.' He thought it should be, believed in availability or what else were the police for? Many of his colleagues saw this as stupid. People came looking for police officers occasionally, to settle up. He wished he had a list of recent jail releases with him now. And gangs came looking for police officers too, and especially a drugs gang on a corporate high when celebrating some festival, like Good Friday or knifing of a competitor.

'What time is it?' Denise asked.

'Nearly two a.m.'

'Col, we ought to have a security drill for this kind of visit.'

'We have.'

'What is it?' she asked.

'I fearlessly go in my fearless style to see who it is. If I don't come back, you dial 999 and mention my name to the

Control room. They'll act, unless an enemy's on duty. Better than fifty-fifty chance they'll respond.'

'You're scared, are you?'

'Of bloody course.' He was dressing.

'If I phone, who do I say I am, for God's sake?' she asked.

'A discriminating sleep-around, crabless, younger friend of C. Harpur.'

'Younger than whom?'

'Most.'

'They wouldn't believe it – the discriminating part. How would I be sleeping with C. Harpur?'

'Stay here,' he replied.

'That's what I mean – we should have a security drill involving me.'

'We have: it's you stay here,' Harpur replied.

He put on no lights and stepped barefoot for quietness down the stairs. In the hall, he dropped on to hands and knees behind the coat-stand and stared at the front door. There was a dim glow from street lights and he made out two figures in the porch. One might be a woman, rather burly. The other was more shadowy, hanging back. Two in the porch, how many elsewhere? What was happening? Informants always came alone. It was not a team trade. No snout livery company.

He heard a sound behind him and thought, God, yes, how many of them? He cowered, moved his head abruptly to the right, in case of a blow. After a moment, he glanced around. There was enough light from the street lamps for him to see both his daughters in pyjamas coming down the

stairs, faces in caring mode. They spotted Harpur crouched
on the floor in the shadows and stopped half-way. He made
small frantic waving movements with one hand, telling them
to go back to their rooms. They were targets on the stairs.
They ignored him. He was about to stand and get between
them and the porch when the younger girl, Jill, descended
a few steps further and gazed at the front-door glass. 'It's Mr
and Mrs Lane,' she said.

'What?' Harpur said.

'Can't you see?' She walked past him and opened up.

'Oh,' Sally Lane said. 'I didn't ring, because I hoped not
to wake you and Hazel, dear. Only your daddy. Isn't he here?
Out? Surveillancing again, the tireless man?'

'Behind the umbrellas,' Jill replied.

'Colin, forgive us, do,' the Chief said. He was in one of
his brownish suits. His round, doughy face seemed to sag
with worry. He looked like a poor actor doing the end of
someone's tether.

Hazel came down the rest of the stairs and stood very
near Harpur as he straightened up. 'Is this about your morals,
Dad?' she whispered. 'Surprise vice inspection? Have they
come to catch you with Denise, above the age of consent
but immature? Will your career be what's called "in schtuk"?
But you're a widower. Isn't it OK now, I mean regardless of
before?'

Harpur said: 'Come in, Mrs Lane. Come in, sir.'

'It's a terrible hour, but Chief was suddenly so anxious,
so anxious,' Mrs Lane replied. 'I didn't think I could cope

alone.' She had a long, heavy, handsome face, bright with excitement and resolve now.

'It's to do with Iles,' Lane said. He sounded appallingly weary, and not just from a lost night's sleep: weary as a way of being, weary as a fate. The suit clung tragically to him, like an exhausted mother arm-cradling her dead child in an earthquake.

'Chief could not rest,' Mrs Lane said. 'I knew you would not mind, in the circumstances, Colin. Perhaps you are even used to late-night calls.'

'This place is called Finks' Haven,' Jill said.

'To do with Mr Iles?' Hazel asked. 'What?'

Jill said: 'Hazel's interested, you see. The thing about Des Iles is he really . . . well, he really sort of *notices* Hazel. Do you know what I mean, *notices*? She quite likes it, in her way, but plays fed up.'

'Button it,' Hazel replied.

'You can go back to bed now, girls,' Harpur said.

'I thought I'd make some tea, Dad,' Jill replied. 'And there's them rock cakes.'

'Those,' Harpur said.

'She talks loutish to suit her peer group and deny bourgeois roots, Mrs Lane,' Hazel said. 'I've done kids like her in Sociology.'

'Bed,' Harpur replied.

'I should think out in the middle of the night Mr and Mrs Lane need a warm drink,' Jill said. 'Even a Chief Constable.'

He took the Lanes into the big sitting room. The children would have followed but Harpur closed the door and stood with his back against it until he heard them go upstairs. Then he produced a litre of whisky, some glasses and a couple of bottles of soda water from the cupboard. For himself he brought out the gin and a half-full flagon of cider to mix. He poured and the Chief and his wife sat down with their drinks.

'Yes, suddenly tonight Chief grew pathologically alarmed, Colin,' Sally Lane said. 'He's never comfortable about the ACC, as you know, I'm sure, and with unassailable reasons, but tonight it was so much worse. It's this undercover matter. I grew worried about Chief's . . . about his mind, yes, the very state of his mind.'

Lane said: 'Oh, Sally, really, I'm not going to—'

'One genuinely feared a relapse, Colin,' she said. 'I could have called the doctor. But . . . well, we're here instead. I felt it would be more helpful. Within walls.'

The Chief had only just returned to work after a bad breakdown. Lane saw worldwide evil on a triumphant roll and believed he alone could stop it: believed he personally *had* to stop it here, in his domain, or it would wildfire on throughout the cosmos. Iles called this 'chaos theory': the notion that some small incident in one continent could produce disaster in all the others. Eternal anxieties about his solitary mission hammered Lane, and they had hammered him into illness.

'When I say undercover, I don't want you to think Chief has told me anything about the details of this impending operation against the drug gangs, Colin. Heavens, no! That would be unforgivable. Chief never discloses sensitive matters, even to me, and even when he is not feeling one hundred per cent. But the generalities of the situation. And the Iles factor.'

'Only the generalities, believe me, Colin,' Lane said.

The Chief made a slow circling movement with one arm to illustrate exactly how general what he had spilled to his wife was. Often, Harpur felt appalled at how much she knew and her influence on Lane. The power behind the clone, Iles termed her.

'His motives, you see,' Sally Lane said.

'Mr Iles's motives?' Harpur asked.

'There's a terrible deviousness to him, Colin,' Sally Lane said. 'I don't feel this is putting it too strongly.'

'Iles would love to be called devious,' the Chief said. 'Ascendancy by any means possible – this is his constant objective.'

Lane's shrewdness made him seem even frailer: although he spotted what was happening, this could not profit him against Iles.

'Ascendancy is yours, Chief,' Sally Lane cried, gripping his brown sleeve maternally for a moment, 'as of right. Yours by achievement, yours by general esteem. Isn't it so, Colin? It's because I knew you recognized this that I assured Chief you would not object to our calling at such an hour – that it would be more effective than bringing out the doctor.' She sat back, the long face grave. 'Tell me this, Colin: why is it that, having for so long opposed undercover operations, Iles suddenly favours them?'

'You'll see the way our mind is going, Col,' Lane said.

'Clearly it's something I wouldn't want to discuss at head-quarters. His influence there is pervasive, virulent.'

'He puts a girl into one of these drugs firms with the concealed hope that she will fail,' Sally Lane stated. 'That's the long and short of it. Why? Oh, so plain, so plain. He deems this will prove his own quite different preferred way of dealing with the scene is right. It's non-stop manoeuvring, Colin. Well, I know you see it, too. Constant politics. And what *is* his preferred way? Why, tolerance of two or three local syndicates, so as to keep invaders out. "Better the devil you know" – that sort of thinking: a permitted criminality, allegedly in the cause of peace on the streets. Blind-eyeing as policy. But I have to ask—' She paused and blushed mini-mally. 'Yes, I have to ask something Chief could never bring himself to ask outright, though he might suspect – and nor, probably, is it something that you, yourself, Colin, would actually articulate, I imagine, much as you, too, might wonder about it – but I – I am not bound by these loyalties, this culture of solidarity – I, I have to ask has Iles . . . well, has he an, as it were, a *link* with one of these evil syndicates? Yes, link. And, not to draw back from exactitudes at this point, I will say it, yes – financial links, backhander links? Is it even conceivable that having helped choose this girl whose name I certainly would never mention – not even here in the confidentiality of your fine family room, Colin – aware as I ever am of the dangers – but is it possible that having selected her he would notify the firm of who is to be planted? Do any of us know, truly know, Desmond Iles? I put these as questions – do no more than that.'

'Sally is . . . is heated, Col. Yet, it is true, he yearns to destroy me.' Lane's head fell forward for a moment, as if all the strength of his body had been stolen. His sandy hair seemed drained of glow. The sofa arm propped him and needed to. The Chief was noble and doomed, cripplingly fractured and toweringly honourable. The evil was too much for him. The job had grown too much for him. Iles was too much for him. Perhaps these last pair were pretty much the same. Iles would have been too much for anyone except possibly Ho Chi Minh, but especially too much for Lane. Harpur wished the Chief would retire or get promoted to the Inspectorate of Constabulary while there was time. The Chief tonight was dull-eyed and crushed, both his hands tight around the whisky glass, like someone grasping a rosary or lifebuoy. Occasionally, his morale could hurtle down irreversibly like this.

Mrs Lane said: 'Don't imagine, Colin – now, *please* Colin – don't imagine that, because I mentioned . . . because I happen to know it is this woman officer who's been selected, please don't imagine Chief has been careless and given me the whole picture. Not at all.'

'Not at all, Colin,' Lane said.

'I'll say again that, as a police wife of many years' standing, I hope I know that any kind of gossip about this sort of operation – yes, any at all, even among the most responsible folk, even among family – *any* kind of gossip is dangerous. Chief is at least as concerned about security and the girl's safety as you are yourself, and I know this is to say a great deal. This was just a very, very general hint Chief gave that the officer currently preferred is the young unmentioned woman. Perhaps, this choice of a female is, so to speak, an attempt to exorcise that terrible precedent we all have in mind, Detective Constable Raymond Street. And, oh, I do wish her well – the courage, the skill, the determination.'

'Proud of her,' the Chief said.

Harpur knew he should feel rage to hear how Lane had been blabbing. And he *was* angry. Did Sally Lane have Naomi's name? It sounded as if she might. Who would have it next? Yet Harpur also felt a kind of understanding and a kind of hopelessness. Lane had never been able to settle in his post as Chief – had never been allowed to settle, by Iles, and by Iles's tough expanding cohort. Lane was isolated at the top. The Chief had nobody else to speak to about big topics but his wife, nobody else he trusted. Once in a while, like tonight, he might confide in Harpur, because for a spell Lane seemed able to believe that Harpur was not wholly sold to Iles and devoted to Iles, as other high-rank people certainly were. The cohort. Those in it worked always for the ACC, not always for the Force and hardly ever for the Chief. The terrifying certainty that his own people aimed to destroy him had helped drive Lane half mad. His wife stayed feverishly loyal, so, of course, he leaned on her, talked to her, listened to her, answered to her. Yes, talked and talked to her.

Sally Lane glanced around the sitting room while Harpur poured more drinks. 'I like what you have done here, Colin.'

When his wife was alive, the room had been lined with books. Megan was into reading and so on. He had known this when they married, of course, but not the scale. After a respectable time, Harpur and the children had disposed of her library – to Iles, as it happened. Harpur didn't go much on books, especially in quantity. They had made the room seem schooly and dead, full of famous titles with nothing to say to him or to the girls, except a book on boxing and *The Orton Diaries* which Jill had been fond of and kept. The sitting room was brighter now, and *like* a sitting room. *Edwin Drood* or some name very close to that was the one title above all that used to get Harpur right down.

'Chief believes – believes, absolutely, Colin – that you would be honest with him.'

'Absolutely, Colin.'

'If Iles were scheming against your Chief Constable in this despicable fashion, Colin, would you know? Would you in that case be prepared to let Iles proceed, perhaps destroy a good man? Perhaps destroy a young woman officer, too.'

Hurriedly, Lane declared: 'That, obviously, is the main concern, safety of—' He had seemed about to speak Naomi Anstruther's name, but stopped and then said: 'Of this officer. My position, career, is of very secondary signficance.'

'Of course, Chief,' she cried. 'Against a life, of course. Yet it is not merely Chief's career and reasonable pride. It is a matter of his health. I say his health, Colin, and yes, his . . . Well . . . And, then again, I regard his personal health and condition as something symbolic of something far wider, something—'

The door to the sitting room opened slowly and Harpur saw Denise wearing an old C&A navy raincoat of his from

the coat-stand and carrying an umbrella thrust out in front
of her as a weapon. It must mean she had come down the
stairs naked. Mrs Lane heard the door but from where she
was sitting could not see who was there until it opened fully.
'Ah, your daughters again, looking after you, Colin. How
thoughtful! How lovely!'

'Are you all right, Col?' Denise asked. 'I didn't dial 999. I
could hear the voices. It sounded peaceful. But then I began
to worry.' She came into the room, still with the furled
umbrella like a quarterstaff. Her body could do nothing for
a raincoat this size.

Lane stood and gave a small shifty bow. Harpur saw him
fight not to cave in to shock. The Chief had wonderful
inborn decency.

'Here's a friend of mine,' Harpur said. 'Denise, this is Mr
and Mrs Lane. The Chief and his wife.'

Denise put the umbrella on to her shoulder, like a rifle. 'I
come over sometimes to help out,' she said. The bottom of
the coat was almost down to her feet.

'A kindness,' Mrs Lane said. 'We hear much of the problems of one-parent families – as Colin's so regrettably is
now.'

'Is something very wrong?' Denise asked. 'So late.'

'Mrs Lane likes the changed room,' Harpur replied.
'Denise helped with the wallpapering, up and down the
ladder a lot.' He mixed Denise a gin and cider and prepared
another for himself. He gave the Lanes no more. It was time
for them to go. He walked to Denise with her drink and took
the umbrella from her.

31

'Is something very wrong?' she asked again. 'So late.'

'Yes, we think something *is* very wrong. There is at least one life at stake. Integrity is at stake,' Mrs Lane said. 'I don't think that is putting it too strongly, is it, Chief, is it, Colin? But you'll understand, Denise, that these matters have to remain confidential. Police matters.'

'There's all sorts that is confidential goes on here,' Denise replied.

'You visit on a regular basis?' Mrs Lane asked.

'I live in a student flat at Jonson Court. But Col needs plenty of help – the single parent aspect you mentioned.'

When the Lanes had left and Harpur and Denise were lying alongside each other again in bed she said: 'Avaunt the missionary position.'

'All right,' he said, 'it can be avaunted, but only as starters. I finish on top. This is a power thing with you. Christ, I rate enough to get a Chief Constable and his wife here for discussions in the small hours, so I'm not someone to be casually straddled.'

'This won't be casual.'

'Just the same.'

'You're such a cliché, Col.'

'Many clichés contain established wisdom.'

'Oh, Jesus,' she replied. 'Some variety of sex position and you think it's a female takeover.'

'I *like* sexual variety.'

'I've noticed.'

'Thanks. But—'

'There's a book called *Women On Top*, you know,' she said. 'It's to do with the gender war.'

'Well, there you are then.'

'What's that mean?'

'There you are.'

'It's a title that sends up your kind of stone-age thinking,' she said.

'Sharon Stone on top of Michael Douglas bound hand and foot in *Basic Instinct*. Shirley Anne Field on top of the squeaking Indian tycoon in *My Beautiful Laundrette*. It's control, subjugation.'

'Your face looks better from above. Less coarse,' she said.

'Is that true?'

'Marginal,' she replied. 'But, yes.'

'Oh, all right then.'

'Were they satisfied?'

'Who?'

'Mr and Mrs Chief. I'm not sure which is which.'

'What are they to do with this? I can't discuss police matters with you,' he said.

'Nuts. Is it a drugs trade thing?'

'Why do you say that?'

'Most police things are these days, aren't they? Most big police things.'

'I can't discuss police matters with you.'

'There's all sorts of aggro among the drugs firms, isn't there? The girl in the next flat to me at Jonson Court – she's had some trouble. Yes, she's in a bad way, off and on. Can't get her stuff. Her regular pusher just disappeared.

Disappeared. This is in confidence, Col. Look, I'm not snitching. No names. I sleep with the police but I don't talk.'

'Being the police, I expect I could find out who's got the next room to yours.'

'But you won't, will you?' she said. 'I knew that, or I wouldn't have spoken.'

'Who's disappeared?' Harpur replied.

'So, she's all over the place – mentally, I mean. Hallucinating. All that cold turkey stuff. That's why I promised her I wouldn't stay away the whole night.'

'You what?'

'She likes to know I'm there, in my room. In case of crisis.'

'What about me?'

'You'll be fine. We'll have our crisis together first. Were they satisfied?'

'Who?'

'Mr and Mrs Chief.'

'They think Iles . . . They think Iles is trying to get a girl killed.'

'So, that's impossible?'

'One of our own girls,' he said.

'So, that's impossible?'

'This is Iles, we're talking about, for God's sake. An Assistant Chief,' he replied.

'Yes.'

'Of course it's impossible.'

'Well, everything's OK then, yes?' she said.

'Yes. Yes.'

'You'll go ahead with it?'

'What?' he asked.

'Whatever it is where Iles is not trying to get a girl killed.'

'Of course. The Lanes are over-jumpy about him.'

'Yes?'

'Yes.'

'So forget it now.'

'Yes,' he replied.

She climbed on to him: 'I won't hurt you.'

'Nice,' he said.

'Isn't it?'

'But at a certain point I'm going to turn you over,' he replied.

'Which certain point?'

'Not yet.'

'No.'

'What's that mean?' he asked.

'No.'

They went quiet for a time, more or less. She crouched forward to put her face near his. 'You,' he said, 'you look unmatchable from above or below.'

'I do know you believe it, Col. You lack all charm, so it has to be true, not just bed chat.'

'Now,' he said.

'Yes, this seems like a certain point. But don't come out when we're turning.'

'I should think not. That would be so damned inconsiderate.'

Eventually, he slept, that fine, wholesome safe-feeling kind of sleep he always had – had eventually – when Denise was in the bed. The other side of this contentment, though, was that if she got up he always awoke at once. He did now. It was still dark, but he could make her out on the other side of the room. She was dressing. 'God, you meant it,' he muttered. 'Listen, Denise, the girls like you to be here for breakfast. *I* like you to be here for breakfast.'

'Priorities, Col.' She switched on the light and began fiddling with her hair in front of the mirror.

He sat up. 'Which pusher disappeared?'

'I can't discuss non-police matters with you.'

'This could be someone's life, Denise.'

She came and sat down on the bed. 'You'd go and look for him?'

'As you said, there's some trouble in the trade at present. Firms trying to score off one another.'

'Killing?'

'Could be,' he replied.

She stood again. 'Oh, God, this is one of those genuine moral dilemmas, like in philosophy. If I stay quiet it could be wrong. If I talk it could be wrong.'

'Nobody's ever going to know you talked.'

'I'd know. That's the point.'

'Yes, it is. And you might know you've saved a life.'

*

No, she would not know that, Harpur thought as he gazed on Gladhand Mace.

Denise had left Harpur's bedroom an hour ago without disclosing any more. Then, as he was folding down into sleep again, she pushed open the door and breathed the name once. He had rolled from under the duvet immediately and dressed. Denise did not wait. Harpur drove across town. Mace had been in and out of crime for years and Harpur knew his address, had called there two or three times to do some questioning.

It was a small, spruce-looking semi on a small, spruce-looking private estate, the Dome. Mace had been married, but Harpur thought this might be over now and he lived alone. When Harpur arrived it was just after 6 a.m. and the house was dark. He had driven past, parked, then walked back and turned into the drive. A Ford Fiesta was parked there, guarded by a big yellow anti-theft bar across the steering wheel. Gladhand had always been careful. His nickname was one of those jokes.

Harpur rang the front doorbell hard three times and waited. It was an hour when official police visits often happened, so as to get the householder at a dozey disadvantage. Old pros like Mace knew the procedure and would often lie quiet, at least until they heard the sledgehammer. Harpur's bellwork produced nothing. He tried a plastic card on the lock but that also failed.

He decided to break in, though not by sledgehammer. Looking for the easiest way and to check there was no alarm, he had done a quick tour of the outside. People like Mace did not go in for alarms, no matter how careful they might be, because a siren could bring all sorts of helpers to your house. People like Mace might not want helpers in their property looking about, and especially not helpers who were police.

Harpur was a competent burglar, not more than that. He hated leaving signs of forced entry, but once the plastic card had let him down, he was generally pushed to smashing a window or shouldering a door. Now, though, he found that he might not be the first to try Gladhand's house. The window to what looked like a utility room at the rear seemed to hang slightly askew. When Harpur went closer he saw it had been jemmied open and the catch torn from the wood. The window had been closed – probably from outside – to hide the splintering. Harpur pulled it open and prepared to go in.

Generally, he adored this kind of work – the secret intrusion on someone's home. Even the ordinary domestic layout could tell you so much, often more than interrogation. But he felt none of that joy as he hauled himself up and into the utility room. He was not here to read character in someone's décor and possessions. He was here to find Mace, and the forced window said he might find him in a poor way. Possibly whoever had done the window was still inside, lying low after the din from the doorbell. Harpur was not keen on guns but he would have liked to be carrying one now. That could not be. He was here privately and illegally. Guns were not issued for his mission.

Harpur had feared from the start, of course, that Mace was in peril: why he had jumped from bed as soon as Denise spoke the name. He had known as he climbed into the house that the peril was almost a certainty.

A certainty. Looking at him, Harpur thought that death had probably come quite fast, or, at least, unconsciousness had. He was sitting in his nicely arranged living room in front of the TV and the first blow to the head would almost certainly have knocked him out. The following ones were to make sure he wasn't *only* unconscious and would never come round. Harpur saw a lot of dried blood on Gladhand's shirt and trousers and in front of his chair on the tasteful green and gold fitted carpet.

For a while, Harpur stood still alongside the body, listening. The house seemed silent. He decided to trust his first feeling that the utility-room window had been pushed to from outside and that whoever had been here and done this was now gone. He went through Mace's pockets but someone else had perhaps been there already and he found nothing helpful. Swiftly, he went over the rest of the house, again with no result. He left through the same window and reclosed it, then drove home and went to bed.

*

When he next saw Mace thirty-six hours later, Iles and the Chief and a couple of scenes of crime people were in the living room, too. It was about to be sealed. Apparently, a girlfriend with a key to Gladhand's place had called on him, found the body and dialled 999. Lane would often turn out on cases he thought spoke some general message about the situation in his domain, especially its downside. This was downside all right.

'A nobody pusher, sir,' Harpur told the Chief, 'who took his goods from Ember and Shale.'

'Goods? My God, goods! You mean drugs, Colin. And this was tolerated? Blind-eyed?'

'We've done him once or twice, small amounts, small sentences. He's learned to be a bit cagey – tended not to carry stuff but made the deal then delivered at some safe spot.'

'I want to know these safe spots,' Lane said.

'They change, sir.'

'I still want to know them. And if he's so small-time, why is he dead?'

Iles went closer to the body and studied the head damage. 'He was a dear, unassuming, neat lad. He'd loathe all this shambles.' The ACC straightened. 'Have you been here before, Col? The usual scenario.'

'This would be a warning death, Mr Lane,' Harpur replied. 'We've had others – Eleri ap Vaughan. Maybe the London team asked Mace to take his supplies from them and he refused. The killing tells others that *they'd* better not refuse.'

'I will not put up with warfare,' Lane declared. 'The need to destroy these people, *all* of these people, all these so-called *firms* – the need to destroy them through undercover becomes inescapable.'

A sergeant in white dungarees and with plastic coverings over his hair and shoes was trying to get them to leave.

Iles said: 'Alternatively, we re-establish peaceful coexistence based on that civilized agreement between Panicking Ralph and Shale.'

'And on a corrupting agreement with *us*,' Lane replied. 'Some people cannot understand how you feel able to recommend such a solution, Desmond.'

'I'd certainly hate to bewilder you, sir. Or Mrs Lane,' Iles replied.

'My wife is not concerned in this. I've already assured you of that,' Lane hissed 'But many, many, are surprised at your attitude.'

'Do you meet any of the many, Col?' Iles asked.

'We must quit the room now, sir,' Harpur replied.

'But you *have* been here before, haven't you, Col?' Iles said.

4

When she stopped going in to work Naomi Anstruther had a couple of phone calls from friends at headquarters asking if she was all right: asking if she was all right, and asking more than that, naturally. After all, these were cops. They looked for angles.

'I got some leave,' she said. 'Don and I are going to Torremolinos.'

All the callers replied something like, 'God, why there?'

'Nothing else available in the time. It will be all right. There's a beach. There's wine. There are bars.'

All the callers replied something like, 'Why the rush, anyway? How did you wangle leave so fast?'

Obviously, they were right. It had been made too easy. Iles or Harpur had done the fixing. They could fix anything, especially Iles. People would read a meaning into the pace of things: might even realize these were standard bits of run-up for undercover. Did Raymond Street get sudden time off before going where he went and where he failed to come back from? She said what Harpur had told her to say, about a Special Branch course and the need to use up leave entitlement before it started. Did anyone believe this? It troubled her to know nothing was confidential, nothing secure. She had known it before. Now, though, she knew it in the way you would know you had colic or cramp, a bullying ongoing pain.

She lied when she said nothing but Torremolinos was on offer. Naomi chose the resort carefully from the agent's full range. Normally, she would have opted for anywhere but. Now was not normal. She had to get used to being someone else. The idea intrigued her. Yes, that was the word. Intrigue beckoned. She would not mind ditching Naomi Anstruther for a while, or even longer. Naomi Anstruther would have been too snobbish to select Torremolinos, like Naomi Anstruther's colleagues.

And like Don. At first, he did not believe it when she said where they were going, regarded it as one of Naomi's jokes. That showed how he thought of her. It had taken him some skill and push to get time off at such notice, and he clearly doubted if he should have bothered. On the aircraft to Malaga Naomi wondered for a couple of moments whether there might be an ending between her and him on this break. Yes, break. Sad, sad, after two years, but she did wonder. It was not anything he said at this point, though he had already said a lot she did not much like before they embarked, and would probably say a lot more she did not much like before their return. Simply, though, he sat alongside her on the Boeing civil enough but tense with disapproval and puzzlement. He was in good holiday gear and looked as fanciable and handsome as he ever did, but seemed closed off, locked into that trim and logical managerial personality he and others were building for him.

As antidote, she hit the drinks a bit and let her mind float and memory stroll. She thought of Harpur. He had the ability she craved of being able for a time to turn himself into someone else. Once, only once, she had been with him on an illicit break-in at some villain's house. She suspected Harpur often made such entries, but generally alone. A fluke had placed her with him that night. She watched a brilliant pleasure come over Harpur as he took on the flavour of the place, breathing the sour room smells, stroking bits of the crap furniture, fondly lifting a dirty cup to his nose and mouth, as though all of it were precious to him and spoke to his core. For, say, an hour then Harpur had seemed to move into the being of that target to learn its thinking, its tastes, its possibilities, whoever he or she was: on the Boeing, Naomi's strolling half-boozed memory would not stroll into specifics. She had been thrilled to watch him. She loved this aptitude, this willingness to leave one's self behind. Donald did not have it and would not want it. He had other qualities – grand stability, fine certainties, eternal focus. Stuff them. They were leadership qualities and hemmed him in, narrowed him down. She believed in escape, at least now and then. Now.

Torremolinos turned out more or less as bad as they said and as she would have guessed. It was one bright, endlessly convulsive noiserama, full of British and Dutch, too cheap for Germans and Americans. Even the bullfight she went to in the first week was tatty. Dud matadors kept almost getting caught by dud animals. She had seen bullfights before in Madrid and Seville and loved the grotesque elegance and vicious artistry. She could understand how the sport had captured Ernest Hemingway. Now, though, in the Torremolinos arena that evening, she saw why people might find the spectacle disgusting: no elegance, no artistry, incompetent viciousness. Spectators screamed contempt and threw their hired cushions. One charmer stood on his wooden seat, pulled out his dick and peed towards the ring, scattering folk in front of him.

Donald had stayed in their hotel. He did not go much on bullfighting, good or bad. In fact, he did not believe there could be 'good' bullfighting. So, she went with a group of young Brits who had been on the plane with them, encountered later around the bars. In one way it was unwise, she saw that. On her own with them she was likely to be drawn closer and it would be natural for them to ask where she worked. In Britain they lived more than a hundred miles from her, and there was probably no security risk, but all the same she had come abroad to lose her cop identity for a while and did not want to declare herself one. She had to practise being something else. That was the point, though, wasn't it: joining in with this group might help her become someone else?

They were from Cardiff, full of saved cash and lilting talk about the trip they would do next year to 'Vegas'. Two girls and one of the men worked in a toy factory, and three men and two girls were clerking civil servants. As far as Naomi could make out there was no established pairing between any of them. The group seemed to grow or shrink from day to day as other holidaymakers from the clubs or the beach attached themselves, or as some of their own party joined other groups for a while.

They drank white rum or Spanish brandy or beer, never 'cough-cure' sangria. They did pot, nothing stronger. Don and Naomi smoked some with them. He liked the group, though not as much as Naomi did. She loved their ease, their little solemnities, their aimlessness – except for Las Vegas – and their gentle wit, mild cheek and dodgy tolerance: a couple of the men thought the free-range pisser was what they called 'beyond'. 'Worse than a rugby international at the Arms Park,' Lyndon said. They had asked Naomi and Don some personal questions, but only out of polite curiosity.

'Don, he's against bullfighting is he, Naomi?' Lyndon said, when they had all moved into a bar from the ring. 'There's a lot like that. They're entitled.' He was one of the factory contingent, tall, thin, fair, in an azure T-shirt with the word MANTRA on it in gold. 'My sister's against. "Barbaric", that's her word. She got it off of a pamphlet. Are you together a while, you and Don? Manager in a Sainsbury's I heard. That's something.'

'Yes.' She stood by with lies.

'Some of the others are white collar – Esmé and Paul and Ifor, with an f, being Welsh, but you say it v. I expect fuck in Welsh is vuck.'

'Vantastic.'

'Oh, I like it! Humour is a favourite thing with me. What do you do, Naomi?'

'Between jobs.'

'Signing on?'

'Yes.'

'Talk to Ifor. He works in dole. Knows all the tricks. But before, what were you?'

'Here and there. Worked in a shop. The receptionist – switchboard.'

He went to the bar and bought brandies for himself and her and a couple of the others. When he came back and sat by Naomi again he said: 'Do you know what I thought – your job, I mean? Now, don't get mad, but I thought—'

She waited, longing and fearing to learn what signs she had flashed without knowing, hoping he thought wrong, although it hardly mattered: he would not be around when she went back to work – though not back to work.

'Well, I thought maybe a teacher – the way you talk, putting things tidy in the way you talk, like a teacher.'

'No.' They were a little apart from the rest of the group. Esmé grinned at her, as if to say, 'Yes, he's nice, isn't he?'

Yes, he was nice. Yes, he was the kind of boy-man she saw little of these days. Yes, she wished she could be more like him – the rambling harmlessness, the high contentment with a low future – but she couldn't. A mission was what she had been picked for.

'Would it matter if I, like, kept in touch when we got back?' he asked. 'I mean friends, that's all. Nothing to get Don going.'

'You're a long way off in Wales.'

'A postcard, that's all. Open. He could read it, welcome.

Friends. Or I could maybe take a car or hitch and come there, just a jaunt.'

'I don't know where I'm going to be,' she said.

'Oh? I thought you and Don had a place and—'

'If I get another job,' she said.

'Right.'

'I mean it could be a job away from where I'm living now.'

He nodded and held up his hands, like surrender, his face hot with apology: 'Right. You don't want me to write because it would be awkward with Don, even only friendship. Nor a visit. Especially a visit! I can understand that. I don't think I'd like it, a girl of mine getting cards, even only friendship.'

'No, it's nothing to do with that. But I'd hate you to write and get no reply because I never received your card. And if you came, worse.' Yes, a lot worse, if he started looking, street asking.

'Ah,' he said. He lowered his head towards hers and started to talk in a heavy whisper: 'No, not a teacher, maybe SAS, something like that – secret. No address given, for security reasons. Wearing a balaclava to hide your face every time you go out.'

'That's it,' she replied, and they had a good laugh together. Esmé gave her a grin through the crowd.

'But *I* could let you have *my* address?' he asked.

'Why not?'

'And I'll never hear a dicky bird.'

'Perhaps when I'm settled,' she said.

'What, you might not be living with Don?'

'Perhaps when I'm settled,' she said.

In the hotel afterwards she told Don about the drab bull-fight and the drinks. 'Do they ask about your job?' he said.

'I don't think they're interested in jobs. They're here on holiday. That's as far as they think. It's good.'

'But if they did ask you?'

'I'd tell them. Why not?'

'I don't know. I wondered.'

'What?'

'I don't buy this tale about a special course,' he replied. 'You can spot that, I expect.'

'I'm lucky to get on it.'

'It's balls, love. So stop trying to con me, will you? Everything too hurried, so scrappily arranged. It's not believable, not for an organization like the police.'

'You think too much of their organization – because you believe in organization. You're good at it.'

'How do I reach you when you're on this course? I can phone?'

'It's not like that, I've told you. This is a course with a security rating.'

'Where?'

'Don't ask, Don, please.'

'I can't ring.'

'I'll be in touch.'

'Do you get weekends? Leave?'

'Not at first.'

'How long's that?'

'Please, Don.'

He held both hands up, palms towards her, signalling that it was plain he had things right: 'I do think something secret – well, clearly – but not a course. I think they want to plant you somewhere. Spy games.'

'That'll be the day,' she said, and sniggered.

'And you'd do it. These people – Harpur, Iles – they could talk you into it. Perhaps they wouldn't even have to. You admire them. They're the real winning soul of police policy, aren't they?'

They were in their hotel room, Don sitting on the bed, she on a pink and blue wooden upright chair. She went and took a place alongside him, trying a moderately seductive walk, nothing farcical. He put an arm around her shoulders and they stayed silent for a time, still sitting up. Then she said: 'I'm going on a Special Branch course. Not many make it, and even fewer women.'

She could tell he was keeping his voice patient: 'You told me they lost someone undercover.'

'Undercover they might have. Not on a Special Branch course.'

'They don't strike me as capable, those two,' he said.

'Which?'

'Harpur and Iles. I mean, the story they give you to tell – cock-and-bull Special Branch thing. This sudden holiday. A few weeks' absence and everyone's supposed to forget you were ever a cop. Mad, Naomi. It's – well, it's criminally incompetent.'

She slipped out from under his arm and stood.

'I worry about you,' he said.

'I know.' She would have liked to remain held by him, but some comforts came too pricey.

He said: 'I feel as if all at once I don't know you properly. As if those two have taken you over, transformed you. And don't ask me which two.'

'It's the way to advance my career,' she replied. This was the kind of pious, management-selection wordage Iles had suggested in case of argument. 'You can sympathize, surely, Don. You know about getting on.'

'There's getting on and there's being used by a system.'

'Special Branch training on my cv can't be bad.'

He stretched flat on the bed suddenly and spoke up at the ceiling, not looking towards her: 'Oh, look, fuck off, Naomi. You're only proving what I said: they've taken you over, made you lie, made you different.'

He might be correct. Of course he was correct. But she had had enough of this: 'If I'm someone different now, perhaps you—'

'Yes, I've thought of that,' he said. 'God, it makes me damn miserable, Naomi, but, yes, I have thought of that.'

5

He stayed a week and then flew home. Like her, Don was booked for a fortnight and there would be no refund. In fact, he was lucky to get on a flight at no extra cost. To the travel people he pleaded a bereavement in Britain. Naomi went with him by taxi to the airport and waved at what she thought might be his face at a window just before take-off. Although there was no response, it was as good a face as another to wave at. She would not be seeing him again. He had agreed to move out before she returned: not that she would be returning to the flat until after the undercover job, anyway. In the taxi and in the airport lounge and bar they had been totally amiable with each other, even fond. But she had known it was a finale and saw that he did, too. She found she *wanted* it to be a finale. Whether he did, she was uncertain. She hoped so. No point in prolonging pain.

Naomi watched the tailplane out of sight, as though afraid he might somehow return and start the questioning and pressurizing and pleading again. Afterwards, she went back into the bar, ordered another Pernod and sat trying to put herself together again: sat trying to put herself together so she could then take herself apart and have a go at becoming someone else. She still loved that notion: the scope of it. She could dodge out from the

narrowness Don had tried to fix on her, in his caring, indomi-
table style. Well, domitable: hadn't he given up and
vamoosed?

If she'd had a joint with her now she would have lit up,
though you never knew how Spaniards would react. There
were still relics of the old regime in uniforms. Pernod could
do the trick just as well, almost. She recalled a television
interview with Mira Sorvino who won a best-support Oscar
playing a tart in Woody Allen's *Mighty Aphrodite*. As preparation she said she had dressed up flashy and gone to walk
one of the most famous hooker beats, though, naturally,
taking no clients. This was it, this was what Naomi liked the
thought of: getting into some other mode of life, some other
personality. Mobility. Great! It freed you from your genes,
your class, your predestined psychological shape. For a time.
And possibly for more than that. Perhaps she should have
been an actress herself. She was *going* to be an actress. She'd
tested for a role and landed it. Don thought she would be
no good. Two fingers to him. No, be fair. He thought *nobody*
could do it. Basically, he believed crooks smarter than police.
That meant not just smarter than Naomi but smarter than
the power clique who had devised and would run the operation, Harpur, Iles, Lane. They did not come up to his notion
of an executive. Now, he foresaw general perilous disaster,
and especially disaster for her. He couldn't approve. He had
opted out. He was showing his principles. So, yes, two fingers
to him.

She crooned to herself:

> We were intelligent people.
> No tears no fuss,
> Hurrah for us.

But she wondered whether she had been only destructive. Why this parting, after two goodish years, and sometimes very good? Don was probably right and the cover fiction given her by Harpur and Iles had dangerous holes. If her police friends would not believe it, why should Don? Had she wanted him to *make* himself believe it, even pretend to believe it? Yes, pretend, probably. It would have harmonized with how she felt. She was preparing herself for a long session of pretence, and preparing herself with joy and bright anticipation, plus a lot of terror. When Don complained he felt as if he no longer knew her properly, she had been upset for a moment, only for a moment, and then delighted. She did not want him to know her properly. She wanted to be various, plural, at least two-faced and possibly more. Of course, everybody was various, plural and at least two-faced and possibly more: how life ran. People would not usually admit it, though, or even recognize it. She admitted it and recognized it and meant to make it a career move. She could not be corralled by Don's wholesome notion of her. *Goodbye, Don, it was lovely, really.* Perhaps he thought that by walking out he would make her change. No, he definitely did not know her any longer.

With Lyndon and the rest of them back in Torremolinos she stuck to the bereavement tale for Don's departure, but saw nobody believed this, either. While she and Esmé shared a smoke in the Ladies' at the Lowlife Bar one night, Esmé said: 'Split for keeps?'

'Like that, yes.'

'I think you're a strong one, Naomi – won't take shit from anybody – or maybe only take the kind you can mainline!'

'I still like him. A lot.'

'But he wants to tell you what's what?'

'Like that, yes.'

'Sackcloth. You've done well, kid.'

Naomi slept with Lyndon for the last three nights of the holiday. As he said, why waste a double room? Being in bed with him was cheery and consoling and not quite meaningless. She had been careful to put no address tags on her luggage, but she made a last-minute check before letting him into the room. True, he might be able to find out something from the hotel or the tour operator, if he was that interested. He would not be. A holiday was a holiday. Yet he did keep on about wanting to be in touch.

'I thought you and your friends just drifted,' she said. 'Nothing long-term. No dealing in futures.'

'Yes, well I might just want to drift along to see you again,' he said.

'Not on. I'm a shifty piece.'

'Is that why he went?'

'Like that, yes.'

'Won't you ever settle down, like come to rest?'

'RIP? I hope not.'

6

As per instruction, Alfred did the research and reported, yes, there would be undercover. Even the Chief's wife knew. Well, of course, Manse Shale did not need Alfie to tell him he was right, but Shale really praised dear Alf's work, anyway. The thing about Alfie was he was bloody brilliant at confirming what Shale had already picked up by feel. Here you had the difference between leadership and Alfie Ivis. True leaders were equipped with what could be referred to as antennae, like the animal world, meaning able to pick up things early. Alf had skills, definitely, or why salary him? – skills to go out and find what someone had told him was there, like dogs with shot birds.

On the side, Alfie picked up another item, also obvious – that it was London invaders who had hit poor Gladhand Mace. He had been only one step up from a nobody in the trade, true, but he always behaved all right and did some steady, miniature bits of selling with stuff bought from Shale or Panicking. Crucial to get some wipe-out moves going against London and against the undercover very soon. This was strategy, another leadership matter.

Shale decided he'd raise these topics at the next confederation get-together with Panicking Ralph Ember. Luckily, one was due. Shale liked a formal business meeting with Ralphy two or three times a year, meaning by formal the lot – dinner jacket and black tie for all the mains taking part and, for him and Alfie, anyway, cummerbunds, Shale's own being azure. He liked delicate colours, not violent. Generally there were four present: Mansel and Ivis from Shale's outfit, and Panicking and Beau Derek from Ember's. Christ, that Beau, though! The red cabbage skin and slippery voice. But Panicking seemed to rate him as something, so Shale kept polite and told Alfie Ivis to offer Beau respectful comments now and then. Beau did not do a cummerbund. That might be sensible. No way could you think of Beau as a cummerbund person.

Shale and Panicking acted host turn and turn about to these meetings. That is, one of them picked up the bill each time. Alfred had located a grand venue, so secure and, at the same time, dignified. They always had a tidy meal with some bright wines accompanying, plus liqueurs and so on, so on being mainly rum for Beau who could not get total burn-out from Remy Martin, fine champagne, cognac or tia maria. A lot of the early talk was about how this filthy murderous London troupe hung on and even conquered new bits of territory, regardless. It was slow, the spread, and stop-start, but it was happening, and it could get swifter and no stops.

Gladhand's death showed how fast things were going now. This cockney kid, Lincoln W. Lincoln – Jesus, even the crazy fucking name was an insult to anyone decent thinking – well, Lincoln W. Lincoln might need to have something timely done to him, as a message for his chieftains. What Shale's mother used to call, a word to the wise. This word to the wise would be 'buckwheat'. That was a famous family term in the US. Well, not family, *family*. It meant finish someone in the most painful, slow way there was, so other folk, and especially their top folk, would eventually see the messy bodybag result and wonder if it was worth it, and if they were next. Oh, Lincoln's friends would put on a stately funeral in Metropoland, fifteen grand behind the bar, but not even the finest coffin style blurred that kind of message.

They were at a huge old table in the banqueting room of Agincourt Castle, a room that Shale reckoned could not have more fucking distinction, including minstrels' gallery. This eatery, out just beyond Georgeboon village in wide grounds, never did real work as a castle, definitely, not hurling back hordes. It was built as a house for someone who cleaned up in industry a hundred years ago when castle wars were definitely over. One of the breweries had turned it into a restaurant now and they did medieval feasts, with girls serving like wenches and showing plenty. Alfred knew the management and could get it for their dinners on a Monday, when it would usually be closed.

Although the castle was through-and-through fake, it had a good little stone tower and real wood panelling around the banqueting room, plus great coloured paintings on the ceiling and more top-class art in the friezes and dados. The colours were that delicate kind Shale adored – pink, blue, tan – and, as far as he could see, none of the paintings was shag-based or oral – not like some carvings in ancient Italian or Indian spots, including stiff dicks, but you had to be tolerant in this day and age.

It cost, yes. This was opening up the whole building and

bringing the chef in special on his day off. Shale did not mind paying when it came to him. This was a place that had style. One waitress was enough and Shale had told the management from the start there was no need for costume, just proper clothes. These were relaxed occasions, but not raucous.

Beau Derek said: 'Coming late into this trade, I've got to say these few months have been an education for me – cooperation between the two firms, the atmosphere of continuing peace, the give and take. I read the Press – places like Manchester, Liverpool, let alone London – they've got open battles between trafficking firms non-stop, shoot-outs, limb reprisals, God knows what. Yet here, a decent business atmosphere where trade can thrive, and moments of true conviviality like tonight.'

Shale said: 'Peace, yes. Sort of. Mace is peace? That kind of violence could get usual. They're switching tactics. Maybe you feel it, too, Ralph.'

'London? Lincoln W. Lincoln?'

'He been put in here by masters to buy what he can in the way of pushers and runners, preparatory. We've all watched him try, haven't we? Mace said no . . . so . . .'

Ember waved a hand to show he personally was not too worried, the smug prat. He said: 'One or two respond. That's all. Eleri did, and look what happened to her. Most people know it's so much wiser to stick with us, even taking Gladhand into account. They appreciate our clout, Manse.'

'Of course they do. That's what I mean.'

'What, Manse?' Ember asked.

'This boy, LWL, been told to recruit. If he can't do it by buying – which he can't, not enough, as you truly say – but if he can't he's going to try something else. He's started at it with Mace. More to come.'

'All round heaviness?' Ember asked.

'He'll start hurting more people, frightening people. Otherwise he's in trouble himself, having fucked up. So where's peace then?' Shale said.

Ember gave a couple of very kindly nods and wagged his profile, like to say, *I'm listening to it and it's cock but you're definitely entitled to a point of view, Manse.* If you did not know him and you looked at him now, with the nice drop of Pomerol in one hand on its way to his mouth above the jaw scar, and his eyes so calm and thoughtful, you would never think he was called Panicking Ralph. Shale could tell Ember had something special to say, but he was sitting on it until his big brain whispered, Now, Ralphy. A lot thought Ember looked like Charlton Heston in the young days, *El Cid* days or even *Touch of Evil* days, that nose and the shoulders. Once, they used to say he was like Charlton Heston without the money, but somehow Ember *had* the money now. The panics did not stop him collecting. 'Lincoln W. Lincoln to turn violent as standard policy you believe, Manse?' Ember said. 'This is certainly one possible scenario. But perhaps the worst-case scenario, do you think? I wonder if we need to embrace it quite yet.'

Oh, Jesus, the lingo.

'This undercover,' Ember said. 'Why do you think they're putting her in, Manse?'

How he would do it, a sod like Panicking. Just slip in something like that – let you know he knew, but no big moment. Panicking must have learned a lot of ploys sitting on the wrong side of police interrogation. Although they all said he was never convicted, Ember must have faced a ton of questioning, and it was such a famous fucking interrogator trick suddenly to bring in a bit of information you thought was confidential, and to talk about it like, of course, it was fact, recognized by both parties, and needed no show or arguing. Then he would watch you. Ember was watching, and Beau. This bit of information was not just he knew about the undercover but he said 'her'.

'You want to knock over Lincoln W. Lincoln, Manse, but before we expose ourselves like that I think you should ask why would they plant Anstruther,' Ember said.

'Trying to read beyond the immediate event or appearance, you see, Mansel,' Beau said. 'This is a search for their thinking, so typical of Ralph. Deduction not just observation.'

'Certainly to wipe out Lincoln W. Lincoln is one option,' Ember said.

'I want it done meaningful,' Shale replied.

'And, on the face of it, to kill Lincoln is not by any means an unproductive option,' Ember replied. 'But I feel what we must do is recognize it is only *an* option among several.'

'If there's one thing Mansel believes in it is to keep the whole range of options before one when devising policy,' Ivis replied.

The talk died for a time then. Once or twice Beau looked

like he might restart it, but he seemed to have run out of horseshit. Then, when Shale, Beau and Ivis had cigars going with the coffee, Ember said: 'Desmond Iles is famed for hating undercover, fearing undercover, because of Street. Now he's suddenly for it. Why?'

'He been overruled,' Shale said. 'The Chief wants it.'

'Iles doesn't get overruled.'

'Lane got leadership,' Shale replied.

'Manse has an almost mystical view of the power of leadership,' Ivis said. 'Understandably. Is he not a brilliant exponent himself?'

Ember did a spell of fingering his jaw scar. Some said it was a bank raid wound. Some said he fell on his Ovaltine cup.

Shale said: 'I heard the Chief is really hands-onning, really telling them what got to be done.'

Ember ignored that, the ponce. 'I don't think Iles is completely evil, Mansel,' he said. 'I always try to defend the ACC when I hear people speak of him in those terms.'

Iles would be fucking delighted to hear some eternal dross like Ralphy was acting his friend and backer.

'For instance, Manse, I don't believe that in order to convince Lane undercover cannot work, Iles would put a girl like Naomi Anstruther into your firm or mine – just so she will get caught and eliminated,' Ember said.

'I hear this is Mrs Lane's view,' Ivis replied.

'Me, I'd say there's quite a few fragments of honour in Iles,' Ember said.

'Manse has always shown a very considerable respect for both Harpur and Iles,' Ivis replied. 'He is not one who—'

Beau held up one hand, thumb pointing, like a teapot spout. You would not think someone with such slob fingers could do safes, but that was where he started. 'I think you'll find Ralph wants to put forward quite a deep reading of this situation, deep and very convincing. Being Ralph, he would not say this himself, but—'

'So what we got to fucking do, Ralphy, welcome this Anstruther, let her see how the whole lot works?' Shale asked. 'So she can go back and feed Harpur and Harpur can feed a jury?'

Ember looked around the big room, like bothered about listeners. 'Now, please don't mind my saying this, Manse, but you do rush to extremes.'

'So what we got to do with her?' Shale replied.

Ivis said: 'Not so much a rush to extremes, Ralph, as the ability to focus on absolutely essential factors. This is Mansel's flair, central to leadership.'

'If we deal heavily with the girl, where are we?' Ember asked. 'Iles, Harpur, but especially Iles – they'd be fierce to avenge anything like that after Raymond Street.'

'This would be she disappears dead, wouldn't it?' Shale replied. 'We don't leave no signs for Harpur and Iles.'

'Iles doesn't need signs. He'd see what had happened and deal with it in his own way – deal with us in his own way. Perhaps you feel you can cope with that, Manse? Do you?'

That meant, *No you fucking don't, Manse*. 'So you say put up with this girl?' Shale replied.

'Put up with her but there's more to it, much more to it,' Beau replied with a gorgeous chuckle. 'There's some subtlety, some psychology.'

'Fuck subtlety,' Shale replied. 'And fuck whatever. This is our business you're talking about, Ralphy. Livelihood. Life.'

'Ralph,' Ember replied. 'Not Ralphy.'

'Ralph hates that dangler on the end,' Beau said. 'It's not in keeping.'

Ember said: 'I don't really think we're at variance on anything basic, Mansel. Our reading of the prospects are probably similar and it's only a matter of approach.'

'Just don't let Beau make out I'm short on subtlety, that's all.'

'Not what he meant, Manse, not at all,' Ember replied.

'Definitely not,' Beau said. 'I was only—'

'Subtlety I was famed for from birth,' Shale said. 'My mother would tell you that. She noticed it.'

'When subtlety is required, Mansel can be supreme in subtlety,' Ivis said. 'When directness is required, nobody is more giftedly direct than Mansel.'

The girl brought in the liqueurs and Beau's rum. Shale paid her. She and the chef would leave now. Alfie promised to lock up. It would really give him a hard-on to be king of the castle. That was a harmless little dream. A castle was a move up from a has-been lighthouse.

Ember said: 'I stick to my conviction that what Des Iles wants is what counts. Nobody else. Not Harpur, and certainly not Mark Lane. And what Desmond Iles still wants is a good and well-ordered business scene in the hands of responsible local folk, folk with fine pedigrees that he can recognize – you, Manse, obviously, and perhaps one's self.'

'So he tries to destroy us with undercover,' Shale replied. 'And we're supposed to let him, yes? That your subtlety, Ralph?'

Beau said: 'Ralph admires irony, even when apparently used against him. He has the maturity.'

'Iles's target is Lincoln W. Lincoln, Manse,' Ember said, slowly, gently like a teacher with the thicko class. 'He wants him finished as much as we do. This is an intruder who does not know our ways, does not know Mr Iles's ways. Lincoln is a force of disequilibrium and will menace the happy, tranquil pattern established by our understanding with the police and theirs with us. He's already started to do it through the death of Mace – he or someone he paid.'

Beau held up that porky mitt again. 'Here's the subtlety, coming now,' he said, joyously.

'Thanks,' Shale said. 'We might have been too dim to notice.'

'That's not how he meant it, Manse,' Ember said.

'How *does* he fucking mean it?' Shale replied. 'How come you got to keep on interpreting this sod? He a white Zulu or something?'

Ember said: 'What Iles wants is to plant this girl with one of us so she gets cred. Entirely that at this first stage. People would see her doing trade, perhaps using a bit, too. Maybe Lincoln W. Lincoln sees her doing trade. And he tries to buy her over. That's what he's here for, ahead of his masters, isn't it? And this one, Anstruther, will go to him – like Eleri ap Vaughan. That's her orders. And it would be believable for her to go. Lincoln promises bigger discounts, better lawyers if there's trouble, better protection on the street, better quality material. Only promises, yes, but they could persuade a girl. They persuaded Eleri. Once Naomi does go, Des Iles has an observer inside the target firm. He can wipe out Lincoln W. Lincoln. He and Harpur will be fed evidence by Anstruther. We're a transit camp and training ground for her, Manse, that's all.'

'The beauty is we don't need to do a thing,' Beau said.

That was always the sort of plan Panicking liked. Let the other buggers handle the work and take the risks. He would just haul in the benefits.

'Iles is not interested in our operation, Manse. He *needs* our operation. Our joint operation is peace and safety on the street, and he wants it to be joint with him, too. The girl won't be interested in our operation, either, except as a route to dealership credentials.'

Beau said: 'So Iles will seem to be doing things how the Chief wants – i.e., the undercover. But really he'll be doing it *his* way, as ever, because the undercover will be used to get rid of Lincoln W. Lincoln and whoever's behind him. And thus we're back to the happy conditions of mutuality between us and the police. Ralph's right, it's joint.'

What you had to wonder when you heard Ember go on like this so definite about police plans and calling Iles Des was if someone had put a word or two about the future in his ear, say someone like Iles. Was there another alliance? Was Iles already nice and joint with Ralphy? Ember had all

sorts of connections, was famed for it. This could be quite a
worrying idea. Ember was saying Iles yearned for a peaceful
life with their two firms controlling all business. Yes? Yes?
Maybe Iles believed it would be better if only *one* firm ran
things, a true monopoly. That would be fucking Ralphy's, of
course. Ember said he wanted this girl let in as a plant so
she could go on and destroy Lincoln W. Lincoln and the firm
behind him. But what if she came in and learned the total
lot about Mansel Shale's business on her way to Lincoln
W. Lincoln, so eventually she could destroy both? That was
just the sort of pretty arrangement Iles would love, and
Panicking.

All right, Shale would watch to see which firm the girl
tried to join for her apprenticeship, his or Ralphy's. If Iles
and Ember had a scheme going, that would be an indicator.
And if she had a big try to get into Shale's, he would know
something a bit private was going on, private to Panicking,
Iles and the girl, plus possibly Harpur. In that case, she might
have to be taken out somewhere deep and permanently lost.
It would sadden Shale, brutality of that sort, especially to a
girl, even a fink girl, but you could not let a nice business
just go fuck itself, could you? This was the kind of work
Alfie should have been able to take on – so simple, and
he really knew about handguns. But he always said when
something like this had to be handled that it was a long
time now since he used a pistol and maybe it would be
better if Denzil Lake took the duty. The sod knew Lake had
no proper gun skills, he was just Shale's fucking chauffeur,
and what Alfie was really saying was, if Shale wanted that

sort of task done he ought to do it himself. Probably, he would.

'I like it, your reading of the situation, Ralph,' Shale said. 'Convincing.'

'I was certain you'd see the point, Manse. It has a logic to it, a kind of inevitable sequence.'

'Long views are what Ralph is so good at,' Beau said. 'This is a university-trained mind, and can't you just feel it, though?'

Yes, for a while big brain Ralphy had joined one of the local colleges, the same one where Harpur's bird with the tits, Denise, was a student. Shale said: 'We had the Anstruther name, of course. But do we know yet which firm they're going to put her into first?'

'I believe the whisper says yours, Manse,' Ember replied. 'Does the whisper say Manse's, Beau?'

'That's what the whisper says.'

'But it's of no significance,' Ember explained. 'Could have been either, equally.'

'I appreciate that, Ralph.'

Ivis said: 'When it comes to long views, Manse is as talented as any. Isn't the organization of his firm glistening proof of that? This girl could not have a better place to pick up the essentials of our business.'

This was the thing about Alfie – he could not see what were known as ramifications, not even if they were right in front of him like a fucking placard. Look at him smiling away there now like Daft Clarence while Ember and Beau were cutting his and Shale's throats.

7

Harpur was doing breakfast for himself, Denise and his daughters when Jill came into the kitchen and said there was someone to see him. 'He's what some would call dishy, Dad. Twenty-five, six? Tanned. Holiday abroad, maybe. He seems worried. He said your address is in the phone book, which is true, so that's a good start. I don't think one of your grasses. Not smarmy enough.'

'I didn't hear anyone knock.'

'Saw him coming up the front garden path. I went at once to open the door. It seemed to me he needed help.'

Harpur's daughters often offered callers help. It could be awkward. Hazel was fifteen, Jill thirteen, and their idea of help was not always . . . helpful.

'What name?' Harpur asked.

'He wouldn't. All right, that sounds like a fink, but no. Not whiny and looking over his shoulder. More like . . . more like urgent.'

'Where is he?'

'In the sitting room. Hazel's looking after him – doing the hostess thing that greasy way she has. What she calls *bringing him out of himself*, you know?'

Jesus. Harpur said: 'I'll be with them now. I'll just finish here.' Thank God it was a school day.

'Is this to do with what Mr and Mrs Lane came about?'

'Why should it be?'

'What *did* Mr and Mrs Lane come about, Dad?'

'They were passing,' Harpur replied.

'The middle of the night?'

'They're allowed out in the dark,' he said.

'OK, OK. I can do the rest of the brekker, if you like.'

'No. You go back. Give the message.' When he was at home in the mornings, Harpur liked to cook the girls a full breakfast. He hoped that one day they would remember him as a good single-parent provider, and it was easy to score with breakfast. As adults they might recall the happy smell of black pudding and bacon in the pan, and think well of him despite admitted shortfalls. He was in a hurry today. The Chief wanted a formal meeting first thing this morning to discuss how to place Anstruther once she'd done the Hilston Manor course, and if she survived it. Normally, Lane disliked formal meetings: preferred drifting in on people as if for a casual chat. But undercover was special, damned uncasual.

'Where's Denise?' Jill asked.

'Still in bed.'

'Shall I take her up some tea?'

'Get Hazel to go.' It might shift her from the visitor, whoever.

Jill said: 'Is Denise getting up for breakfast? What I mean, Dad, do you want this caller to know you're – ? I mean, do you want this man to see her?'

'Why not?'

'The point is, I gather she also came downstairs while Mr and Mrs Lane were here the other night.'

'So? Anyway, *how* do you gather she came downstairs while Mr and Mrs Lane were here?'

'Heard.'

'Earholing. Don't you sleep?'

'Do you want this kind of . . . well, you know?'

'What?'

'People knowing.'

'My reputation?' Harpur said.

'Yes, that's the word. I couldn't think of it right off. As I see it, Dad, so many people sort of . . . well, sort of bumping into her here.'

'Denise doesn't mind. I don't.'

'Right. If you say. And it is the *same* girl each time, as long as they all realize this. But I'll tell Hazel to ask her to dress a bit carefully. Buttons done up. You know how she is sometimes at breakfast. That's Denise, I mean.'

'On second thoughts, bring him into the kitchen,' Harpur said.

'Is there some for him?'

'I'll do more.'

In a while, Jill returned. Harpur recognized Donald McWater from pictures in Naomi's undercover file. 'I've got to talk to you privately, Mr Harpur,' he said.

'You are?' Harpur replied.

Hazel came in from upstairs. 'Denise is ghastly hung-over.'

'No surprise,' Jill said. 'What time were the two of you up

till, Dad? And that crazy singing. The same Marilyn Monroe number twenty odd times – *Running wild, lost control.* Your theme tune?'

'She's staying in bed,' Hazel said.

'That means enough breakfast for the four of us,' Jill said.

'Oh, no, no, I mustn't intrude,' McWater said.

'There's plenty,' Hazel replied. 'But Dad wouldn't offer it without being pushed. He's police.' They all sat down and began to eat. Jill poured tea. For a while there was no talk and then Hazel said: 'We get all sorts here. Dad can usually sort it out. He's not nearly as crude as he looks. It *is* a business call, is it? Dad hasn't been . . . It's not about some girl you know, is it? Your wife even? People who come here – well, all sorts of grubby reasons.'

'Of course it's business,' Jill snarled at her. 'Why say cruel things, Haze?' She turned to McWater. 'This with Denise upstairs is like a nice settled thing for Dad now, lately. He doesn't need anyone else. OK, like, so she throws up after a boozy night. That's how students are, though.'

'You're well fed now,' Harpur said. 'Get moving.' The girls did some bent-double bowing and backed slowly out.

'Harpur, as you know, I live with, lived with, Naomi Anstruther,' McWater said. 'I bet you thought I was in Spain with her.'

'Naomi's in Spain?'

'Oh, come on. You'd know her movements.'

'People take their leave where they like, Mr—?'

'You've been all over her dossier, for sure, and I'm in it,

with pictures. She stayed on out there. I'm going to Heathrow this morning to meet her.'

'Was there something wrong here you had to come back early for?' Harpur asked.

'No, something wrong *there*.'

'I'm sorry,' Harpur said.

He heard what could be a scampering to the bathroom, and then the sounds of distress. He wondered if Jill might be right and he was corrupting Denise on all fronts.

'Naomi won't be expecting me,' McWater said.

'You'll make it up with her? Good.'

'I want to tell her you're taking her off this undercover rubbish, Harpur. She'd get back to being someone I know then.'

Christ, she had talked to him, despite all the instructions and promises. If she had, he certainly would pull her out: she was a weakness. Lane and Mrs Lane talking could not be helped, but this was the girl herself.

McWater said: 'I've heard the tale she's going on a course, so don't try that. She keeps brickwalling me with it.'

'Perhaps she brickwalls you because it's true.'

'She brickwalls me because you and Iles have told her to brickwall me.'

'Yes, she's going on a course,' Harpur replied. 'It's a very good chance. There are certainly confidential aspects to it. Are you confusing that with undercover work? Something different, believe me.' So, a girl's love life was shattered by this job even before it started. Occasionally, Harpur had doubts about policing.

'You'll get her killed, Harpur,' he said. 'They'll spot her, the way they spotted that other one. Street? These things can't be kept secret, and you can't look after her. *I* have to look after her. You're putting her among viciously dangerous people. Look what happened to Mace. And you catch nobody for it.'

Harpur read true worry for her in McWater, but did he also scent a lover's jealousy? McWater fought against handing her over. As Iles had said, going undercover involved close dealings with her Controller. 'I don't think Naomi would want you to come here and talk like this,' Harpur said.

'I *know* she wouldn't. She thinks I've gone from her life. I've moved out of the flat. But I can't write her off.'

'It's admirable in you.'

'Don't shit me, Harpur.'

'Look, I—'

'She can't think when you and Iles are at her. She caves in, does whatever you say, like hypnotized.'

Yes, perhaps jealousy. McWater was tall, slim, dark, groomed: probably first-class management potential. Good pushiness, too. He had a lean, nicely balanced face and his eyes glinted now with fright for Naomi, or with hate for Harpur and what Harpur stood for. When McWater spoke about what he saw as the abuse of her mind, his voice thinned to a horrified squeak.

'I've seen her alter,' McWater said. 'She seems out of my reach. She didn't want me with her.'

'As I say, I'm sorry. But she won't want you at Heathrow, either. Not if you're trying to dissuade her from this Special

Branch course. I'm not supposed to tell you what it is but I'll risk it – because you're so worried and mixed up.'

For a second it looked as if McWater would spit on the carpet. 'You won't stop her undercover work – even though I know about it?' he said. 'That's why I came – to show I do know. God, how can you go on now? Where's security?'

Yes, where? Yes, how could it go on? Harpur said: 'Not to be rude, but you know nothing. And if you meet her and bully her Naomi will tell you the same.'

As when the Lanes were here, the door began to open slowly and Denise came a few steps into the room. She had put on her jeans and a check shirt. There were what could be vomit flecks on the lower right leg of her jeans and the right arm of the shirt. She was drinking a bit hard lately. News of Mace's death had upset her badly. She imagined a sort of link to him through her neighbour at Jonson Court.

'I feel worse in bed, Col,' she muttered. 'I'm going out to lie on the grass in the back garden and breathe some helpful air.'

'It's raining,' Harpur replied.

'Good. Are you scared I might be seen by the neighbours?'

'A bit. Oh, more than a bit.'

'Col's pathetically prim. Is he looking after you all right?' she asked McWater. 'I'll breathe a while out there and then die or go back to my flat. You look full of angst,' she told him.

'It's a personal thing,' Harpur said.

'They're the worst,' Denise replied.

*

'I always love this room, sir,' Iles cried. 'Well, suite, I suppose. Of course, it rightly has the scale for your rank, and yet it is a modest room, plain and to the point. Somehow "suite" seems almost grandiose in the circumstances. Don't you think the Chief's room is plain and to the point, Col? Do you feel "suite" a word somehow full of inappropriate clangour?'

The ACC did like answers to his questions. Harpur said: 'It looks as if Beau Derek's been recruited as a permanency by Ember. We're pretty sure he was at the last Saltmead Castle session and perhaps previous ones. That's a very select invitation list. Policy-making responsibilities for the cartel.'

'Beau's a good solid lad,' Iles said. 'Ralphy Ember's always shrewd on staff selection. This is two very nicely established outfits in sane combination now – Ember and Beau, Shale and Ivis.'

A couple of reddish rage spots showed in veins which had suddenly surfaced on the Chief's normally tolerant, puffy face. He said: 'It becomes increasingly urgent to attack one of the firms from the inside. They will reach a point where they're *so* what you call "established", Desmond, that they grow impregnable. I will not countenance a return to the kind of "established" drugs villainy that prevailed with Oliphant Kenward Knapp. We resist, we attack. No further blind-eyeing in my domain.'

'I hope Mrs Lane is well, sir,' Iles replied.

Harpur said: 'We might have some problems with—'

Iles said: 'I get unofficial word from a friend in the Met that two upper echelon lads from a London south-east trafficking firm will arrive soon to help Lincoln W. Lincoln here. No names yet. It's the pattern, this move out from traditional centres of drugs commerce. Things grow tough for outfits in London – outfits in Manchester and Liverpool, too. The competition's brutal. And the police there have learned how to be heavy.'

'And we . . . we shall learn how to combine finesse with resolve,' Lane declared. It was said without yelling but clipped, even confident. They were seated around the Chief's big conference table. He was in uniform for some luncheon later, and looked as always catastrophically unkempt. Also as always, he had chosen a nondescript spot at one side of the table. Harpur had never seen him sit at the head. Lane craved recognition of his leadership, yet despised leadership's status. He seemed for a moment now to slip into a kind of trance, gazing constantly towards the chain-of-command diagram on the wall opposite him. On this his post appeared as a thick-lined scarlet rectangle at the top, with the letters C.C. in regal purple at the centre. Perhaps he needed reassurance. When he spoke, it was as if he had programmed himself to say the words, or as if they were coming from him pre-recorded, like the floor voice in a lift. There was a kind of strength to it, and a kind of terrifying feebleness. Harpur could not decide whether Lane had reached that resolve he just mentioned, or was on the run-in to collapse.

Harpur said: 'As to undercover, I'm sorry but I don't think we—'

'No, this is not my wife speaking through me, not, not, not,' Lane cried. 'Oh, I hear your imputation, Desmond, but no, never. My views of undercover are personal and are above all positive. I love the notion of these damn filthy firms having within their very being the germ – our, planted germ – the germ to destroy them. They might look as if they will last for ever, and yet they'll contain their own defeat.'

He glanced at Harpur then at Iles, craving confirmation. Harpur remembered the Chief when he was a brilliant detective on the neighbouring turf. Several times they had worked together successfully then. But promotion had brought Lane low. Iles often told Harpur the Chief illustrated a well-known career tragedy: talented people rose to a point where they were no longer capable of the work – 'like St Peter'. Iles said they stayed stuck at that level, but at that level could do foul damage, 'like St Peter'.

Lane continued, powerfully, for him: 'Once we have this girl in place, law and order will begin eating away at the evil of gangdom. One is proud to have a part in eradication of a plague, the violence and greed plague that killed Mace. And I say "One" with intent, Desmond, Colin. I, I am that one, not my wife, splendid as she may be as my loyal, endlessly supportive companion. That companionship does not, cannot, infringe upon the fundamentals of my role as commander here.' His voice faltered. 'Desmond, sometimes I wonder whether you understand the kind of marital interdependence which Sally and I have – its sweetness, its solidity, its boundaries.'

Iles watched Lane throughout and remained silent when the Chief finished. Harpur had seen this kind of speechlessness disable the ACC a few times before over the years. Now and then the ACC seemed to find Lane so frail he could not bring himself to give further pain. Somewhere in the ACC there definitely lived slim elements of tenderness.

'And yet you, too, have a lovely wife, Desmond,' the Chief said.

'You don't have to take my word for that, sir. Ask Harpur, or Francis Garland. They've both had the body tour, though at different times, I believe.'

Lane swallowed. 'A wife who, I am sure, is always there to offer you her, well, guidance and encouragement.'

'What Sarah offers is seasonal, sir,' Iles said.

A moment ago Harpur had started to say that the undercover project must be killed, at least with Naomi Anstruther as the plant. It had become too perilous. Now, though, he found himself unable to continue. Like Iles, he could not bear to threaten Lane's fragile spell of glorious stability. How would it be if Harpur insisted the operation must be shelved because Naomi's boyfriend had guessed its existence, and because McWater's fear there had been a thousand leaks might turn out true – some of the leaks from Lane himself? The Chief would disintegrate. Lane's soul and entire philosophy were tied up in the undercover scheme: his spiritual mission of good against evil. If the plot were aborted, not even a fiercely supportive wife could hold him together.

Most likely Lane would suspect an agreement between Harpur and Iles to crush him by killing his pet proposal. The Chief's old crippling sense of isolation at the top – isolation and victimization – would come tearing back. Also, to speak now about McWater's sharp guesses would drop an unbearable moral dilemma on to Lane, perhaps shove him this time into permanent mental confusion. He would have to decide whether to guard his pride regardless by continuing the plan, or to withdraw it because of appalling risk to Naomi. The Chief was a good man and would not want to send Anstruther into blatant danger. But the Chief was also a man in frenzied late-life search for dignity, and with Mrs Lane to answer to. Harpur prayed that when McWater met Naomi off the plane today he could persuade her into pulling out of undercover work, terrorize her into it, if necessary. Lane's stratagem would be at an end then, but none of the blame Harpur's.

The Chief said: 'From the outset I've favoured placing her in Shale's outfit, as you know. Ralphy Ember's too damn bright. There *is* an argument in favour of Ember's, of course: I don't believe either Ralphy or Beau Derek would kill, not close up and in cold blood. Shale might be different. And Alf Ivis. Just the same, I do think on balance, Mansel's. And she'll probably be able to pick up something useful about Ember even when she's with Shale. They're working very closely now, aren't they, Col?'

'How it looks,' Harpur replied. 'Manse and Panicking were both at the Saltmead Castle meeting, of course. Principals.'

'And then, all right, there's a possiblity that Lincoln W. Lincoln, Lovely Mover as I believe he's dubbed – there's a possibility that Lovely Mover will try to poach Naomi for this new, apparently expanding London unit. Well, that's fine, fine. This is to kill two birds, perhaps even three, with one stone.'

Iles seemed to have recovered some of his malice and brought a notebook from the pocket of his grey-suit jacket and with a gold propelling pencil made a show of writing down, *This is to kill two birds, perhaps even three, with one stone.* 'I hate to lose these phrases, where our role is so effortlessly encapsulated, sir,' he said. 'Once they're in my, well, Commonplace Book I can savour them and take intellectual nourishment at leisure.'

Lane said hurriedly: 'Of course, not that I think of the girl as a stone. Hardly.'

'Nor as one of the dead birds,' Iles replied.

'She is a life in our care, so very much in our care.'

Iles paraphrased this addition, speaking it aloud as he wrote. Then he read the complete entry to himself, silently now but forming the words with his lips and nodding with appreciation bordering on reverence.

'My understanding is that the girl has been as it were losing herself abroad pre Hilston,' Lane said.

'Yes,' Harpur replied.

'This is good. I insist on every precaution.'

'I'm glad, sir,' Iles replied.

Harpur said: 'I've told Naomi she may withdraw without prejudice at any time before the operation actually begins.'

'Of course, of course,' Lane said. 'Might she?'

'I don't know,' Harpur replied.

In the corridor outside, when he and Iles were returning to their own rooms, Iles said gently: 'I'll kill the sod if we lose her, then you for losing her, Harpur, then whoever did it. Yes, in that order. But you've put her up to backing out, have you, you devious saint, Col? Was that what you were telling him?'

'She'd never quit.'

8

In the plane on the way home, Naomi began to wonder whether Don would be at Heathrow to welcome her and to put things right between them. She wanted him to be there. It amazed her how much she wanted him to be there. Turning up after their squabble was just the kind of thing Don would do. It was that, wasn't it – only a squabble? In the past, they had had quarrels, would break with each other for a while, and then one of them – it worked out about fifty-fifty which – one of them would reappear white flagging and they would talk it all out, perhaps eventually make love – well, *always* eventually make love – and their good partnership would resume. That was the point – it *was* good: sensible, passionate, solid. It would have been crazy to lose everything because of some flurry of bad temper and wacky ideas about self. And maybe crazy to lose it because of a job.

Sitting there sipping gin alongside Esmé, Naomi decided that the way she had been thinking of herself lately was farcical – that crap about wanting to be 'liberated' from her identity, transformed into something 'other'. Oh, God, just psychobabble. This 'other' picked a trite spot like Torremolinos for a holiday, and had a few nights of hotel romancing with a lad like Lyndon: a nice-natured and amusing lad like Lyndon, but one who could have nothing to do with her life back in Britain. When she thought now about the dangerous play acting she had to take on very soon, it no longer seemed like something that would magically bring her freedom, newness, escape. She was about to stick her head in a hole and the animals living there might bite it off, the way they bit off Raymond Street's. She saw now what she had been trying to do – to turn the dirty skills of spying into a brilliant mystique. But they were nothing more than safety equipment. Today she abruptly realized that when she moved into the deceit and shiftiness of undercover she would need more than ever the assurance that Don was still around for her: Don as familiar Don, clear-headed, formidable, loving, and waiting for her return: Naomi as Naomi, not some daft girl pushed off balance by a career chance, and imagining herself to be whatever she wanted to be whenever she wanted to be it. Pathetic.

Lyndon and the others were hitting the trolley drinks pretty hard, as antidote to arrival and the unfriendly prospect of work. She was on her second large gin and tonic herself, and ordered another. Yes, the prospect of work did need blocking out, pro tem. There was some singing, but not *Viva Espana*. Nobody had drunk that much yet. Esmé was seeing off a run of brandies. 'We'll miss you, Naomi. Pity we can't all join up again for some fun one weekend.'

'Well, yes. I'll try and send a card. Fix something.'

'We can't reach you?'

'Not immediately. But I've got Lyndon's address.'

'He'll miss you most.'

'Oh, I—'

'He doesn't generally fall like that. It's the mystery around you.'

'Ah, my mystery!' She gave it a big, self-mocking voice. 'Oh, yes. I work at that. Men drool.'

'Yes, you do work at it, don't you? That what wowed Don, too?'

'Obviously not enough, was it?'

Esmé finished her fourth drink and then got her lips organized for a serious statement: 'Well, I have to say it, he didn't seem your sort. Very cool and lovely looking and with a future, yes, but not your sort.'

'What's my sort then, Esmé?'

'You like more laughs.'

'Don can laugh.'

'But I don't say you're sort of giggling crazy, not like some of us! Not like Penny. You – you're into good order, I think, deep down.'

'That's me,' she whooped. 'Don't I just *love* good order, though?' She might have said she was on good order's payroll, but even after the gins knew she had better not.

'I expect he'll come looking,' Esmé said.

'Who?'

'Who do you think?'

'Who?' Naomi asked.

'I meant Don. Did you think I meant Lyndon?'

'Yes, Donald might come looking, I suppose. These stupid little battles.' Perhaps when he met her she would admit at once that he had guessed right and there was no Special Branch course. It was the cover tale which had seemed to hurt Don most – the screaming phoniness of it, as if any old yarn would do for him. She would tell Don, tell him straight away on arrival, that infiltration was no more than a tough workaday duty, not some enormous spiritual journey. It would last a while and then end without changing her essence, and especially would not change her feelings for him. And he would accept then, wouldn't he, that she must do what she had promised to do? Of course. He would willingly adjust his life to fit the requirements of secrecy, knowing that her security would depend on it – her security and the prospect of picking up that good, loving partnership, once her guest spot with a gang ended. They would both want that.

Esmé said: 'I thought maybe a cop.'

Naomi laughed, but without any give-away excess, she hoped. 'Lyndon can do better. He thinks SAS.'

'Not just because you like good order. Your eyes. They're beautiful, really beautiful, but you don't miss much, do you? They're all round the place, like observing, like making a case.'

Esmé scared her, made her dribble some of her drink. Christ, was the mark really so clear? And, Christ, if it was, what could she do about it? If she looked as though she was making a case when she was not making a case what would she look like when she was with Shale's lot or Panicking's or Lovely Mover's and really had to make cases?

'I've got nothing against cops,' Esmé said.

'Know many?

'A few.'

'Not me,' Naomi said.

'No?'

'I hate uniforms.'

'Not all of them wear uniforms. Some lurk about acting ordinary. Watching.'

'I'd hate that, too.'

'You'd be good at it.'

'How can you tell?' Naomi asked.

'I can tell.' The booze gave her solemnity and excused her from explaining herself.

Lyndon came slinking down the aisle with a bacardi miniature in his hand. He wanted Esmé to swap places with him. She stood, a bit shaky: 'Naomi's sad. No good to you. She's dreaming of the four-square Donald.' She moved off and Lyndon sat down.

'That right?' he said.

'Would you like to go to the toilet?' she replied. 'I'll follow.'

He gasped. 'Isn't that sort of . . . well . . . a bit obvious? Risky?'

'Yes, it's risky.'

When she joined him he was sitting naked apart from his Disneyland T-shirt on the closed lavatory pedestal. She locked the door and undressed completely. She straddled him. 'God, you're wild, Naomi,' he muttered.

'Not yet I'm not,' she said, moving slowly on him. 'But I will be.'

'Yes. Don't just disappear afterwards.'

'I'll try not to.'

He had both hands flat on her shoulder blades pressing her down. There was a mirror and she could see her face. It looked rule-busting and pleasured – how she wanted it to look. She thought she felt the aircraft bank a little, changing course: it would do instead of the earth moving. Someone tried the door and they ignored it for a while yet. When the someone tried again she pulled her lips off his, turned her head and yelled: 'Get fucking lost, will you?'

'Is this love, Nai?' he asked. 'It is, isn't it?'

'Don't call me Nai. I'm not a horse, and I'm not a vote.'

'What? Oh, neigh? Vote?'

'Ayes and nays in Parliament.'

'But is this love, Naomi? It has to be, hasn't it?'

'It's a fuck in a toilet above the clouds,' she replied. 'Isn't that enough?'

When they were dressing he whispered, 'It's going to look bad when we go out. Very disorderly, you know.'

'Yes, good,' she said.

Don was not at Heathrow. She came out alone from the customs channel and looked urgently about for him, keen to rebuild the old status quo. Lyndon and some of the others caught her up. 'So, when do I see you?' he asked.

'I'll be in touch,' she replied.

9

Donald McWater must have failed to persuade her. Harpur
waited for a visit from Naomi to say she was pulling out. He
would act hurt and feel happy. Iles, when he heard, would
not even act hurt. But Naomi did not show. So, what the
fuck was wrong with McWater? Couldn't he convince her
the project was mad, suicidal? Supposed to be executive
material, yet not up to a simple bit of man/woman management? Didn't he care enough to browbeat her into safety, if
that was the only way? Didn't he know that Harpur himself
could never try to frighten her off? A senior police officer
did not get between a volunteer and a job, no matter how
doomed the job might be. Yes, McWater would realize this.
Hadn't he stressed that only he could look after Naomi? So,
why hadn't he, didn't he? Had he given up? Feeble jerk. But
Naomi was a tough one. Harpur would not have picked her
otherwise.

He had to assume now that after her holiday she travelled
straight to Hilston Manor for what was known officially as
the 'Familiarization Module'. Those had been Naomi's
orders. She was not to return to her flat. Before she left for
Spain Harpur had given her road directions to the Manor to
be memorized, plus a credit card in the name of her new
identity, Angela Rivers. Whoever thought up 'Familiarization
Module' as title had genius. It was the reverse of what went

on. Officers were in fact *de*familiarized – defamiliarized from their own personality and given another. In a way, Naomi and Harpur had spoken the truth when they told McWater she was going on a course. But it was not the long Special Branch training. At Hilston she would receive two weeks learning undercover drills and get used to shelving her standard self. A fortnight was as much as it took. Undercover work had to be almost all natural instinct, natural caginess, natural tenacity, natural inventiveness.

Harpur telephoned the Manor now to check that Rivers had booked in. They were not too forthcoming with information: said they might ring him back if it was 'appropriate'. That is, they would check whether he was who he said he was. After half an hour they did call and confirmed they had a guest named A. Rivers. 'I'll be coming there myself,' Harpur said. They liked to see the operative and Controller together for a couple of days of the course. The Manor's psychology wizards reckoned they could judge how two personalities might work paired in the special stresses of undercover work. Possibly. Astrologers did the same sort of forecasts from zodiac birth signs, and might be just as accurate, or wrong. The whole Hilston Manor programme was new – post Raymond Street, and perhaps *because* of Raymond Street. Before Street, those going undercover were required to think themselves into a new personality more or less overnight, dress themselves into a new personality, maybe coiffure themselves into a new personality, perhaps slouch, limp, grin, frown, pad or drool themselves into a new personality. Elementary, but sometimes it had worked. Harpur wondered whether Hilston Manor would do better than sometimes. 'Yes, I'm due the day after tomorrow,' he said. 'One of your mid-week breaks.'

There was no response to this, though the receiver at the other end had not been replaced.

'Is Rivers all right?' he asked. 'Moduling with panache?'

And then the receiver at the other end *was* put down. They were entitled to their games. People working at Hilston probably read a lot of John le Carré. As Harpur was replacing the receiver himself, he heard a very tentative knock at his door and, when he called 'Come in', Lane entered shoeless and in shirt sleeves, his trousers tied up with what looked like tasselled pyjama cord. Lane loathed military smartness, and never approached it, especially when in uniform. 'We are civilians, only civilians, always civilians, not Sandhurst and the Guards,' he would intone. His careful scruffiness was answer to those who demanded chief constables should be ex-army officers, as under the old system.

Today, Lane's untidy face radiated almost a gleam. Intensity and concern flashed from his brown eyes – friendly eyes Iles had once described as 'fatally humane, culpably humane'.

'Ah, Colin,' he said. 'Good. I wanted to catch you alone.' He sat down in Harpur's armchair and crouched forward as if eager to confide, and eager for attention. 'I was wondering about your daughters. And my wife, she was wondering about them.'

Harpur had been wondering about them, also, but did not say so.

'This is of some delicacy, Colin. Please don't hesitate to close the conversation if you feel one is, well . . . infringing.'

'Unlikely, sir.'

'Kind. We wondered – we both wondered independently of each other, and then were astonished to find we shared the same anxieties . . . well, independently, we both wondered, Sally and I, about the wisdom of leaving your daughters in the house alone when you are away at Hilston Manor. I take it our girl is installed there now and this, will, of course, entail a compatability session for you. I know it's only a couple of days but . . . Oh, look, I'm sure your daughters are entirely capable, but . . . well, they *are* still quite young, Colin!'

Harpur said: 'Yes, I've been wondering what—'

'Iles,' the Chief said. He sat back in the chair now, the guts of his message out.

Yes, Harpur had thought about Iles but said: 'The ACC, sir? I'm not sure I—'

'Obviously Desmond is going to know exactly when you're away from home. It's his role to know. Ordinary police work might occasionally keep you away from home overnight, certainly, but this is different – this is something strictly timetabled by the Manor, and the Assistant Chief would be privy to that timetable. We both found we were wondering – this was quite separate from each other believe me . . . as I say, independently entirely – Sally and I found we were wondering whether it was wise to leave young girls in the house alone in those circumstances, Colin. Desmond is a fine, loyal officer, but . . . You see, he would have a totally valid reason for calling on them while you were away, as if to make sure they are all right. Represented as welfare. As I've said – delicate, but Sally has noticed in company once or twice that the ACC is certainly . . . well, is certainly *aware* of your older daughter. This is Hazel, isn't it – a lovely child, but a child, Colin.' Lane's words began to race. 'I know that Desmond is married and is a father of a daughter himself and in some senses devoted, I would never deny it. But one does wonder about . . . well . . . some aspects of that marriage – I mean, even on the basis of what he says himself, Colin – one does wonder, and the ACC does have this . . . I have to mention it . . . this leaning towards rather young girls. I believe that's true.'

'Did, possibly. But, as you say, sir, Mr Iles himself is now—'

'We wondered whether it might be wise if your daughters came to live with us for the duration of your absence, Colin.'

'It's very kind, sir, but I don't really think Mr Iles would ever—'

'Desmond, as you know, is one of those people whose presence in a police force . . . in *any* police force or, come to that, yes, in any organization concerned with administering the law – whose choice of a career in a police force is not altogether easy to explain. There is to him what I don't think it's unfair to call an unbridled element, even anarchic. Tarts, of course. Some ethnic, most very young. Backs of cars, upright in shop doorways, probably, building sites. With protection?'

'I'd thought of asking a friend of mine to stay with the girls,' Harpur replied.

Lane raised a finger. 'Ah. So you had yourself seen possible danger from Iles?' He sounded triumphant for a second. Then he became grave again: 'This friend? A woman? The student girl?'

'Yes.'

Lane wagged his head sadly. 'A young, pretty student girl. Do you think that's sensible, Colin, if Desmond is calling there? This dastardly energy.'

Harpur had wondered about that, too. 'This friend has—'

The door was pushed open, no knocking, and Iles entered.

'Sorry,' he remarked, 'sir, Col. I'd no idea you were here, Chief. Please go on, Harpur. You were saying, Col. *This friend*. Which is that, Col? The multi-talented undergrad?' Beaming, Iles turned to the Chief. 'Have you ever caught a view of this one, sir? She's a girl with, apparently, quite a brain and yet an untiring devotion to Harpur. She *is* untiring, isn't she, Col? Wonderful cheekbones and general uninhibitedness. I'm not sure whether that's your taste, sir, uninhibitedness, but that is what she has, isn't it, Harpur?'

'Naomi Anstruther is in place at the Manor,' Harpur said.

'I looked in on Colin for an update,' Lane said. 'I do want to keep a close personal contact with this project, Desmond.'

'Does Naomi get gun training?' Iles replied.

Lane made a small, pitiable cry, like an animal mildly hurt but fearing worse. 'Guns? Why would she need a gun, Desmond?'

'Hilston has a firing range?' Iles asked. 'Armaments people?'

Lane said: 'But no, Desmond. I certainly would not have thought so. Hilston surely focuses on psychological aspects, not street combat.'

'I don't mind a bit of psychology,' Iles said. 'Many would bear me out on that. Can *we* give her gun training, Col?'

'How could we train her, even if it were necessary?' Lane asked. 'This girl is surely now in quarantine as far as we are concerned. That is the set process. She must have no contact with us, except by the given undercover methods. We certainly cannot have her on our range. But, guns, guns?' The little chorus fluttered weakly in the air like a sick moth. 'No need, surely.'

Iles had remained standing just inside the room. He stared at Lane for a while and then at Harpur, as though debating whether this kind of audience was worth further notice. He had on a fine lightweight navy-blue suit, the jacket broad cut despite his lean frame, and wore a silver tie decorated with lines of small, mauve shields, probably signifying some decent London club. Seeing Iles in civilian clothes, few would take him for a police officer: perhaps an inspired chiropodist to the well off, or vice chancellor of a new university. He decided to stay and went to sit on the corner of Harpur's desk, nosing through some of the papers there while he spoke. 'I've names now for the people coming from London to join Lovely Mover's operation,' he said. 'Apparently these are quite considerable folk. They're accustomed to success, will look for success here. As you always suspected, sir, Lincoln W. Lincoln was sent ahead to prepare the way – like John the Baptist, I think you said. I prize wit.'

It was a blasphemy Lane would never have spoken. Iles liked to confer embarrassing statements on others, and especially on the Chief. In fact, Lane had never even said he thought Lincoln was only a forerunner. The Chief longed to discount any London threat, not inflate it.

'This is Tommy Mill-Kaper and Corporeal Digby – Digby Lighthorn,' Iles said.

Harpur had heard a little of both. The little was not heartening. They had always been a long way away, though, and he had not needed to know more. Perhaps Iles was right and things would change now. The ACC could be good with information, had talented contacts in other forces, including the Met. Or he might be manufacturing the threat, to frighten Lane and force him to abandon undercover, even so late, because of the supposed extra threat to Naomi.

'From whom, Desmond?' Lane asked.

'What, sir?'

'From whom do these names come?'

'Lincoln W. Lincoln has been prepared to work quite modestly until now,' Iles replied, 'dealership scraps, hardly more than that. Oh, perhaps someone taken out of the scene here and there, but not major, not really disturbing. But with Mill-Kaper and Corporeal present – why I say get our girl some gun training.'

'It's crucial we know the status of all information about these two people, Desmond,' the Chief cried fiercely gripping the arms of his chair.

Iles said: 'We are confronted by a basic irony, aren't we, Harpur?'

'Mill-Kaper's the grandson of someone very distinguished, isn't he?' Harpur replied.

Iles said: 'The more effectively Anstruther gets herself absorbed by Manse Shale's team, the more likely she is to become caught up in street battles for territory once these two laddies and their back-up arrive. I'd like to know she has some defence.'

Lane took a while to think about this. Then, sounding almost harsh, he said: 'But this is alarmist hypothesis upon alarmist hypothesis, Desmond. We have moved from the possible arrival of these Londoners to street gun battles and thence to peril for Naomi Anstruther.'

Iles had been swinging a foot gently in its soft black leather slip-on. Now, he stopped this, perhaps to signal awe: 'There is always an eloquence and pith about the way you analyse a situation which I concede is very hard to resist, sir,' he replied. 'It's a damn long time since I heard the word "thence" used at all, let alone so devastatingly. And yet . . .' Iles gave a superbly modest shrug inside the wide jacket and lowered his head slightly, as though troubled by his own doggedness. 'You'll forgive me, Chief, but my anxieties about likely street carnage will not leave me alone, despite your elegant scepticism.'

Lane said: 'Even if we gave her arms training, how could she carry a gun? Suppose it were found by Shale or one of his people. Where is her cover identity then?'

'Her cover identity would be fine, absolutely fucking fine,'

Iles replied. 'Once the London group get their storm troopers on the streets, every dealer will carry something, and every dealer will be ready to use it. If he/she isn't, he/she will have no fucking identity at all, sir, except chiselled on a headstone.'

'*All* dealers?' Lane cried. 'Guns? My God, Desmond – a wholesale proliferation of weapons? Do you accept this forecast, Colin?'

Iles said: 'Harpur's not really in a—'

'Do you accept this forecast, Colin?' Lane asked.

Iles said: 'I don't mean Anstruther should be brought up to marksman level. No time. But she needs to know how to point something and how to squeeze not pull.'

'Have you heard anything of the arrival of these two – this Corporeal and the other one, Colin?' Lane asked.

'I hate the notion of their parading your domain, sir, in their disgusting vicuna garments,' Iles replied. 'Cecil Rhodesing as they disgracefully call it in the firms.'

'What does that mean?' Lane asked.

'Colonizing,' Iles said.

'Never.' Lane stood. Perhaps he felt he should be on his feet to combat Iles. 'I certainly do not dismiss your appraisal of Anstruther's situation, Desmond. Incidentally, didn't we have a gospel preacher called Anstruther involved in a case once? Related?' The Chief loved to seem encyclopedic on detail. It was harmless.

Iles said: 'Possible. Not probable. The Revd Bart Anstruther was black the last time I heard. That sort of thing tends to run through families.'

'No, indeed, one feels by no means dismissive of your appraisal, Desmond,' the Chief replied. 'Yet I don't believe we should change our intentions for Naomi Anstruther at this stage – and I, of course, stress "at this stage" – this is an operation to be kept under continuous review – but no need for change, as I see it, at this stage, nor for what I would consider a rather rushed attempt to give her arms training. I will definitely bear in mind your forecast that gun use in our streets might increase, Desmond, but I consider it would be hasty to anticipate that as a certainty. I do appreciate we must cater for the possible worst. I think, though, I would prefer to act on things as they now are, rather than as they might be, and I would like you, Colin, to tell Naomi Anstruther of my admiration of her dedication and assure her that all possible safeguards will be in force to protect her.'

'This will buttress Anstruther, sir,' Iles said. 'The white one. Might I suggest, Chief, that she would be even more bucked if you could couple your wife's name with the message of admiration and reassurance.'

Lane waved a hand slightly behind him, as though feeling for the chair, in case he wanted to retreat into it. 'I don't believe that is possible, Desmond. My wife cannot be told anything of this kind of work, so could hardly offer congratulations to Anstruther for taking it on.'

'Oh,' Iles replied.

'Absolutely not,' the Chief said.

'These details of security precautions slip from my mind sometimes, I'm afraid,' the ACC said. 'Do pardon me, sir.'

Lane nodded very briskly. 'That's all right, Desmond. I

would have no objection to Harpur giving Anstruther a general message of goodwill from my wife, making it clear that this is a message Sally directs to all members of the force.'

'As one of those members, thank her for me, sir, do. Harpur, I hope you've got that. You may give Anstruther Mrs Lane's best regards, but while making clear that it cannot be a specific greeting for security reasons but encompasses all, you included.'

Lane left then, shuffling out with slow, unsmart dignity.

'What did the sly wreck want with you, Harpur?' the ACC asked.

'Companionship.'

Iles said: 'With travel, I make it you'll be away three days, two nights.'

'The Chief and his wife would like my daughters to stay with them.'

'Oh? Did he mention my name?'

'I'll be interested in the psychological profile Hilston produces for me, sir,' Harpur replied.

'Now, don't let it demoralize you permanently, Col, if they're pedantically accurate about your intellect and drive. You've got other passable things going for you, though not that fucking suit.'

10

At Hilston Manor, Naomi quickly picked up a ripe odour of bullshit and thought: *Ditch this bloody undercover assignment now. Get out. Get out.*

The Manor staff made the spy role sound a doddle, really worked at it. Christ, they had to *sell* the job. They could not find enough people to wear the risk. This place trawled for suckers.

According to the gurus Naomi here could not be more suited to the work. Rockmain, their main man, said he'd never come across anyone with such brilliant 'liberty of persona, excuse the trade talk'. As far as she could make out, that meant she had no character of her own at all, but could become whatever she felt like. Rockmain, this fair-haired kinky magician, aimed to flatter into final commitment anyone who showed a fragment of interest: interest, not talent.

Yes, final commitment, possibly – damn final. As to talent, they thought they could kid you into believing you had that. She wanted to get scarce. She would not let Rockmain con her. From the beginning at Hilston she had found him disturbing – over-rehearsed, over-pleased, deep into phoney confession.

First session

'I'm here to find out about you, Naomi, or Angela as we must call you now, and it would be absurd to pretend my role is other than that. But I feel you are entitled at the outset, as quid pro quo, to know something about *me*. These meetings depend on interchange, and there can be no equality of interchange if only one of us is making revelations.'

This would be his little set-piece, decently phrased and delivered in a mild, ardently modest style, manufactured to disarm. He needed to disarm. His role was creepy. And he had his own personal creepiness, inbuilt, undisguisable by the humility act.

'Who am I, then? Some question for a psychologist! My first name is Andrew, the rest you know! I am thirty-six years old, mainly of the heterosexual persuasion, at present single and unpartnered. I am a police officer, with the nominal rank and actual salary of a Commander in the Metropolitan force. I joined the service in the normal way and was then selected for accelerated promotion. After eight years, and in the rank of Detective Chief Inspector, I took a career break and did a psychology degree at Cambridge. I was awarded a starred First of course and considered an academic career. Then the Home Office asked me to return to police work, but in the particular role that you see now. I found it attractive because of its challenge and its usefulness – the fact that it was psychology, but *applied* psychology.'

Without any change of tone Rockmain suddenly said then: 'I've looked at some of the brilliant written test answers you did here this morning and yesterday and my impression, Angela, is that you might actually resent feeling confined in orderly fashion to one particular let's for the moment call it *self*, shall we?'

'I fucked a lad in an aircraft toilet because someone said I reeked of orderliness.'

'How?'

'How what?'

'The position.'

'You being dirty-curious, Rockmain?'

'Oh, yes, yes, indeed. I'm always dirty-curious. Sex detail – you can't beat it in this job. If, for instance, you were standing, this would certainly suggest urgency, but perhaps not absolute frenzy.'

'He sat on the toilet. I climbed aboard.'

'Was the toilet lid up or down?'

'Oh, God, you're not turning this into a thing about potty training as a babe, are you? My late protest against strictness?'

'Was the lid up or down?'

'Down, of course. He had to have something to support him.'

'All the same, I like it,' Rockmain said.

'You're not getting it.'

'You suggested it to him?'

'Certainly.'

Rockmain said: 'This *is* quite wild.'

'Yes, but I was conscious at the time it was quite wild.'

'It's best you were conscious it was quite wild. If it was

simply wild wildness, that might be the kind of personality you have, permanently: wildly wild. But this was a calculated wildness. This was you as something other than you.'

'What's that mean? I *needed* to be other, for Christ's sake. A girl had deduced I was cop.'

'Of course you needed to be other,' Rockmain replied. 'Still need. Why you're here. Why you were picked.'

'Look, I'm not schizoid, am I – always in terrified flight from my True Self?'

'Ah, you've read *The Potted Home Guide To Psychiatry*, have you? I don't object.'

'Sweet.'

'No, not schizoid. You don't feel alienated from your body, do you?'

'I didn't want to be locked in.'

'In the toilet?'

'No. I *did* want to be locked in the toilet with him, obviously. Yes, obviously: I didn't care who knew about it. But I didn't want to be locked inside a police identity.'

'You crave freedom from your self. It's natural. Such an impulse is crucial for undercover work.'

*

Second session

Rockmain said: 'Anstruther. Anstruther. Tell me what that name *means* to you.'

'Means?'

'What do you see, feel, hear when the name is spoken?'

'Do I feel it's forever me?' Naomi replied.

'Well, plainly not. You're Rivers now, aren't you?' Rockmain said.

'Do I still feel Anstruther is my identity? That what you're asking?'

'Identity is a term we don't much care for,' Rockmain offered.

'Who?'

'Oh, you know, my profession. That's my *psychologist* profession, of course, not my police profession. Police believe in identity, for sure. They bring relatives to morgues to establish identity. But "identity" suggests a precision that many psychologists don't consider helpful. There's a term coined by Allport – the "proprium". Heard of that? Don't be scared of the jargon. It's what he calls "the self-as-known". The "me" bit. Better? Or Kierkegaard's lovely limpid stuff about an individual being "constantly in process of becoming". Then there's dear old Jung, wanting nothing that is "eternally fixed" or "hopelessly petrified" in someone's nature. I think these views will please you, chime with your own feelings.'

'But you gave me *your* identity – clever, hetero, thirty-six, name of Andy.'

'I gave you something. Is it really who I am?'

She said: 'If I think of the name Anstruther, I see a black gospel preacher.'

Rockmain did some jolly work with his yellowish eyebrows. 'Well, here's a surprise. Are you sure?'

They used a big, bare white-walled room for these conversations and sat opposite each other on a pair of beige, low-backed sofas. It was like the president of a company's office, the décor kept simple and the furniture comfortable and minimal, so nothing should distract from quality brain work.

Naomi said: 'One day I saw billboards announcing special services to be given by the Reverend Bartholomew Anstruther near where I lived. They intrigued me.'

'And you went?'

'I found I wanted to see this other Anstruther.'

'Ah, so suddenly the reassuring exactitudes in "Anstruther" were shaken?'

'Bart Anstruther was wonderfully warm and vibrant as a preacher.'

'Did he preach instant conversion – complete upheaval of the personality?' Rockmain asked. The possibility seemed to thrill him.

'First time I went he talked about Saul becoming Paul.'

'Yes, absolutely yes! All in a moment, on the road to Damascus,' Rockmain said. 'And you – you were converted? Yes, it's like what we want. The "me" can change.'

'I admired him.'

'You were converted?'

'I came out of that Gospel Hall different.'

'You had counselling after the meeting, and then a new life? Brilliant. I'm not surprised. It's so . . . it's so *you*.'

'What's so me?'

'It's so you to be capable of instantly becoming somebody else. You're brilliant.'

'It didn't last,' Naomi replied.

'Of course not. Nothing lasts. Nobody lasts. The best undercover people prove that mobility.'

*

Naomi hated the look of Hilston, outside and in. So stately, so clean, so wrong for its smartarse trickery. There seemed to be four or five other officers getting 'familiarization', but the habit of secrecy had already fallen on Naomi and the others, and they did not mix much. In fact, socializing was discouraged. They never came together as a class. They were not a class. The work was for solitaries and group dynamics irrelevant. Hilston ran on one-to-one sessions, like the tutorials Rockmain would have had at Cambridge, if he ever went there. Meals were good. You ordered them by internal telephone from a menu. Civilian waitresses brought the food to one's room. There was no bar, no library, no reading room, no TV lounge, though she had television and radio in her bedroom. Naomi watched *The Manchurian Candidate* on the Movie Channel, a film about the takeover of war prisoners' minds, and wondered whether those who ran Hilston Manor should have somehow blocked it from the guest quarters.

Third session

Rockmain said: 'So you backslide eventually after the episode with the Reverend Bart. You had changed and then you changed back. When that happened, didn't you need some other means of dodging out from the life-script dungeon? Drugs?'

'No. People say I look as if I once had a habit, I know. I see why. Sometimes my face appears sort of out of focus. But no.'

'No nice trips where you could become someone else, amend the self for a while?'

'No.'

'Look,' Rockmain said confidentially, 'since you were obviously able to get past them at selection for the service, I'm not going to broadcast you once had a habit, am I? It might be super-useful undercover.'

She stared at him for a while. Then she said, 'Yes, I did a bit.'

'What?'

'Crack. Ketamine.'

'Ah, yes, Special K. That would bring hallucinations for you, thorough displacement of the self. Grand. You could shuffle off the inconvenient tedious N. Anstruther for a while, could you?'

'For a while.'

'Like conversion.'

'More expensive.'

'That why you stopped?' he asked.

'I'll still do a bit of grass.'

'Doesn't everyone? But nothing seriously trippy now?'

'I'd be a fool,' she said.

'There speaks that True Self you mentioned.'

'It doesn't exist, does it?'

'I'm not sure. Sorry, but I'm not,' Rockmain replied.

11

Rockmain said: 'I think she wants out.'

Harpur felt delighted and hurt.

'She believes she's being soft-soaped into peril,' Rockmain said. 'One can read these things.'

'There's peril all right. I don't know about the rest,' Harpur replied. This huge bare, pretentious room was a giggle: just a couple of sofas in it, as though only a few very select folk would ever get to sit here. Well, he was one of the very select today. But so was Rockmain, and that hit shit out of the whole idea.

'Pity if she does quit. You might have been OK as a teaming.'

'Not better than that?'

Rockmain stroked his elegant little face a couple of fond times. 'Your force sent on your previous psychometric test results and, of course, I have this morning's.' He did a brisk evasive laugh. 'Oh, I'm sure you're sceptical about psyche measuring. Best means we have, though. Anyway, yours are . . . sort of middling – beta/alpha. There are doubts. None about her. Only you. Age is a bugger. We build tendencies, deficiencies.'

'So, she's *not* being soft-soaped?'

Rockmain stood and took a few paces on the dark-blue fitted carpet, a shoe-flashing aid to emphasis. He was a mind man, but he clearly liked garb, too. His denim toned, and Harpur thought of a small, neat, blue-sailed boat at sea on a good day. Rockmain cried out, confidingly: 'She's uniquely suitable. I've told her. But she distrusts me – finds me false and manipulative, which, inevitably, I am. Qualities basic to the job.' He intoned the frankness. Harpur got himself further on guard against this bright-eyed conjuror. He felt proud Naomi had rumbled Rockmain, yet absurdly sad she might discard Harpur's recommendation of her. 'I am capable of speaking the truth, though, when appropriate,' Rockmain went on. 'At present, she can't see that. Anstruther/Rivers has admirable scepticism herself – is a fine, disbelieving ordinary cop, as well as a potentially supreme undercover cop. If it was you who found her, you've done well. And yet when I look at these tests – yours – oh, I do get an uneasiness. I wonder if you can be wholly committed to using her. I wonder whether you're wholly committed to undercover operations as such. Am I adrift? Or, tell me, do you have bad doubts? Why?'

'As you said – peril,' Harpur replied.

'Policing is a peril career, isn't it?'

'Standard policing works by getting more trained personnel to the spot than the enemy. Undercover's the opposite.'

'Well, the enemy? I don't think we have enemies, do we? We're not the army or a political party.'

'Yes, we have enemies,' Harpur replied.

'I'm not going to note that,' Rockmain said. 'I'd prefer you thought about it privately.'

'I *have*, often, and will. Enemies.'

Rockmain did impassivity with his reputable features. 'I've read about Raymond Street, naturally.' He was able to bring some proper solemnity, even grief, into the words.

'I picked badly,' Harpur said.

'And you fear with Anstruther you might have done the same again despite what I—?'

'Ray Street's a shadow on me.'

Rockmain said: 'Perhaps a degree of serfdom to the past in you? The tests do hint at that. Small c conservatism? Why you're stuck at DCS?'

Harpur thought he might stand, lean across and take hold of this flimsy denim poem by his flimsy neck. 'Have you ever killed a colleague, *Commander*?' he replied, still seated.

Rockmain chortled. 'How justified you are to lampoon rank in this setting! What does a house as historic and lovely as this care about our distinctions? But, yes, you *are* crucified to a degree by the past.'

'Have you ever killed a colleague, you fucking backroom bit of grey matter?' Harpur replied.

Rockmain made a note now on his wrist in green Biro. 'I don't think so, Chief Superintendent. Killed? Such a term! I don't think I've ever killed *anybody*. I might have been incompetent here or there and someone might have died violently because of it. That's regrettable but not blame-worthy. And it's the same for you. You didn't kill Street. Perhaps you were at fault in selecting him or made errors in running him as an operative. As I recall it, he was killed by a couple of known villains. You dramatize the past, sentimentalize it. Things have moved on since Street. It's what I mean about cherishing previous error, Harpur.' This lad had Iles's lovely flair for using your name as an insult. 'These days, we can lower the likelihood of disaster. Although I certainly would never say we can eliminate tragedy, improvements have undoubtedly taken place. There's the Manor now.' He spread his arms to proclaim Hilston's skills and scope.

'And there's you,' Harpur said.

'There is applied psychology, yes.'

'The job is still a matter of hoping nobody recognizes you from your previous cop existence – and of hoping you won't get spotted and greeted by a former neighbour while you're supplying in the street – and of hoping you can get away with taking just enough stuff to seem one of the outfit and not enough to make you do something or say something that proves you're not. Psychology and psychometrics might not help.'

Rockmain summoned more signs of sympathy. His eyes darkened with care. 'Ah, the tests are right, you *do* obsessively fret. You wonder – and have wondered and wondered, in your conscientious, numbing way – whether you should have pulled Street out. And now, if Angela Rivers went into a firm, you might pull her out *too* soon. That's what I mean when I say your tests provoke some questions. Unadaptability-stroke-panic. It's why I'm only partly happy about the likely quality of your teaming.'

'It doesn't matter, does it, if she's going to withdraw?'

Rockmain turned and stood square on to Harpur, a teaching position: 'As a Detective Chief Super you worry about the safety of subordinates. Admirable – in some ways. You hesitate to put them into what we've called peril, a peril which exists, undoubtedly, but which is also an indulged and dramatized item from the past. An only partly relevant item. Then, as a subordinate yourself, you have to accept the intructions of a superior who has a different view of leadership. He insists that a set task – destruction of a drugs gang – must be accomplished, and by the means he has chosen. It is what policing is for, as he sees it, and he is right. You suffer role conflict. It results in almost crippling ambiguity, and a bewildered indecisiveness.'

'My Chief's sanity could depend on this project going ahead. I have to look after him.'

Rockmain sat down again, tidily, opposite. His denim rustled faintly, like a mobile. 'I can bring Anstruther back to enthusiasm for the job. Turn her definitively into Rivers.' He glanced at something written on his small palm. 'I've changed her timetable slightly. The Wildcountry Survival Exercise doesn't usually come until towards the end of the stay here. I've advanced it for Rivers so that she's away today and half tomorrow. It seemed best you shouldn't meet her around the building.'

Harpur said: 'Wildcountry survival seems so right before infiltrating a city drugs firm. They'll want to test how she clay-bakes a hedgehog.'

'Self-reliance is self-reliance. You're obstructive, Harpur, *de*structive, Harpur. That shadow from the past moves with you. You radiate enslavement. I cannot have these hampering her steps back to clarity.' His voice rasped.

'Clarity meaning she can't see the risks?' Harpur asked.

'Clarity meaning she can see the risks and can also see how to handle them in the cause of commitment. Clarity means intelligent, watchful resolve. Sadly, it's impossible for me to isolate her altogether from your regressive influence. The programme here stipulates a joint session. That will be tomorrow evening. I would find it unforgivable if you said anything to reinforce her doubts at that time. And I'm sure your Chief would also find it unforgivable, and shattering to his mental balance, if it were reported that you had sabotaged his project.'

'And, of course, it *would* be reported,' Harpur replied.

*

In the evening, Harpur telephoned home. Jill answered. 'Seen anyone?' he asked.

'Denise looked in twice and helped with homework. She's better than you at French. Not so good with Religious Knowledge.'

'Few are.'

'Mr Iles was here last evening.'

'Oh?'

'To see how we were. Just friendly and nice,' she said.

'To whom?

'Both of us,' she replied.

'What time did he go?'

'Not late,' she said. 'Honestly.'

'Are you sure he left?'

'What do you mean?'

'Are you sure he left?'

'We went to bed at the same time.'

'Who?' Harpur asked.

'Who do you think? Hazel and me.'

'*Whom*. Hazel and *I*. Did you?'

'I know he wasn't still around,' she said.

'Yes?'

'Of course. How is it with you, Dad?'

'I miss the two of you.'

'Don't worry. We're really fine.'

'Yes?' Harpur replied.

12

Ralph Ember had a summons down to see his bulk supplier at The Wharf. As usual, the phone call came early in the morning and meant, Get here today. 'Some unpleasant indications your end, Ralph,' Barney said.

Often this jaunty sod talked as if he knew the region better than Ember. 'Oh?' Ralph remarked.

'Oh, yes,' Barney replied.

'I can assure you things are in hand. The arrangement with Manse Shale goes swimmingly.'

'Any bad factors reach you they reach me, too,' Barney replied.

The bugger's favourite song.

Ember said: 'If you could let me have an idea of what's bothering you, I might be able to give reassurances more fully.' For security, Barney always came through on the public booth line in The Monty, Ember's club. He knew Ralph would be there first thing cashing up from the night before. Mad: if the police or anyone else tapped the private phone they would tap the booth as well. But Ember accepted the procedure. And he accepted another which said he should not call Barney by name in these conversations, point no fingers. But Barney would call him Ralph, or sometimes Ralphy, the patronizing shit.

'Perhaps you could make it to us for luncheon,' Barney said.

'That's kind.' Oh, Christ, to eat food prepared by those two women of Barney's while sitting with those two women of Barney's.

'The least one can do, Ralph. You'll bring your new partner, naturally. Beau, I believe?' He spoke the name like a joke which, all right, it was. Take a look at Beau.

Always some insult came when dealing with Barney. The 'naturally'. *Bring your new partner* naturally. Barney would never acknowledge that Ember ran the firm more or less solo and any 'partner' was just a handyman with knobs on, no real dimensions or boardroom clout or investment status. What firm would want to show off Beau, for Christ's sake? What firm would want him in policy meetings with big out-siders? 'I'm not sure Beau is about,' Ember said.

'Yes, we're all greatly looking forward to meeting this new principal,' Barney replied. Probably he knew Ember would hate that word 'principal' for someone like Beau: it alleged parity. 'So vital to know a whole outfit, not just the founder, crucial though the founder certainly is in your case, Ralphy. Maud wants a word. She's on one of the extensions.'

Maud said: 'We hear a damn dangerous expansion of let's call it the London tendency in your area, Ralph.'

'There's some expansion, true. I don't feel it's at all dangerous. No point in getting alarmist.'

'Smug. Inert,' Maud replied. 'These are *London* people. They take business seriously and kill people who mess them about. Was there someone called Mace?'

Her voice came out of the receiver like a flick knife from its base. In the booth, Ember began to sweat, but a sort of half power sweat only, fairly private, nowhere near one of his full public panics. 'I hope we all take business seriously,' he replied. 'London? I don't roll over and shout "Surrender!" just because people come from London, I trust. It's a place, like this is a place.'

Maud said: 'No, it's not a place like this is a place. Camilla wishes to speak.'

'Ruthlessness, Ralph. Another dimension, another scale – this is these London folk. Phlegm – oh, one admires your phlegm, in the old sense, of course, of calmness of character. One has always said, and Maud will confirm this, I know, that phlegm in a man is a prime quality, one I would place above charm or an unflabby arse. Yet one has to wonder whether, in the matter of a London incursion, such phlegm is warranted.'

Maud said: 'Get here, Ember. Both.'

Barney said: 'Regard it as a refresher, Ralph, in your own case, at least, though obviously something different for Beau – an introduction.'

Barney was into boating and had a voice that could crackle like a storm or lilt like a shanty. Months ago when he first said his address was The Wharf Ember thought it must be a kind of working dock, like something near Valencia Esplanade. No: Barney lived in Hampshire west of Southampton and the Isle of Wight, a nice little river village with its own landing jetty where three or four yachts worth up to a million each and belonging to salty locals were generally moored, waiting for Cowes or the Caribbean. At least one of them would be Barney's when Barney was ashore. Barney had a boat called Modesty, which echoed his personality so nicely. The Wharf was the half dozen huge houses looking out on the river over their bright lawns – as Ember remembered it, two with croquet hoops, so fucking old-money, what!

At luncheon in what Barney called the Games Room he said: 'The word is two *formidablos* from the Everton Esta Osprey group up there in London will be transferred on indefinite secondment to your area, developing and consolidating whatever their early man, Lincoln W. Lincoln, has built. I hear the likelies are Thomas Mill-Kaper, the old Victoria Cross holder's grandson, and Digby Lighthorn – Corporeal, as they call him, he's so thin.'

Ember thought the meal not too foul after all. When it was something put together by Maud and Camilla you would expect bits of drab wool from their cardigans or whiskery ear wax to have dropped in, but this was quite a harmless veggie load served on plates he had definitely seen worse than in some spots.

Barney said: 'Mill-Kaper and Digby are major distribution experts, Ralph, each with a specialization, each with distinguished jail form. Well, you'll have heard of them, naturally. Digby takes the professions mainly – solicitors, media, doctors, pinball arcade directors, dentists, super-pimps, ballet folk, a few academics, major plumbers and roof insulators. Plus full county people and above, of course. So, it's mainly coke for moneyed nostrils, but some H and freebase. Mill-

Kaper is more street level and disco dumps, despite the hyphen. Did you hear of the grandfather? Memorable gallantry with Wingate, I think. Tommy's going a different route and will probably never even get an MBE. He's doing freebase, rocks and a lot of grass. This is an important career move for both of them, sort of ambassadorial role. They'll be eager to excel on your terrain and impress Everton and the Right Hon. through good trade and profitability.'

Beau said: 'Barney, we feel the Assistant Chief in our area will blot these invaders the minute they show.'

'Iles?' Barney asked.

'They'll mincemeat him,' Maud said. 'Or buy him.'

'Iles doesn't take,' Beau replied.

'Oh, my!' Maud said.

'What's that mean?' Beau replied.

'It means oh, my!' Maud said. 'Prick.'

This was why you did not bring someone like Beau to a meeting at such a level, unless forced. Gauche. He left himself open.

'That's a hasty judgement, perhaps,' Beau replied.

'How would you two sleepwalkers know what haste is?' Maud replied.

With Barney and these two women you had to edge along rather than shout your views straight off. Beau was not used to class. How could he be? Finesse Beau had never heard of, except if you had a safe to undo or accounts to be translated. Thank God he had ditched that brown leather jacket he used to wear, but there were still his teeth and the soup-kitchen face. His name was Derek and they called him Beau because of an actress, Bo Derek, but they changed the spelling to Beau, meaning beautiful. It was damned unkind. Ember said: 'As you know, I work in cooperation, and beautifully effective cooperation, with the firm run by Shale and together we certainly—'

'Fuck Shale,' Maud replied. 'What's Shale? We don't supply Shale. We supply you and Beau. Once you're wiped out where's our business quotient in your realm? If these London people get dominant, they're not going to buy from us either. They've got sources already. Be as casual as you like about your own bloody outfit, Ralph, but don't ever be casual with ours.'

'Dominant? Never,' Ember said.

'Precedents, Ralphy,' Camilla declared. 'We've seen this kind of situation – by which one means a mountingly trying situation, oh, *mountingly* unless stopped – we have seen this happen before in big provincial centres like yours. One thinks of Hull, Newcastle, Stoke, Huddersfield. Attrition, Ralph. Collapse, Ralph. Splendidly established local cocaine, hash and Ecstasy dealers – firms with venerable histories stretching back three, even five years – these firms worn down by conquerors from London, worn down and worn down until . . . until collapse. Some esteemed folk terribly injured, and not just limbs. Real central damage. And, yes, Ralph, several even dead. Intemperate – we live in an intemperate and unprincipled age. Even those who avoided the maiming or worse were forced to burglary or running girls or extortion to flesh out the dole.'

It always amazed Ember that neither of these two rough

chunks, Maud and Camilla, obviously ever had one sex thought about him between them. Hurtful. He was not used to indifference from women. There were times when he would have *liked* indifference from women. He thought now he had better put on a bit more tension and vigilance to satisfy these three edgy business folk: 'Naturally, I've been monitoring the Lincoln W. Lincoln enterprise since its very beginning. Opened a file.'

Beau said: 'Ralph's not one to allow a development of that sort to go unnoticed, yet, at the same time, is certainly not one, either, to tumble into, well . . . panic because some Londoner arrives.'

The dim bastard. Ember hated to hear that word, 'panic'.

'This girl they're going to put in,' Barney replied. 'The one at Hilston now, learning to be unseen and anonymous and safe: here's another aspect we're not happy about.'

Beau said: 'This also is very much on our agenda, Barney. This is one where we're taking a longish-term view, though.' He held out his plate to Camilla for more high fibre. At least Beau did know how to fit in as to food. And he was smart not to show shock at how much Barney knew.

Maud said: 'We heard you were taking it *so* lightly, Ralph, because they would be placing her in Shale's outfit, not yours. To which I say, so fucking what? You and Shale are linked like sweet brothers, as you said, and this girl will see right through both firms, no question. This is a girl with a bright little brain and bright little eyes. And when she sees through yours she sees as far as us here. Understand the ramifications? It's a triple threat you've got there, Ralphy.

You could get blasted by Mill-Kaper and Corporeal. Certainly will if you don't come out of the coma. Or the police could wipe you out on evidence from the girl. And then the last threat is the one that would hit *us* – police start working outwards from you to all your contacts, including your supplier. Barney won't countenance it, Ralphy. I won't countenance it, nor Camilla. This could be ashes. There's a quality of life to be preserved here and a dear man who's come up through the ranks, from street pusher to major importer.'

Barney was knife and forking some big friendly looking lump of pumpkin and had his head down waiting for the kill like a matador, but he sidelined the fork for a moment, glanced up and gave Maud a humble little smile of thanks for this description of his rise. He had a broad, small-nosed not too amiable face, a face where boredom, greed and fear jostled one another, boredom winning most of the time. He put his hand into the pocket of the garment he had on – some kind of kimono or sheikh gear in purple and green, and brought out a piece of paper. He began to read aloud: 'Naomi Anstruther, Detective Constable, two commendations, pre-assignment leave in Spain, tutored by Rockmain personally at Hilston, household boyfriend Donald McWater, possibly estranged at the moment.' He put the paper back and resumed eating. 'She's wavering but she'll do it. Of course she'll do it. This is *gloire*.'

'Obviously the kid has to be neutralized, I regret, Ralph,' Maud remarked.

Beau said: 'Mansel was of that view at first, I must admit, but once he heard Ralph's arguments for a more subtle—'

Camilla said: 'Difficulties, certainly. Death of a young woman – not exactly what Maud calls a kid, but what, twenty-six, twenty-eight? – death in execution circs, undoubtedly a hellishly trying prospect, Ralph, Beau, especially if Harpur is involved there in more than the Controller sense. He can bear a grudge. And yet perhaps removal of her is inescapable. One fears so. Oh, we're all affected somewhat by the famous and seminal Raymond Street incident. Again a young life. But no business firm can tolerate that kind of inner menace. It's part of the culture, surely, that a discovered fink has to be countered. Ralph, I know you're not one who would wish to run against standard folk wisdom. How do we survive if such attacks are not properly dealt with?'

Ember let Camilla have quite an intimate smile in reply but her face stayed stiff as a breadboard. These two ragged pieces, Maud and Camilla, saw him as a small-time business parasite, nothing more. Yet many women had told Ember about the Charlton Heston resemblance. Usually, they adored Ralph's jaw scar and some would finger it heatedly, as though seeking a short cut to his core and psyche. Not Maud and Camilla. If they'd had a tradesmen's entrance to the house they would have told him to use it, whereas really attractive women offered him entrance unconditionally. He did not think they were gay. Ember had always assumed they catered for Barney all round, not just cookery and nosing into the commerce. In fact, Ralph had decided recently that Barney might have some genuinely aristocratic blood, after all, because he put up with such lumpy old bed mates, like the upper classes.

'Shale spotted the full hazard, did he, Beau, Ralph?' Barney asked. 'Manse is a lad with flair, I've always said so.'

'There's a different way of looking at the matter, if I could point it out, Barney,' Beau replied.

'Oh, this is that mighty Iles again, is it?' Maud said.

Beau said: 'We think – and I know I carry Ralph with me on this – we think that Harpur and Iles will place her with Shale merely as preparation—

'To get her into Lincoln's outfit,' Maud said. 'Corporeal would sniff her out the minute she started dealing. Corporeal was shopped once by undercover himself. He's sensitive.'

'Perception, Ralph. Corporeal is famed for that,' Camilla said. 'In fact, those closest to him call him Perception rather than Corporeal. He's not keen on being dubbed Corporeal because of his physique, any more than, say, Ralph, you care for people referring so ill-advisedly to you as Panicking.'

They were eating from a trestle table that must have been put up especially for the meal. Ralph was between Camilla and Barney, which could have been worse. A dartboard hung at one end of the Games Room and a high-backed church pew stood against one wall. Never at any meeting with Maud and Camilla had either of them done the slightest fondle of his scar, nor even ferreted around under the table with a free hand for intimacies when they were seated in convenient placings, as he was with Camilla now. He was sure he had done nothing to cause such coldness. There was no other permanent furniture in the room, no games equipment other than the dartboard and no carpets. The floor was covered with battered cream linoleum that still had traces of a swirling brown and grey pattern more or less visible. Ember had been in the room on earlier visits. Always it made him think that Barney was bored with money. He had bought the house and the boat and probably a car or two, but then lost interest and could not be bothered to fit the place out properly or use the wealth to attract some decent young pussy, above all young. Ember had come across such apathy among the rich before. It seemed tragic. And yet Barney obviously worried about what he had, or why all this agitation to do with the London boys and Anstruther? Barney he could not really sort out.

'So we're sceptical about the long-term aspect, Ralph,' he said. 'We think she has to be taken out early and discarded efficiently. Now, I gather from what Beau mentioned that we are in accord with Mansel Shale on this, and possibly with Ivis, too. I feel this is conclusive.'

Camilla went out and came back with some big yogurt job on a lopsided serving trolley. There were side dishes of celery and raw rhubarb. 'Ah,' Beau cried, 'no wonder Barney looks so wholesome – meals like this day in day out.'

'You've got pressure, Ralphy, I can see it,' Barney said.

Yes, there was that: pressure from these three, pressure from Shale, and this novice undercover girl with him in the middle of it.

Beau said: 'Ralph lives with pressure. It's his habitat, you could say.' He got down to the yogurt, clutching at his spoon with those big, gnarled fingers. Beau lived with a nice broad-faced woman called Melanie. Ember wondered sometimes why she stayed with Beau. Although getting on, she kept some loveliness. She would definitely be worth an approach soon – very soon, while she still had it all in place more or less.

13

Fourth session

Rockmain said, sort of considerately: 'Observing you over these several days, looking at what you've written in the tests and taking into account the reports on you of others here, Naomi, I'd say you want to pull out.'

Oh, sod, here's another one – more than one – who thinks that he/they can read me, categorize me, contain me. He tells me there's no settled self, but then reckons to find mine. A deferential smile sat square on Rockmain's goldfish face. It made him look steely, a steely goldfish. Did people's psyches unfold for him the way a carcass did for a butcher? No matter how she'd been thinking until now, she must resist his cocky claim to see into her, and to tell her how her mind, brain and will functioned. 'That's rot,' she replied. Yes, she had wanted out, but never if he tried to direct her.

Rockmain put his head back and spoke confidingly to the high pale-blue ceiling, as she imagined one of his supposed Cambridge tutors might have sat relaxed, floating a spicy thought. 'It's a paradoxical situation we do run into at the Manor very occasionally with people who seem at first exceptionally suited to undercover work,' he said.

They were once more in the same large empty room, opposite each other on the sofas. He wore denim again, but different denim, just as stylish and expensive, yet more faded, more free-spirit-student, a tattier, stronger denial of his rank and power.

Rockmain said: 'We assess such candidates and tell them they have unmatched natural abilities for the role. But of course these abilities contain two elements – two elements which quite possibly fight each other. On one side, there's a flair for adapting to whatever the prevailing conditions might be where they'll work. No undercover detective could operate without that. Against this, though, is a capacity to view those conditions very coolly, as if by an outsider. No undercover detective could operate without this, either. After all, the planted detective *is* an outsider, though pretending not to be. As a result of this second factor – this cool detachment – some of our potentially best officers come to suspect they are being merely flattered when told they excel. You see, Naomi, they apply this cold, cold eye to *us*! They believe we want to dupe them into accepting what on the face of it at least is a very dangerous spell of duty.'

It enraged her to hear him interpret her so brilliantly, the prat, bracket her so justly with others. If he had looked different – more sexy, or sexy at all, or more solid, or solid at all – his astonishing sharpness might have disgusted her less. 'Not me,' she replied. 'I don't think you're duping me. You couldn't, ever. I know I'm good, know I'm right for it.'

'And because of their reaction they move from having been wonderfully suitable for undercover to entirely disqualified. Such a loss! But it's one we have to accept: they would go into the assignment with their confidence self-destroyed. No good to anyone. In the trade it's known as the Alain Pajot Syndrome, after a French psychologist who charted it all first. Probably you've heard.'

'Are you telling me I'm disqualified?' Naomi felt desolated to think she might be dropped by this stinkingly gifted sod. Christ, how had he picked up that she wanted to quit? *Had* wanted to. Not now. She must not get tearful in front of him.

Rockmain said: 'An attitude of distrust is, of course, crucial to an undercover operative – life and death to an undercover operative – but is to be exercised against the host gang where he/she is ultimately placed, not against those at Hilston whose only object is to diagnose and develop an officer's attributes.'

'Please,' she repeated, yelling almost, 'are you telling me I'm disqualified?' But she did not give him time to reply – rushed on. 'Now, don't, don't say that. I don't mistrust you, honestly. I know I can do the job, and do it better than anybody. My confidence is still here.'

'I don't make the decision on your suitability alone, you know, Naomi,' he said with fish gravity.

'Oh?'

He laughed. 'Of course not. Hilston looks at a spectrum of qualities and skills. Psychology is one section only – and there's more than one psychologist.'

'But you're senior.' She was aware of his eyes going over her quickly now and then, nothing to do with psyche. Perhaps his job brought him occasional successes, despite everything. Women did fall for their analysts, and he came close to being that. He would definitely need some advantaged starting point. At times, the fish resemblance faded and she could visualize him instead in a cage pecking away at one of those big lumps of stuff meant to sharpen beaks. 'You think I'm shit scared, don't you?' she asked.

' "Scared" isn't a term we'd use here, shit or otherwise.'

'What term *would* you use?'

'We'd talk of an awareness of risk, quite possibly an *intelligent* awareness of risk. There *is* risk, damn it. Are you shit scared?' He did not pause and said: 'I'm wondering if it's something between you and the boyfriend.'

'If *what's* something between me and the boyfriend?'

'The decision not to go on.'

'I told you, I haven't decided not to go on. The reverse. Haven't even thought about not going on,' she said.

'Yes, you told me that. He was – is – against?'

'Are you asking whether I want to return to what you called my True Self?' She boomed the jargon.

'That fixed, comfortable, knowable thing – not to be despised. An established co-habiting relationship. You hankered – hanker – for restoration of that value. You found that a quick casual shag with someone on a closed aircraft lav was no proper replacement?'

'It wasn't quick, not especially,' she replied. 'That was the point. People were kept waiting. It had to be disruptive and obvious. It wasn't casual. I'd already slept with him three times. He's nice. I might see him again.'

'Don't you want to get back to Donald, but know you can't if you go through with this?'

'No, I don't want to get back to him. No.'

Quietly, oozingly, he said: 'One "no" might be enough,

then. Are you surprised he finished with you – came home early from Spain as I understand it? Are you surprised and hurt he's made no effort to reach you since? Has he?'

'No, I'm not surprised and hurt. It was agreed.'

'Might you have expected him to be at Heathrow, for instance?'

'That wouldn't have made sense,' she said. 'We'd agreed it was over.'

'I wonder if—'

She twitched on the sofa, brought her feet down with a bang on the carpet. 'Stop fucking wondering or pretending to wonder, will you?' she screamed. 'I'm here because I want to do this job. I can do this job. I wouldn't let anything stop me doing this job. OK, *you* can stop me doing this job, I know. You, personally, could stop me, I see that. You don't need some committee of other experts to discuss and confirm.'

Rockmain said: 'Yes, I could stop you. I won't.'

14

Harpur was surprised and disappointed to get the invitation to a three-way meeting with Rockmain and Naomi Anstruther. He expected her to have withdrawn by now – hoped she had withdrawn, as promised. Rockmain must have worked something. Had he told her he thought she wanted to quit? That would antagonize Naomi, challenge her, make her fight back in denial. Rockmain said: 'What will you call Harpur during this operation?'

'Control,' she replied at once.

'Oh, you've already thought it out, have you?'

'Control,' she said.

'This is a very close relationship. I wondered if first names might be more natural,' Rockmain said.

'Control,' she replied.

He put on a mighty frown and held up his short denim arms in blue surrender, like the wings of a small bird, say a blue puffin. 'What will *you* call *her*, Harpur?'

'Is it important?' he asked.

'What will *you* call *her*, Harpur?' Rockmain replied.

'Angela.'

'Is that all right with you?' Rockmain asked.

'Can I stop him?' she replied.

'Do you want to?' Rockmain said.

'What is all this crap?' she said. 'Names? Are we back to

that? What's it matter? It won't be my real name, anyway, not my soul or self.' She was in a grey and red tracksuit and trainers. Harpur thought she looked miserably confused. He felt confused himself. Rockmain would be pleased, if he spotted it, and he probably would.

'Is there some sexual primness involved in avoiding Harpur's name?' Rockmain asked. 'Colin, isn't it? What's wrong with that? Naomi, are you trying to make distance between you – defining the degree of closeness allowable, professionalizing it, for fear it should develop into something else?'

She was sitting alongside Rockmain on one of the sofas. Harpur faced them. He tried to think of some way to warn her off this job even now, though not a way Rockmain would pick up. Difficult. Rockmain did pick up a lot. Even on a quick view of him you could see he might not be a total jerk. And when you really looked you observed genuine wiliness and maturity and resolve in the small jumpy face. 'How about you, Harpur – does it piss you off a bit that she should choose to arms-length you by use of the title only?'

'I *will* be her Controller,' Harpur said.

'Obviously it's important to know whether there are any sexual tremors in this kind of very sensitive relationship,' Rockmain replied. 'Tremors either incipient or actual.'

'None,' she said.

'None,' Harpur said.

'How did you choose her?' Rockmain asked.

'Her dossier. Her attitude,' Harpur said.

'Really?' Rockmain replied.

'What do *you* think?' she asked. 'Tits? Are you saying I haven't got the aptitude for this job and he picked me only as a fuck prospect?'

'Well, choosing is a complex thing, you know,' Rockmain replied. 'Harpur could be someone who shags around and on the look out.'

'Could he?'

'Do you shag around, Harpur?' Rockmain asked.

'Don't the personality tests tell you?' Harpur replied.

'Oh, tests,' Rockmain said. 'Neither here nor there. I smell sex between the two of you, either incipient or actual.'

'Maybe you bring it,' Harpur replied. 'Jealousy.'

Rockmain gave a little nod and did some thinking. 'Ah, transference, as we call it,' he said. 'Not impossible. I'll have to ponder. Look, are you already banging each other?'

'Don't the personality tests tell you?' she replied.

'Sex can be a bugger in undercover,' Rockmain said, 'using "bugger" loosely.'

'We're both in other relationships,' she said. 'Or, I *was*. He still is. How could there be anything sexual?'

'Look, are you already banging each other?' Rockmain replied. 'Not here. We'd know. But prior and continuing. When you say you'll call him Control, is that to fool me? Not primness at all – cleverness?'

'*How* would you know if we were doing anything here?' she asked. 'Are the rooms bugged? The rooms *are* bugged? Jesus, what sort of a place is this.'

'That sort of place, obviously,' Rockmain said. '"Control" – it seems the sort of term you'd run a mile from, Naomi.

You're looking for freedom from definition, from curtailment – from control.'

'It's the name of a fucking job, that's all,' she replied.

'Not a *fucking* job, Rivers,' Harpur said.

'Moot,' Rockmain said. 'There are going to be tense, intense, very secret, very inter-dependent meetings between you. These will have the kind of emotional charge more usually found in a love affair.'

'Have you been talking to Iles?' Harpur asked.

'Ah, Iles,' Rockmain said.

'What?' Harpur replied.

But Rockmain left it there. Did he? Rockmain said: 'Daughters – they're a problem. Now, this is a job that will bring you together, and a job that will arbitrarily separate you. Understand?'

'Understand what?' she asked. 'That there will only be certain set times when we can make contact? Naturally. It's how undercover works.'

'And between those times, what?' Rockmain asked. 'We're putting a pretty woman with, as you say, Naomi, tits, into an outfit of male villains – mostly male, at any rate. There are certain obvious hazards besides the actual life and death ones, aren't there? If a girl's Control is also her lover, he's going to be in a continuous sweat about what might be happening to her when she's out of reach – I mean sexually happening to her.'

'I think we got that,' she replied.

'Ah, *we*,' Rockmain said. 'So, there *is* rapport.'

'I meant any half wit would have got it, and Mr Harpur and I are both at least half wits.'

Rockmain said: 'A lover in continuous turmoil – does this make for an efficient operation? Will he be able to keep away, leave her to deal with things on her own? If he doesn't, where the hell is secrecy? The Controller nosing in, wanting to protect not just her life but her pussy.' His eyes shone. 'Likewise, a girl isolated in one of the firms is going to be wondering what her man is up to while she's unable to get to him.'

'None of this applies,' she answered.

'None of it,' Harpur said.

'Well, good.'

'It gives you a little dick buzz, does it, to think of her in sexual peril from heavies?' Harpur asked.

Rockmain thought about this, too. 'Yes, I suppose it does.'

'You started to sweat on your chin when you were talking about it, and the pile on your denim stood up, even though so old,' Harpur said.

'You want my job?' Rockmain asked. 'My chin's always been a damn give-away. Psychology hasn't done much on chins. Jung on chins might have been useful. Yes, I do think I'm into sex at one remove. Fantasy sex – much to be said for it. Done direct it's so enmeshing and intricate, isn't it?'

'Why make yourself look so damn irresistible in that gear if you're not after real women, then?' Harpur asked.

'That's a point.'

'Is it fair on them?'

'Right,' Rockmain said. He made a note on his wrist.

'Now, Harpur I want you to think for a moment that *you* are the officer going undercover and that Naomi is your Controller. And ditto for you, Naomi – you're Controller, he's the operative. It's what we call role play.'

'Is that right?' Harpur asked.

Rockmain said: 'What would you ask her, Harpur, if she was your Controller? I'd like to hear you put the question in proper form.'

Harpur did a girlish voice: 'Control, do you think there's a real chance of getting me into this outfit undetected and keeping me undetected?'

'Am I right to read here a question that invites the answer, No,' Rockmain said.

Yes, that was what Harpur hoped Naomi would read into it, anyway, and decide to bale out.

'It's that word *real* chance, isn't it?' Rockmain said. 'This would seem to imply there was only an *un*real chance. And then comes the apparent suggestion of mounting unlikelihoods: as if *getting me in undetected* might be just about possible but *keeping me undetected* went beyond rational hope.'

Naomi said: 'So much bloody analysis you fall over yourself. I don't hear the question like that. I hear a question expecting the answer, Yes. I hear optimism and positiveness in that "real chance".'

'So, as Controller, you would give that answer – Yes, there *is* a real chance?' Rockmain asked.

'Absolutely.'

'And, to turn the situation around: as Controller, what

would you like to ask the officer going undercover?' Rockmain replied.

Naomi tried to turn gruff: 'Angela, how could I have been
so lucky to find someone with your confidence and flair?'

15

Shale said: 'Me, I still feel we got to knock her over immediate and dispose if she comes trying to slide and slime her way into our firm. This is an entitlement. Fair's fair.'

'I do sympathize to some degree with your anxieties, Manse,' Ivis replied, 'but please don't take it badly if I remind you we have a binding agreement with Panicking about Anstruther.'

'Fuck Panicking.'

'We promised patience, the longer view.'

'And fuck binding and patience,' Shale replied. They were in the back of Shale's car, parked close to railway lines on the edge of the dockside, and finishing their tactics chat before going aboard a big floating restaurant moored nearby. There could be trouble here. Shale knew it from something Alfie had mentioned this afternoon, though Alfie did not seem to understand the seriousness. Well, that was just like him. Don't expect insights from Alfie. Don't expect him to see a situation.

It was just after midnight. They could hear music from the bar, some authentic jazz tripe, Shale thought. He hated how jazz took decent old songs and pissed about with them until they were something else, usually every note played six times while they decided which way to go next, known as improvisation. This boat had come as part of the marina

development, and Shale did not mind it too much. The tale
said it had once been a China clipper or fighting the Armada,
something like that, and they had tried to keep it looking
genuine deep sea. Although it was phoney as fuck, obviously, and would most likely sink if they undid the mooring
ropes, Shale liked the portholes and masts and navigation
lights, all that kind of carry on. These did give a dimension,
in his opinion. They were down here now to see Simon
Pilgrim who handled their dealing on the boat and was
making quite a go of it lately, even though you would never
have believed it, he looked such a complete elderflower with
his complexion and sad chestiness.

Denzil was behind the wheel, no chauffeur's cap on
tonight. He acted like he was not listening but he was listening. Although a glass partition had been fitted between
front and back in the Jaguar, Shale only rarely shut it. He'd
hate to seem high and mighty. 'Look at this,' Denzil said,
and pointed with his thumb, that rude way of his, he gloried
in it from ignorance.

Shale said: 'Christ, this is Pilgrim his self, isn't it? Why's
he leaving so early? He got hours to go.'

'He's scared,' Ivis replied. 'Look at his legs.'

'He's always scared,' Shale said. 'What about his legs?'

'Shaky.'

'They're always shaky, and so fucking short.'

'Really scared, Manse.'

'Flash the lights,' Shale told Denzil.

'What?' Denzil said.

'Just flash a couple of times,' Shale said. 'He'll run this way then. He'll know we're friends, a refuge.'

'How?' Denzil replied. 'We could be part of it. That distance, he can't recognize the car.'

'Flash the fucking lights will you,' Shale said. 'Part of what?'

'He's hunted,' Denzil said, but he did signal with the main beam, three long flashes.

Simon Pilgrim may have seen them, or may not. He did not run their way. Perhaps Denzil was right and Pilgrim noticed the lights but would not trust them. Pilgrim worked his stunted self hard and came stumbling down the gangplank, his arms flapping to keep him balanced, hair blowing all ways, no picture. He reached the quay and then turned and galloped in his comical style up towards the marina streets and Blake's Hotel, but Shale saw it was *not* comical.

'Follow him, Denzil,' he said.

Denzil said: 'We won't get there in time. I'll have to go around these rail lines and wagons, and we can't get into the marina from this end. They've got bollards there.'

'So, go round the rails. Get as close as you can. We'll move on foot from there. All of us.'

Denzil started the Jaguar but they did not shift yet. 'Here's the pursuit, anyway,' he said, pointing again, same movement.

Shale saw a man of about twenty-five in a khaki or beige jacket coming fast down the gangplank, sprinting with total ease, even grace. The jacket was beautiful and had grace, too. He kept one hand inside the jacket and was either giving

his heart a life massage or keeping his grip ready on a hol-
stered pistol. You would know this boy was London even if
you did not know him. Shale *did*. 'Jesus, it's Lovely Mover
– Lincoln W. Lincoln.'

'Is this what you expected, Manse?' Ivis said.

'Why we came,' Shale replied. He pulled the HK P9S
automatic from his jacket pocket. Ivis produced a Smith and
Wesson 669.

'I could run him down,' Denzil said. 'He's this side of the
rails.'

'Yes, run him down,' Ivis replied. 'Go for him. Forget Si
for a minute. He'll be fine.'

'The sod knows you could run him down,' Shale said.
Lincoln W. Lincoln had stopped on the quay and was looking
at the car. He turned suddenly and ran back towards the
gangplank, the same powerful lope, his jacket fluttering so
elegantly.

'We're all right, Manse. He's given up,' Ivis said.

Alfie – he never saw all the bits of the picture. Could you
expect it from someone who bought a fucking lighthouse to
live in with those kids of his? 'He don't care,' Shale said. 'As
long as he's got him off the boat. He's pushing Si towards
someone else, someone in one of the marina streets. Maybe
a car. It's schemed. Si will keep going. Fright-powered, you
can't beat it. Lincoln's job's done. Si's another one who's
crossed the Londoners, like Mace.'

'So, what do I do?' Denzil asked.

'Go after Pilgrim,' Shale said.

'Once we're around this bit of railway, he'll think we're trying to run *him* down and go faster,' Denzil said.

This bastard, always damned intelligent argument. 'Just move the thing, will you, Denzil?' Shale replied.

'Keep flashing,' Ivis said.

'On his back?'

'Keep flashing,' Shale said. 'Lean on the horn. If he turns he'll recognize the car.'

'He's not going to turn,' Denzil replied. 'And if he did, he's so scared he wouldn't see anything.'

Denzil did move the Jaguar after Si then, flashing the lights, sounding the horn and laughing that stupid way he had sometimes, shaking his shoulders like jelly on a plate, to make sure everyone knew the bugger was amused in his superior way. So why was he a fucking minder-chauffeur and ugly if he was so choice? They did a half circle behind some wagons to reach the crossing spot over the rails.

Shale said: 'Oh, God, that poor wreck Si. I should have come welfaring him a week ago, more.'

'Don't blame yourself, Manse. I couldn't inform you of developments until today. You came at once.'

'Maybe we should have known sooner.' He had heard only this afternoon, and even then did not cotton fast enough. Blame? He was chieftain, so he would take it like chieftains did, but Alfie had not really told it right. He had told him like casual, like it was just ordinary conversation. Just after lunch they had been taking a couple of gin and peps in Shale's place and Alfie said between some heavy sips, 'It looks as if they're coming in – trying to come in –

on two fronts, Mansel, which is what you'd expect when you consider Tommy Mill-Kaper and Digby Lightfoot's special skills in the trade. Tommy's very inner city, of course, and he's looking at the whole Valencia Esplanade area. Digby is—'

'Don't give me that's his real name, fucking *Digby*,' Shale replied. If Alfie had talked a bit more urgent, Shale would not have bothered about the name, but some names did give him colic he had to admit it. 'A jumped-up fraud like that was never christened Digby – his mother would not have even known a name like Digby to give it to him even if she wanted to – this is some layabout from Rotherham, even Blackpool, most probably a terraced property – more like a fucking Ian or Justin, something like that.'

'They call him Corporeal,' Ivis said, 'owing to his body – skinny.'

'Some of these people use the stuff they sell and never have a true meal. Think of Gladhand Eric, you could see right through him if he didn't wear that Dunkirk army cape.'

Then Ivis said around the side of his gin beaker: 'Corporeal's brief is to look at – well, you'll be able to guess, Manse.'

Shale had tried to stay steady. 'Corporeal? This is the quality trade boy, you say?' His voice went down to an outraged whisper: 'You don't mean he's sizing up *The Eton*?' Suddenly, then, he had felt the gravity, even though Alfie was still talking mild.

'Exactly that, Manse. Bound to be, isn't it? Corporeal hears about a nice floating restaurant with a really brilliant class name, *The Eton Boating Song,* plus fully established high calibre dealing with brilliantly select clientèle, so inevitably he makes a bee line. His métier.'

'Christ, *The Eton,*' Shale had replied. 'You could say *The Eton Boating Song* is our flagship outlet, Alf. This is customers with plenty who always pay and who only want top-crop stuff. We got to look at this. I mean, properly look at it. Me, you, Denzil – tonight.'

'Tonight? Oh, look, Manse, Corporeal's only at the early stages,' Ivis said. 'I don't think we need to rush into—'

'Tonight. Who we got there selling for us?'

'Si.'

'Pilgrim? He wouldn't fight to save his mother,' Shale said.

No, he would run, and he was running now, towards the marina streets and off the dangerous open quay. Denzil might have it right again – Pilgrim was too frantic to look back. He thought this car was as evil as Lincoln W. Lincoln, and he was trying to hurtle his little precious self to safety behind the bollards.

'God, he's dropping stuff,' Denzil said. The flashing headlights lit up two small packets in coloured paper as they fell to the ground alongside Pilgrim, like a medallion for someone's birthday or a watch. 'Ever see that film about Jesse James on TV?' Denzil asked.

'Just drive, will you?' Shale replied. He was crouched forward, bent over the back of the front passenger street, staring at Pilgrim, like a mother watching her boy tightrope Niagara.

Denzil said: 'It's terrific. The posse's after the James brothers, so they scatter stolen money. Everyone stops to collect. Si's scattering coke at a hundred quid a gramme.'

'My coke,' Shale replied.

'You want me to stop for it?' Denzil asked.

'No. Get to him. He needs us.'

They reached the row of tubby black bollards and left the car. Pilgrim had disappeared among the smart little houses and flats somewhere. Shale had a flashlight. He told the other two to keep the weaponry out of sight but ready and he put the P9S back into his jacket pocket. You could not run around marina-type dwellings with a piece in your hand, for God's sake, even at midnight. These were people in all sorts of calibre jobs, media, fruit and veg stalls, top of the range tattooists, physicians. People like this were very fast on the 999 calls and they would spot it was a crisis if you had three men with pistols scouring their neighbourhood and trying to look kindly.

*

Denzil found Si. He was in like a little bower with his throat cut. It was Alf said it was a bower. This was like a miniature park in the middle of the marina development, with trees obviously left as environmental from some previous time and crowding around a decent little grass space in the middle, sheltering it from sun and wind. Si was on his back on the grass and it might have been silent if it was done very fast, which with throat-cutting it generally was because only people who knew something about it did it, with all those toughish strands to hack through, instead of stabs in the body. Si would be pretty easy to hold while doing it, even by someone as thin as Alf said this Digby was, because Si was small and flimsy and obviously so scared that his strength would be gone, supposing he usually had any. They must have pulled him into this bower. He would never enter a closed spot like that otherwise, not even to hide.

Well, Denzil did not *exactly* find him, but it was important to praise this sod now and then, as any chief should with an assistant. Denzil would not go into that bower by himself, and you could not be harsh with him for this, he was no leadership figure. He had some bravery, or why employ him, but not the kind of bravery that a chieftain needed.

Denzil, Shale and Ivis had split up at the bollards to do the streets, and in a while Denzil came looking for Shale to say it might be the thing to go into this bower, although at that time Denzil called it just wasteground. Denzil had heard something when he passed the trees: 'Like breathing, but hard breathing – fighting for it, real work,' he said. Of course, that noise could be the one who did it, or more than one, still in there doing it when Denzil picked up the sound. It might not have been Si's difficult breathing but the difficult breathing of whoever was finishing him, because of the knife effort. Just the same, Shale still refused to blame Denzil for failing to go in there himself immediately and maybe saving Si and catching who did it. This was a chauffeur, not the SAS.

When Denzil told Shale about the sounds, they went to find Alfie in another street and then the three of them made for the wasteground, Shale leading in under the trees. He had the flashlight on and they all brought out their handguns now, Denzil with a cheapie Rohm RG14. This was when Alfie said, 'Quite a little bower.' The beam reached Pilgrim and Shale was damn shocked, he would never deny it. He had been expecting something bad because of the breathing, but this was disgraceful – the way it had been done and someone as feeble as Si. 'Well, that don't look to me like your long-term view of matters, Alfred,' he said. Pilgrim had always had funny lips, sort of ragged, but they were not so noticeable now, what with all the rest of it. 'Has he got family?'

'I'd have to look him up in the files, Manse,' Ivis replied. 'Possibly a live-in. I don't think children.'

'We'll have to do some compensation,' Shale said. 'I don't know about attending the funeral, in the circumstances.'

'Probably best not,' Ivis said.

He always said best not when this kind of question came up relating to associates. Alfie was not strong on reckoning up a situation, and he was not strong on considerate leadership gestures, either. Why he was stuck where he was.

Shale said: 'I don't know if any partner or family will hear the way he died, but it would be best not, unhingeing Si's head. Don't put it around. The police might hide that from them, too.'

'Someone will have to identify him,' Denzil said.

'Yes, someone will. Perhaps a bit tidied by then. But, in any case, we don't have to spread it, the method.'

Denzil said: 'You want me to strip him, so the ID will be delayed?'

'No point,' Shale replied. 'He's known from *The Eton* and his little legs. Leave him some dignity. If you've had your throat cut you don't want to be found bollock naked as well. I'm not having those clothes in the boot of my car, not even briefly.' He handed the flashlight to Denzil and went down to search Pilgrim. There was nothing much beyond money, a lot of money. He must have been trading well tonight. Shale kept it. This was not because he wanted the cash, although they were takings and due, but it would be wisest if the police did not see what kind of business went on at *The Eton*. Of course, they knew what *kind* of business Si did at *The Eton* but not the scale of it, and it was also better this London crew did not know, although they must have a good idea or they would not have hunted Si like that. They would not get *The Eton*. If Shale thought they might get *The Eton* he would not bother to hide how much the takings were. It would not matter to him any longer. But it *did* matter, because Shale would stop them.

He sorted out some twenties and tens and gave a hundred each to Alf and Denzil, not a drop of blood on any note as far as he could see with the flashlight. 'Bonus,' he said. This work took place in unsociable hours and they deserved something. It was difficult with Alf, giving him the odd hundred, because he obviously liked to think he had a position in the firm and should not have tips like Denzil. But usually he would take them, as long as they were over fifty. 'You might have really turned into something bonny eventually, Si,' Shale said, and bent again and gave a gentle, comradely squeeze to Si's right arm through that quaint, old-style tweed jacket. Most of the blood had gone to his left.

They walked back to *The Eton Boating Song* and stayed together while they searched for Lovely Mover. Obviously, this was another spot where you could not have guns on show, only very ready. There were all sorts here in the restaurant and bars, such as aged people who probably never did drugs at all and were only here for a satisfactory night out afloat either celebrating a golf win or golden wedding, and you could not frighten such folk by flashing armament. The tale was that some of the diners and drinkers who came here had really been to that prime Eton school personally, and would know this boating song from when they sang it in genuine dormitories when there was no sodomy on. Lovely Mover seemed to have left, which you would expect. He and his associates were not going to move into Si's place tonight, it would be too obvious. As soon as that body was found the police would come to *The Eton*, knowing it was Si's career. Shale and the others had a real search, including the Fo'castle as the disco was called and behind capstans and in the Galley, where they did light snacks only with ocean names, like Cape Kisch and Straits Compote of Mediterranean Fruits.

In the main bar, Alfie said a bit sadly: 'This is where Si used to sit, and Eleri ap Vaughan before him. Eleri would have a rum and black in front of her on the table to show she was ready to deal. I don't know whether Si had anything like that.'

Shale said: 'Yes, well, bygones, but people come tonight and he's not here, they're going to be pissed off. Night out, expensive meal, they want something to go on to. They been telling their friends they know this spot where there's the maritime aspect plus coke and it's a let-down for them. This is no good for the business, Alfred.'

Denzil said: 'I could go back and look for those packets he dropped and sit in for him.'

'Thanks, Denzil, but too risky,' Shale said. 'Any minute there could be a posse here. Whoever's in Si's place is on the shortlist for having done him.'

This was a good, loyal offer by Denzil, probably because he thought he fucked up at the bower by delaying and wanted to put it right now. But you could not have someone as crude as Denzil selling stuff to folk who used to be at Eton or other great places. Si had looked bad enough, with his skin and those garments, but Denzil would really upset this sort of people.

'We'll have to let it go for a while,' Shale said.

'I think so,' Ivis replied.

'And then the danger – it's obvious – the danger Lovely Mover or that fucking Digby slip in to this work station. I would bet Digby in the bower with Si, or the other one, or both.'

They left *The Eton*. In the car, Alfie said: 'If we think a bit long-term, just a bit, Manse, it might be an idea to put that girl in there when she comes nosing, nuzzling, trying to get into the firm. Have you thought of that?'

Yes, he had thought of that. Alfie meant *The Eton* was obviously a peril spot from now on, and Lincoln or Digby or Mill-Kaper or all of them would see to her if she tried for *The Eton* business. They would do the harsh work on her and Shale need not be bothered. It seemed dirty to him. It seemed like dodging out, not the kind of behaviour for a leader. If you were going to see to someone you ought to see to them yourself, in a clean, mindful way.

'I'll give it a mull,' Shale said. 'Get me all the detail on Si's dependents and so on, will you, Alfie. Find out about the parents if there are any. He might have been sending them regular help. Even a makeweight like Si could have quite decent parents somewhere.'

16

Iles turned up late one Saturday night at Harpur's house in Arthur Street claiming he urgently needed help – 'Help with something extremely current, Col.' Naturally, at first Harpur believed no part of this and was on guard. Impossible to imagine Iles asking for help from anyone, and never from him. He assumed the ACC had come hoping the girls were in and still up, and especially Hazel. They *were* still up and in the big sitting room with their boyfriends and a few other kids who'd come back with them from the rap caff for more music and whatever else was going. Denise had some academic work to do tonight and was staying in her university flat. Plus, she and her friend were still very troubled about the death of Mace, her friend especially.

Harpur went to the kitchen to prepare a tureen of spaghetti tuna. He longed for these visitors to spread the word when they went home that he was a great single parent – hospitable at any hour, a gifted cook, uncrusty but watchful of his daughters' wellbeing. He'd had a couple of gin and ciders and before the ACC's arrival felt altogether live-and-let-live: the warm tolerance that this cocktail often brought him, and which he could keep in place once it was there by quite moderate toppings up. He heard the front doorbell and assumed it was more of the caff gang. Jill or Hazel would answer. He opened another tin of tuna and threw in a couple more bunches of spaghetti. 'Generous' was a description he would like these kids to take back to their parents, in addition to 'gifted'. Or 'unstinting', even, if they could manage that, but these days youth had no vocabulary. He hated the notion that people might think Hazel and Jill were in any way deprived since the murder of Megan. Perhaps the few days of separation in Hilston plus Rockmain's hints had made him more conscious than ever of home responsibilities. He hunted out another packet of spaghetti and emptied it in, yes, damned unstintingly. This was going to be a feast. A few of the caff lads would want to discuss police policy again, most likely, and he might pick up some ideas.

In a while, Jill came to help with the crockery. 'How many of you, love?' Harpur asked.

'Seven.'

'Right.'

'And Des.'

Harpur said: 'Oh? Iles here? In uniform? A formal call?'

'Don't be silly. The lovely tan bomber jacket. Must be half a grand's worth.'

'Don't talk like that,' Harpur said. 'Oafish slang.'

'Dad, you sound like somebody's mother.'

'Whose?'

'God, you're not going to say again you have to be mother *and* father to us now.'

Counting the plates on to a tray, Harpur said: 'I have to be mother *and* father to you two now.'

'Des has been somewhere, I think.'

'I wouldn't be surprised.'

'The bomber jacket reeks of Rive Gauche. Scratches on his neck. Don't get all edgy about him.'

'What's he here for?' Harpur asked.

'To see *you*. He said he needs help. An emergency.'

'Why doesn't he come to the kitchen, then?'

'He's dancing.'

'Your kind of music, in that bomber jacket?'

She put cutlery on the tray and a tub of Parmesan.

Harpur said: 'You don't have cheese on fish.'

'Some do. It's the newest thing. I saw it in a supplement. Many say you don't have gin in cider.'

'Dancing with whom?' he asked.

'I love grammar. Do you know that old song, "Whom were you with last night"? Not Hazel. Keep calm. Concentrate on the spag. Hazel's with Scott.'

When they took the food in, Iles was dancing opposite and at a proper distance from some girl Harpur did not know to a disc Harpur did not know and did not want to. The girl would be fourteen or fifteen and had on trainers, multicoloured trousers and a man's shirt, collarless and palely striped. Iles, bright-faced with vibes, called out: 'Ah, Colin, a grand evening! To think I might have missed it but for a mere work crisis. If there's one thing I adore it's the smell of ganja off people in their teens. Early teens. Yet, oddly, there's nothing worse than the same tang attached to the middle-aged – then, it becomes only a dispiriting comment on the mustiness of later life. The young bring their own lovely delicate flesh flavours to it, don't you think? Enhancing.' He inhaled happily. The ACC was in shirt sleeves. The grand bomber jacket and a crimson scarf lay on the floor in the window bay, the jacket inside out, his wallet protruding from the breast pocket. Harpur had seen the ACC in this ensemble before. When wearing the jacket and scarf he could have starred in a TV ad for some small, chic French car. 'What crisis, sir?' Harpur asked.

'Something extremely current, Col. Yes, an emergency.'

Hazel said: 'Well, it's what emergencies *are*, isn't it – extremely current? Pearl Harbor would be an emergency when it was happening. Not now.'

'We must go and have a look at it in a minute, Col,' Iles replied.

'Is this to do with gang war?' Scott asked. He and Hazel had finished dancing and were helping dish out the food. 'My mother says this city is run by gangs. Sort of handed over? The new way to keep the peace?'

'I like your mother,' Jill snarled.

'You've never even met her,' Scott replied.

'That's how I like her,' Jill said.

'Yes, you could say a gang aspect,' Iles replied. He gazed about the sitting room. 'I approve what you've done here, Col – the changed décor, new curtains, yet I do miss the shelves of Megan's books.'

'We don't,' Hazel said. 'They were just books. Like heavy.'

'Yes, like heavy,' Harpur said. They had given the books to Iles because he was into all sorts of reading.

'Which gangs?' one of the other boys asked. 'Is it drugs?'

'You really cooked all this by yourself, Col?' Iles asked. He began to load his meal with Parmesan.

'I told you, Dad,' Jill said.

'My mother says that because of the unquenchable demand you'll never beat them – the gangs,' Scott stated.

Iles breathed in the room atmosphere again and ate swiftly. 'This is how life ought to be always,' he said, 'pasta, baby sweat, music, fellowship.'

Harpur mixed him his favourite drink – what the ACC called 'the old tarts' tipple' – port and lemon, and did another gin and cider for himself. His daughters and their friends drank cider only.

Jill's boyfriend, Darren, was stretched out on a sofa, balancing the dinner plate on his chest and shovelling the spaghetti ends to his lips so he could suck the rest in. He stopped for a few minutes and said: 'In a way, this house, 126 Arthur Street, is a true . . . well . . . nerve centre now, and it's exciting. Like Scotland Yard Ops Room. I mean, two top police, planning, preparing, dealing with a true emergency regardless of how late.'

'Yes, drugs firms,' Iles said. 'There's considerable urgency.' He drank and smacked his lips.

Someone put a new compact disc on and the ACC seemed to know the first number and love it. 'Ah, *Bear Hug Intemperance*, yes?' he cried. 'This says everything that *can* be said about inner city rebirth.' He was sitting on the floor, his back against the wall, most of the meal finished. Putting the plate down, he rose quickly and, still holding the port and lemon in one hand, danced alone for a while, lots of head flexibility and circular movements with his free arm expressing insight. 'Oh, man, listen to it, so . . . so *core*,' he called to Harpur, 'so consequential. But do I need to spell it out?'

'You will, though,' Hazel replied.

At the end, the ACC sat down on the floor again, beaming, and finished his supper. He gazed with rapture at his slim legs in good beige slacks stretched out before him, and at his slim brown brogues that chimed with the jacket.

'You don't have to go on some stupid old emergency, do you?' the girl in the striped shirt asked, bending over him, frotting his shin with her right trainer. 'What is it really, now *really, truly,* Des – a plastic counterflow bollard been knocked over? Nothing as perilous as drugs firms at all, is it – now *is* it?'

Standing again, Iles placed his empty plate and glass on the coffee table. He slipped his jacket on, arranged the scarf primly and waved goodbye to the party. Harpur followed him out to the ACC's new Scorpio. When they were moving, Iles said: 'Oh, yes, I can see now why Hazel would find that Scott a bit lightweight, Col. She's reaching out, isn't she? Reaching out all the time. So questing.'

'What emergency?' Harpur replied.

'McWater.'

'Naomi's live-in? Ex live-in?'

'I *think* McWater. I needed you to confirm. In any case, I was a bit tied up at the time.'

'What's happened to him?'

'Nothing yet. Col, I listen to this boy, Scott, quoting his

mother – most of it damn sensible stuff, mind you – *damn* sensible about keeping the peace – boys' mothers can be perceptive, though not my own – but this is a near-man having to rely on his mother for views. He's what, seventeen, eighteen? Obviously older than Hazel. But she'd find someone like that pretty derivative and feeble, I think. She'd be looking around. Serene body odour from her, Harpur.'

'Thank you, sir. But this is a nice steady long-lasting relationship between her and Scott.'

'It *is* nice, something like that. In its way.'

'Its way is fine.'

Iles was driving down Valencia Esplanade, though few called it that any longer. Once, this had been a long row of distinguished houses looking out over the foreshore to the sea and world trade. Now, the area had sunk a bit and more, and 'Esplanade' seemed a gaudy title for these multi-tenanted old properties, farcical. People referred to the whole decaying district as the Valencia. Harpur knew Iles would come down here sometimes – often – for a girl, and presumably earlier tonight. The ACC turned off the main road now, drove a little further and parked on waste ground littered with car wrecks, old mattresses, fridges, bicycle frames and a couple of gutted moquette settees. The streets around were busy with people on their way to clubs, or looking for girls or for pushers, or doing all three. There was a brilliant grim energy to the place which Harpur always responded to. At least a quarter of his work life was spent in this square mile. 'About here, Col,' Iles said. 'I was about here when I thought I saw McWater walk past down Dring Place, a sort of loitering walk, by no means a supermarket chief's strut. I wasn't sure. I was in the back, of course, looking the length of the car and around these fucking headrests in the dark.'

'He's seeking company, that's all.'

'Then he returns,' Iles said, 'same drill, staring about.'

'It's a while since he broke with Naomi. He needs a girl.'

'Think so? My idea is he's seeking Naomi,' Iles replied. 'Imagines this is where she might be working if undercover. To have him questing could be damn dangerous for her, Col.'

'She's not here yet. Still at Hilston.'

'But he doesn't know it, does he? All he's sure of is she's not at home. This thrustful lad is likely to start asking around on the streets for her. And so, the word could be about in advance. You see the peril – I mean, when she *is* put in place. Supposing the sods don't already know she's coming, anyway, that is.'

Harpur slumped down in the passenger seat and pretended to seek a doze. 'You're going too fast, sir. One, you're not sure it's McWater. Two, even if it is, it's just a man needing some sex. You'd understand that.'

'We could ask him,' Iles said. 'We *must* ask him. He knows you, doesn't he? Why I came to your house.'

'If he's still around. He might be fixed up by now. You had to fucking dance, sir, didn't you, and sniff youth?'

'We look for him,' Iles replied. 'Better with two.'

Someone tapped the window alongside Harpur and he saw a very pretty black girl of about seventeen in a red tank top and brief pink cotton shorts. When he lowered the window he smelled Rive Gauche. He tried to spot whether she had some of Iles under her nails. She ignored Harpur and spoke across to him to the ACC: 'Good God, Des, you back already? What's the matter – on hormone tablets?' She did glance at Harpur now. 'I don't do it with two, you know – I mean, not at the same time, in the same vehicle, even police.'

'This is duty, Grace,' Iles replied. 'I noticed something earlier, darling.'

'Right. I thought your mind wasn't really on things.' She stroked Harpur's cheek and ear, and he tensed. 'It's Mr Harpur, isn't it? Are you here in hindrance of trade?'

'No, no, Grace,' Iles replied. 'Ply, my dear. You have commitments. Make your ends meet.'

She walked away. Iles and Harpur left the car and went towards Dring Place.

'This is mad,' Harpur said. 'We're both known around here.'

'Me only by an amiable few,' Iles replied.

'Possibly.'

A top pimp's or top pusher's BMW passed them and then a second-string pimp's or second-string pusher's Saab, both new. They would be on their rounds. These were workaholic folk, tributes to small business enterprise and industry. Iles said: 'Yes, when I think of Hazel, Col, I—'

'There's McWater,' Harpur replied.

Iles looked. 'Yes, so I had it right.'

'You'll be able to put Grace on expenses, sir, as cover. Fifty?'

'Oh, Grace is much nicer than that.'

'Does that mean she'd take less, or is worth more?'

'Look, you talk to McWater, Col. Bring him to the car, will you?'

'He's not fond of me, sir.'

'I never understand people like that,' Iles replied. 'Charm him, Harpur.'

McWater was alone. As Harpur watched, he approached a corner dealer and spoke to him for a while, perhaps bought something. Although the pusher had his back to Harpur, he thought it might be Untidy Graham, wearing the famous raincoat. Harpur walked towards them. Iles turned and went back to the car.

Yes, it was Untidy. Folk called him Untidy because he was, and to distinguish him from Noisy Graham who helped run Seconds, a restaurant. Untidy came and went in the pushing business and for a while had done Born Again Christian after wandering by mistake when high into a Gospel campaign marquee. Harpur had heard him open-air preach outside Marks and Spencer subsequently, declaring with Paul that he had been chief of sinners. Now, here he was again, back at it. He seemed to sense Harpur's approach, glanced behind and then hurried away down Redvers Street. McWater stayed. He looked nervy, though possibly not because of Harpur. 'This your beat, then?' McWater asked.

'Is it yours?' Harpur replied. 'Look, it's not good for us to be seen talking here.'

'Why?'

'I've got a car up the road. Follow me, would you?'

'Why?'

'We can discuss things,' Harpur replied.

'What things?'

'Follow me,' Harpur said and went back towards the waste ground.

When he climbed into the back of the Ford, Iles said: 'So, where the fuck is he, Harpur?'

'He might come. I'll sit with him here. It's nice. The seat's still warm.'

'He *might* come?'

'Only that,' Harpur replied.

'Didn't you tell him he could be endangering his woman?'

Harpur said: 'How's he endangering his woman when his woman is supposed to be going on a Special Branch course?'

'He doesn't believe that.'

'We've got to act as if he believes it. For now,' Harpur said. 'Here he is.'

McWater crossed the waste ground. Harpur pushed open a door and he got in. Iles drove back on to the Esplanade and away.

'You didn't meet Naomi at Heathrow then?' Harpur said.

'I wrote her off,' McWater replied.

'Then you found you couldn't,' Iles said. 'I think that's lovely.'

McWater said: 'So, I'm at the Valencia night after night, searching.'

'Pointless,' Harpur replied.

'You'll lose your cutting edge in the store,' Iles said over his shoulder.

'Who are you?' McWater asked.

'A friend,' Iles said.

'Is this the great Iles, Harpur? The aplomb and bomber jacket and all that.'

Iles said: 'Aplomb is my second name. My mother thought I should use it instead of Desmond. D. Aplomb Iles.' He had driven to not far from where McWater lived on Attlee Boulevarde, and pulled in there.

'You've got me located, have you?' McWater asked.

Iles turned around and faced him: 'We'd like you to concentrate on your career now, sonny,' he said.

'An Assistant Chief and a Detective Chief Superintendent come looking for me, and you still say she's not going undercover?'

Iles said: 'Yes, we're telling you that she's—'

'Of course she's going undercover,' Harpur replied. 'Do you want to get her killed?'

'She'll get killed, anyway,' McWater said. 'They'll know.'

'You actually asked Untidy about her?' Harpur said. 'A mouth like Untidy?'

'Where is she?' McWater replied.

Iles said: 'I for one respect your feelings, McWater. And probably Harpur does, too, though he's incredibly narrow. They're good and noble feelings, for a shopkeeper. I always refuse to listen when people make fun of the Scotch. I say the Scotch have real tenderness to them and compunction. If I hear you've been down the Valencia again, night or day, I'll come and find you myself, you benighted shit, and you won't be any use thereafter to anyone, not to your bosses or to women, and you'll have no functioning nostril to snort the stuff Untidy will have supplied you with tonight.' He leaned across and McWater pulled back hard and frightened from his hand. Iles opened the rear door. 'Off you go now, Donald. Get your head down for a good doze so you'll be forceful around the checkouts tomorrow. I look at you and see a long and distinguished shelf life, given luck.'

When McWater had gone, Harpur went back to the passenger seat. Iles drove him home. On the way he said: 'I don't think I'll come in now, Harpur, thanks. These youngsters will have sorted things out for the rest of the night, I imagine. No, no, I'm sorry. I've got a wife and child to consider.'

'The visiting kids should have gone home. Hazel and Jill will be asleep.'

'I adore order,' Iles replied.

Harpur's house was dark. When he went to bed he found Denise there, snoring cheerfully. He climbed in and she woke up. 'Finished your high-level learning and comforting Miss Withdrawal Symptoms?' he said. 'Now you can fit me in?'

'Yes, I think I can fit you in. Shortly.' Denise put the bedside lamp on. She looked more cheerful than he had seen her for a while. Perhaps after all she was recovering from the shock of Mace's killing. 'But first . . .' she said. There was a book on the telephone table near her pillow. She sat up naked and opened the volume while he undressed. 'Listen to this, Colin. It should make you feel much more comfortable about some of your ploys in court.'

'I don't have ploys and I'm not uncomfortable.'

'You should have been, but now, no. This is Boswell on Johnson, the biog, you know? Not the Jonson of Jonson Court, where I live, which is *Ben* Jonson, playwright, of course. This is Samuel Johnson, with an h, who did the dictionary.'

'Can't we just make love, with an f?' Harpur replied.

'In due course. Listen: Boswell asked Johnson if it was all right for a lawyer to put up a defence in court for someone he knows is guilty and a bad case.'

'All the buggers would be on the dole if they didn't.'

'Dr Johnson says: "Sir, you don't know it to be bad till the judge determines it. An argument which does not convince yourself may convince the judge and if it does why, then, sir, you are wrong. It is his business to judge, and you are not to be confident in your own opinion."'

'Iles says truth is what a jury believes.'

'The other side of what Johnson argues is, surely, Col, that you, the police, can . . . as it were . . . *improve* the evidence a bit sometimes, to persuade. The way I know you do. It used to worry me.'

'But now Dr Sam's put it right for you?'

'If you can convince the court, then it must be OK, mustn't it?'

'Do you think you've been sleeping with the police for too long? Don't answer. You haven't.'

'I'll answer. I haven't. Oh, no.' She replaced the book, put out the light and turned towards him. 'The girls said you'd gone out on an emergency with Iles. Was it?'

'Oh, yes it was that, all right.'

'Did you resolve it?'

'I don't know. *He* might have.'

Just after dawn, the phone rang and, groping for it across Denise, Harpur knocked Boswell on to the floor. The Control Room told him a body with a convincing throat wound had been found in a bit of a park on the marina. The unofficial identification said it was Simon Pilgrim who dealt drugs as successor to Eleri ap Vaughan on *The Eton Boating Song*. Harpur wondered whether they'd ever get anyone into the dock for this and, if they did, whether a possibly terrorized, possibly bribed, probably anti-police jury would convict. Could Dr Johnson help on that?

While he was dressing to go and look at Si there came a knock at the door and Jill pushed it open. 'Are you all right?' she whispered. 'I heard the phone and then a heavy noise.'

'A book fell, that's all.'

'Oh, books. They get everywhere. Are you going out again, Dad?'

'Something's happened.'

'Is this another emergency?'

'Yes.'

'A real one or one of Des's?'

17

Fifth session

'We'll call you only Angela Rivers, then, from now on, since you're definitely committed,' Rockmain said. 'Yes, it's time for you to absorb the name.' He gazed at her, chummily signalling congratulations, and, again, maybe something else: 'Already you look to me more like an Angela than a Naomi. You must be applying your will to make that change. Bravo!'

The inane praise pleased her, so she thought she'd better say something spiky, something that would hold him off. 'I don't know what name you look like to me,' Naomi replied.

'Eternally Rockmain, but a mobile commodity within those limits.' They were in the palatial room again, on the two sofas opposite each other. He wore different denim, but still denim – a longish jacket that made him look like an officer in some underfunded South American army. 'We have to talk about your . . . your romances,' he said. 'I don't mean Harpur.'

'No, you *don't* mean Harpur.' She wondered whether he really did need to dwell on her sex life, or whether this was a personal spin he gave the programme here to get himself going.

'You mentioned having been in a relationship,' he said.

'It's finished.'

'And then there's the lad in the aircraft lavatory.'

'He was a lad in an aircraft lavatory. These people come and go. Look, what's this about?'

'But you said you'd already slept with him. And that you might see him again.'

'I don't know where he is.'

'But he might know where *you* are, Rivers.'

'How?'

'Hotel staff. Luggage labels.'

'I concealed the labels.'

'Ah, you realized he might wish to trace you?'

'Best that things were more or less anonymous.'

'But did *he* think so? What's his name?'

'I know his name.'

'From?'

'Cardiff.'

'You do remember these things, then?' There was a rat trap snap to his voice for this.

'Mr Rockmain, I fucked him four times. At least. Certain basics stick.'

'So he's not anonymous?'

'He's a happy episode, a nice, comforting episode.'

'You *needed* comforting, did you?'

'But only an episode.'

Rockmain stood and paced about in his big-wheel, thin-necked thoughtful style. Perhaps the talk was exciting him too much and he had to disperse some frenzy. She looked to see if his chin was sweating.

Rockmain said: 'At what point did you conceal the labels?

It would be when you were starting something with him, wouldn't it? He could have seen them before. It's possible he'll come looking. I – we – have to accept that there might be two men trawling for you when you're in place with a trading firm.'

'Not Don,' she said.

He had left a file on the sofa as he walked about and now bent down, opened it and read for a couple of seconds.

'Don's the original, long-term one, yes? Management? So, you agree that the lad on the airplane might show? I think you're right. This could be meaningful for him – getting encompassed with the lid down. You did say with the lid down? It probably doesn't happen to Cardiff chaps all that often. He might reasonably hope it was meaningful for you also and feel he should pursue the relationship.' He paused. His voice warmed a bit. 'Oh, I can understand that,' he said.

'There's no relationship.'

'That's twice there's no relationship!' Rockmain replied. He did a comic frown. He was vivid with doubt. 'Rivers, I have to try to assess how you'd behave if one or both of these men were in touch with you again while you're under-cover. Did Don drop you because you insisted on this duty? An anxiety for you that he found intolerable? Or jealousy – jealousy that your work should monopolize you, that you seemed to be moving into a different personality, different personalities?'

'He didn't know what the duty was. Still doesn't.'

'Didn't he? Doesn't he? Does he suspect? He's bright, I

expect: his company think well of him. Might he have finished with you and then regretted it?'

'He didn't regret it enough to get to Heathrow and meet me.'

'You expected him to, did you?' Rockmain asked.

At once she said: 'Not at all.'

'But it's still a grievance that he didn't?'

'No grievance. I've told you, I didn't want that kind of . . . that kind of bond and bracketing any longer.'

'Hence the in-flight shag and previously.'

'Correct.'

'What you call a bond and bracketing is what most people would regard as conditions of a normal relationship, wouldn't they?'

'Oh, do you know about normal relationships, Mr Rockmain?' she asked. 'Really know. You say you're a wanking voyeur–fantasist.'

'Yes, that does sound familiar.'

'You need to be told whether the lid was up or down so you can visualize things right.'

'Certainly,' Rockmain replied. 'Verisimilitude. It *was* down, wasn't it?'

'Give yourself a treat: think of it as not down if that suits better. This is the right job for you, isn't it? You hear a lot of useful stuff.'

'Oh, absolutely,' Rockmain said. 'I'd hate to be sent to Financial Control.' He nodded for a while, then sat back, grew sort of confiding. 'You know, Rivers, people are always turning these conversations, getting me on the end of the questions. Harpur did it. Police are so used to being in the catbird seat.'

'The lid up or down?' She could feel him trying for comradeship and possibly more. It might be interview technique. It might be anything. She stayed dumb faced, her body slumped, as off-putting as she could make it.

Rockmain said: 'But, as is required, let's get back to you. Suppose Don comes to think he has been cruel. I'm sure he's a decent fellow. Of course he is. Would you be involved with someone who isn't? It could begin to perturb him that he's abandoned you to the perils of this duty. All right, he didn't come to Heathrow. That would have been rather soon after the break, perhaps. But, subsequently, would he dwell on things, come to feel guilty? He's not a Catholic, is he? They're big on all that. I don't know his personality firsthand, obviously. I have to project in my head the sort of man you would agree to a relationship with. And, when I do, I inevitably arrive at the profile of a man with a conscience, with consideration.'

Yes, that was Don. 'It's over, Mr Rockmain,' she said.

'For all we know, he might have already been around the trade haunts looking for you, talking, inquiring. A hazard, Rivers.'

'As you say, you don't know him. He wouldn't.' Would he? She grew ratty herself. 'Look, I've told you I'll do it, and you want me to do it, and the Chief wants me to do it, and it's your job to see I do it, so why all this psychocrap?'

'My job is also to make certain you're secure, Angela. They've had one terrible episode with Street.'

'Gone. The past.'

'What I told Harpur.'

'Well, ditch it.'

Rockmain stood once more. He was going to give a grand analysis and needed the height: 'I believe that if, say, Don approached you in the street when you were supposedly working for a firm your instinct would be to respond. You would not have it in you to freeze him, escape from him immediately, not even though your life might demand it. Well, no *might*, it would. The firm you'll be in will have you under watch at the start. Everyone on the patch will be tense after the death of Mace and this pusher from the yacht, Simon Pilgrim. So far we've only got the media version of Pilgrim's death to go on, but his killing seems meant to scare, meant to instruct. Throat jobs are didactic. People will be expecting bad problems. You might look like one, if Don or laddy-with-the-lid-on come searching, come trying to reclaim you – come *identifying* you.'

'I wouldn't be in the least—'

'You could be dead inside a month from now,' he replied. All the posturing had suddenly left his voice. He said it like a bit of informed speculation, matter-of-fact, tentative – the way her father would guess at tomorrow's weather after consulting the barometer. For the first time then Rockmain frightened her. It sounded as if he had previously seen people leave Hilston and find catastrophe and was reminiscing privately.

'You're teaching me *not* to be dead inside a month.'

He stood there for a second with both arms slightly out

from his body, like someone doing semaphore. But there was no message beyond the one he had just given. He looked stricken. For a second, Naomi thought, Christ, he's got a soul, after all.

His tone grew chatty again. 'What I have to decide is whether you have too much what we might call in lay terms *humanity* for this work, Naomi.'

She resented the way he had just almost sunk her. 'Angela,' she yelled. 'Fuck it, my fucking name's Angela.'

The swearing seemed to reach him and he sat down once more. 'Myself, on a personal level, I adore humanity in women,' he replied. She recognized it as a pronouncement that had been building. He leaned forward, though only fractionally, smiling, though only fractionally, and very resistibly, even if he did have a soul.

Naomi said: '*My* humanity is not available for you or for Don or the holiday boy,' she said.

He chuckled and suddenly sat back. 'You won't believe this – naturally you won't – it might appear to be insulting – but I assure you it was not so meant – I came forward like that, smiled sort of intimately like that – I did it all as—'

'As a performance – as a test, you mean?'

'Absolutely,' Rockmain replied, changing the smile to a pertish grin.

'That's fine, then.'

'I had to see whether—'

'My humanity would take over, regardless?'

'I don't know what *regardless* means in that context, but yes. Rivers, you could be—'

She feared he was going to repeat that deadpan forecast.

He hesitated and said: 'Could be unbelievably good at this work.'

'I passed the test, then?'

'With distinction. Oh, no, I could never sensibly expect you to respond to me, could I?'

She did not answer that one.

Rockmain said: 'It would be – oh, absurd.'

'That's strong – say illogical.'

'Harpur?' he asked.

'As things are, I respond to none of them. None of you.'

'Would it be absurd – illogical – with Harpur?'

'Yes. Very.'

'I don't believe you, but I'll—'

'What don't you believe? Which?'

'That you can switch it all off for a job.' He was staring where you would expect someone who lived on a pictorial imagination to stare, or where Iles would stare – at the high inner thigh zone of her trousers. Whatever might happen to her within a month, he could still concentrate his busy lusts on what was alive for the present.

She said: 'I can switch it off. And I can switch it on. The job's not for ever. I can be what I want to be when I want to be. That's human, too.'

He wrote something on his wrist. 'They're lucky to have you available, Angela.'

'They bloody are,' Naomi replied. 'Can I go now?'

Yes, she could. Avoiding her room in case of bugging, Naomi went into the grounds, walked and wept. The fear

Rockmain had raised in her a few minutes ago still stuck hard. Once more she wanted frantically to get out of under-cover work, but knew she couldn't now. When he spoke those words about Naomi's possible death it was plain Rock-main pitied her. For a second he had been so stricken that all his bounce and glibness slid away and he was lost. Unpro-fessional. Well, she could not let these brief, weak, humane dreads of a denim twerp bring her back down. 'I'm Rivers,' she explained to herself in a mild mutter among oak trees, and stopped sobbing, more or less. She could have liked some help, some conversation, but not with Rockmain. If Harpur had still been here, would she have looked to him? No. He was to be her Controller, even though he clearly did not want that, and she had no interest in control at present, perhaps never did. So, instead, when she left Hilston, would she run to Donald, or try to find Lyndon, or both, and see if he/they could steady her? In the past, Don had been able to do that once or twice, and in Spain and on the airplane Lyndon had brought some balm. But, no, not them, either.

What she would have liked was to talk to a woman, one of the women at the Manor for the same purpose: learning to shape herself into somebody else for a tour of duty. Why a woman? Wouldn't anybody here for selection have identical responses to the place? Possibly. She would still prefer to open up to a woman, though. But talking to other candi-dates, men or women, was discouraged, and she understood the sense of that. These people were getting force-fed the habits of secrecy, and in short time. They would not want to disclose anything about themselves, their real selves, especially their fears. That is, if there was any such item as the *real self*. What sort of reception might she get if she buttonholed one of the girls glimpsed around the building and went confidential? There was a woman of about her age in the next room and they said nothing beyond 'Hi' to each other in the corridor. Undercover was an individual job, the most individual job ever, short of being fired from a cannon. 'I'm Rivers,' she muttered again, 'and I'll still be Rivers a month from now and longer, oh, yes. Fret not, Rockmain. Take the lid off those saucy midriff visions and hot up your blood again. Get back to abnormal. I'm not dead yet.'

18

'Of course, none of these svelte marina fuckers saw a thing, sir,' Iles said. 'If it had been someone trying to break into their bits of bijou they would definitely have noted, and would have been screaming at us down the blower. But a pusher with his throat cut on a bit of bosky common ground? They can tell us nothing – don't want the risk, the exposure. Revenge laddies might trample their lawn or piss on their spinnakers or cut *their* throat.'

Harpur had driven the ACC and Mark Lane to this little park on the marina where Si Pilgrim was found. The body had been removed days ago. It was the Chief's first visit. This was another of those symbolic sites. Lane wanted to see the exact piece of ground, and Iles had been showing him, with lavish precision. Now, as the three men stood for a moment staring at the patch of grass in the chilly shade of beeches, Lane suddenly began to break down. Although Harpur was half prepared, it still dazed him for a couple of seconds. 'You are right, Desmond, right,' Lane said. He was trembling, or more than trembling, shaking, and his voice had almost gone. Harpur, standing opposite him a few yards away, only just heard the words. There seemed hardly any spare breath in Lane for speech. He was gasping, fiercely sucking in the cold air, as though suffocating. Nervous phlegm almost choked what he said. The Chief reached out with one hand to support himself against a tree. He spoke again, not any louder or clearer: 'We cannot put a girl into this appalling world, this trade war. No, we must do what you suggest, Desmond, and look for an arrangement with local firms, an alliance in the interests of peace. I see it now. I wish I'd thought of that, proposed that, but . . . Forgive me for—' He did not finish the sentences, dodged the pains of exactness.

Harpur said: 'Sir, perhaps this is not a good place to make—'

'The hazards are monstrous,' Lane said. 'I cannot, cannot ask an officer to undertake—'

Again he did not complete the thought but clutched at his mouth with the free hand, as if to prevent himself recounting what he had previously planned for Naomi Anstruther, and what now sudddenly seemed to him outrageous.

'We should go back to the car, sir,' Harpur replied.

'In a moment,' Lane said. He nodded downwards at the grass: 'I failed this man. I have permitted evil to run where it will, and it has run here and destroyed him.'

Iles said: 'Evil's a biggish item, sir. It's liable to give even you and Jehovah some bother.'

Harpur said: 'We've seen—'

'Oh, I know you'll tell me this isn't the first of these deaths inside the trade,' Lane whispered. 'No, it isn't. No! No! You'll say they are to be expected when evil men battle for supremacy.' He nodded vehemently. 'So, why aren't I able to stop these evil men and this vile pattern – this intolerable, accelerating cycle?'

Behind Lane, and very briefly, Iles put both hands out in front of him, bent foward and moved his feet and legs at mounting pace, as though pedalling to a zooming lead in the Tour de France. 'Please don't treat yourself so harshly, sir,' he replied. 'You'll recall G.K. Chesterton.'

'Oh?' Lane said.

'That essay in defence of detective stories.'

'Yes?' Lane said.

'He argues that law and order, morality, civilization itself, are all quite freakish growths, "a romantic rebellion". He regards morality as nothing but what he calls a "dark and daring conspiracy" against Nature and sees successful police work as only successful knight-errantry. Correct me if I have the phrasing wrong.'

For a while, Lane continued gazing down at the grass, but then raised his face slowly and said in a rush and still very softly: 'Forgive me once more: I should not say why aren't *I* able to stop these deaths. *I, I, I.* Please, do not think, Desmond, Colin, that one regards one's self as . . . well . . . the only *one* who counts in this police force.'

'Certainly not, sir,' Iles replied. It was unclear what this meant. The ACC would like the doubt.

Lane said: 'Oh, I note your comment about my, perhaps, grandiose statement on fighting evil, Desmond.'

Iles picked at the vocabulary. '*Grandeur* is most definitely a quality I would associate with you,' Iles replied. 'But grandiosity? Oh, hardly. I'd like to ask Harpur whether he's ever heard me mention grandiosity in relation to you, sir.'

This was not actually delivered as a question and Harpur could leave it untouched.

Lane said: 'Just the same, I, yes I, personally, must bear the responsibility for this death and for others which have preceded it. I reject your thesis that civilization and its benefits are mere abnormalities. I preside over a decline from legality into chaos, Desmond.'

'People are blind here, and, as you'd expect, sir, and blinder on *The Eton Boating Song* where Si pushed so elegantly,' Iles replied.

'Yes, yes, and here again I have failed,' Lane mourned. 'Why are they silent? Why do they not help me? One knows why – oh, certainly. It is that they cannot believe – simply *cannot*, whatever they would wish – cannot believe in my ability to protect them, should they speak. They see me as alone and dismally, fatally, weak. Yes, Desmond, let us seek allies now, no matter how dubious. Let us find peace, at whatever cost.' He lowered his head again and once more clutched at his mouth, perhaps to silence himself as before. He had on one of his less rag-bag suits and would have looked nearly all right, except for the unique pallor of his face and a continuing shake in his arms and upper body.

Harpur was astonished to find himself almost regretting Anstruther would not after all go under cover. Perhaps she could have done it well. Perhaps he could have helped her and kept her alive. The notion of a blind-eye alliance with Mansel and Panicking still half nauseated him.

The Chief slackened the fingers on his mouth and said: 'Will you allow me to remain here alone for a short while, Desmond, Colin, please? I feel one owes that to the memory of Pilgrim, abominable though he was. Such damned irony in that name!'

Iles said: 'Oh, Simon wasn't all that rotten, sir – now and then afflicted by Giant Despair, as we all are, but he'd certainly have had the grace to appreciate your guarded tribute to his piece of turf.' He and Harpur walked back to the car. 'We can't do it, Col, can we?' the ACC said. 'Anstruther will have to go into a firm. We can't let Lane totally disintegrate.'

'He needs his doctor.'

'This man is a near wreck, a preposterous old slab of mock-epic misery, Harpur. We must stop him falling further. I won't let him plunge the whole distance down and do a Lucifer on me.'

Such bewilderingly fine elements would occasionally glint in Iles. Generally, they stayed capably suppressed. Harpur saw them only off and on. The ACC's wife, Sarah, must see them often enough to make him more or less tolerable some days, and nights. There was a weird upside down battle going on between the Chief and Iles as to who would concede most. Naomi Anstruther was in the No-man's-land. They stood waiting for Lane by the car. 'You knew he was liable to flip, did you, Col?'

'He *has* seemed changed.'

For the Chief to put off his visit here had been alarming. Normally he liked to get early on the site of any crime with overtones, and this one certainly had that. It pointed to pervasive violence and a terrible reversal of progress – reversal of cosmic progress, not just Pilgrim's. 'He sees things in a world context, sir.'

Iles said: 'Well, I often give the world a thought or two, myself. Mainly towards the end of the week. At Staff College I was known as—'

'The fear we'll be engulfed by wrong—' Harpur said, 'that's what the Chief has.' Bad offences on the marina always distressed Lane. To him they spoke of world decline. He longed to regard this new dockland development as an emblem of the future, brilliantly inspiring, brilliantly clean. These pretty streets and boulevards would spread out gradually from dockland and replace the old, villain-infested properties of the Valencia. Likewise, across the earth there would be similar patches of improvement which would spread and redeem the planet. But now this reversal.

'Engulfed by wrong?' Iles said. 'Yes, that could be – if we were all as house-trained tame and eternally sweet as the Chief, couldn't it, Col? But we'll look after him and the fucking universe on his behalf, won't we, Harpur?'

'We get nowhere with this death, sir,' Harpur replied.

'Nor with Mace's. Of course we get nowhere. This is a bit of private knockabout. These marina sweeties know that behind their see-no-evil, pretty whited doors.'

A death like Pilgrim's mocked all Lane's hopes. It said architecture altered nothing. Si and his rough wound had brutal meanings, and Lane's reluctance to come and look at once had emphasized for Harpur something he already feared: the Chief might be hurtling towards fresh mental catastrophe. For days before this outing, Harpur had wondered if Lane's break of behaviour pattern, the unwillingness to act, were dire signs.

Iles said: 'No, Harpur, I will not see Lane destroyed. The dickhead must retain his foibles, and undercover is one.'

'This is damn caring of you, sir.'

'Throw that fucking Eventide Home word, "caring", at me, Harpur, and you won't be around to see the inside of one yourself.' Iles struck the top of the vehicle gently with his palm and said: 'You understand, do you: I'm going to let Lane plant Anstruther in a syndicate after all? That scheme is his whole pathetic being, and he must not be allowed to retreat from it. It would be a retreat into self-extinction.'

Harpur had witnessed such frail unnerving fragments of decency in Iles three or four times before, but he was still disorientated whenever they came. Almost invariably they were to do with Lane. Although Iles spent most of his career attempting to bring the Chief down, he could never consent to wipe him out altogether.

Lane approached from the park, his head still low. Iles said: 'He's not quite so bad now. He'll probably make it home to his pills and his wife without a seizure. Marky Lane is the principality and power that has been put over us, Col – put over us by a committee of drunks but put over us.'

Iles might despise hierarchies, and especially a hierarchy which could set Lane on top, but the ACC was also part of that hierarchy. He would not wipe out the Chief because to do that would be to wipe out the system and Iles needed the system. It had created him, as much as Lane. Harpur thought that ultimately, too, the ACC might doubt his own ability to operate permanently at the very top, despite all his seeming arrogance. Perhaps this was part of the same hidden reverence of hierarchy. When he made it one day to Chief somewhere he might then believe he could do it as Number One. Possibly he could *not* believe it now. Perhaps that indicated he never *would* make it to Chief. Iles might be a supreme dogsbody, apparently subversive, really subservient.

The Chief began to speak before he reached them. His voice did seem marginally stronger, as though he had passed through the worst of his sufferings: 'Yes, it would have been absurd to put Anstruther into one of the firms, absurd and irresponsible. Callous. She has a Drugs Squad background and might well be known on the streets. Her chances would have been nil.'

Iles said: 'Nil, sir? That's unfair to your good self, I feel. Mrs Lane would not want to hear you depreciate your ideas so. Callous? You, Chief, would never have countenanced a callous operation, even countenanced it to abandon it eventually. Nobody outside will recognize her. Harpur's had her in mind for undercover almost from the beginning of her time here and we've ensured her work was in headquarters. She knows the area thoroughly because her job was to collate Squad reports, but the trade there haven't seen her. She's ideal.'

'Just the same,' Lane said, 'I cannot—'

'Both Col and I are convinced that undercover is the only feasible tactic now, sir.'

Lane gave a little lost gasp. Harpur thought the Chief might fall and took half a step towards him, in case he needed support. But Lane seemed to right himself. Surveying this police force quickly in his head then, Harpur saw a stressed Chief Constable whose decisions fell apart, and an ACC who at first helped kick them to bits, and later had to do hurried repairs, or come to pieces himself. Harpur had the conviction that a lot depended on *him*, and much more than he was paid for.

Iles said: 'Impossible to get an enforced peace via accommodation with local syndicates, sir. Pilgrim's death shows the war is too advanced. London is established. We must do it *your* way. We can protect the girl, don't worry. Harpur has a gift for that, although the sod did lose Raymond Street.'

The Chief looked uncertain, and almost pleased. 'Colin, is that really your view about Anstruther?'

'Do you know what I'm going to do now, sir?' Iles replied. 'I'm going to knock a few of these doors and tell the sea-girt sods inside that they had better start coughing what they saw and heard or this whole place will edge into a condition you so rightly called chaos, Chief. And where's the value of their dinky little villas and flats then?'

'Francis Garland and the boys have already knocked doors, sir,' Harpur said.

'Of course they have,' Iles replied. 'But it's a different fucking thing having me on their mat, isn't it, Harpur?'

This *was* a question so Harpur said: 'You take the odds, I'll do the evens, sir. The Chief can wait in the car.' Harpur held the rear door open for him.

The Chief did not move at once. 'And then there are the personality test results from Hilston Manor,' he replied. His voice had almost left him again and he seemed to be slipping back towards defeat. 'They say the girl is a wonderful find but that . . . well, Colin, that you—'

'This is Andrew Rockmain, is it?' Iles asked. 'We ignore that tosser – or the bits about Harpur we do. They're transparent.'

'You know Rockmain, Desmond?'

'Of. Famed as a twisted little ponce. He's putting down poison from fear Col gets to fuck Anstruther as Controller, whereas he can't. Isn't that so, Harpur?'

'It must be a damn long time since an Assistant Chief did door-knocking on a case,' Harpur replied.

19

Naomi came back from Hilston to a flat they had fixed up for her on the edge of the Valencia. She adored it. The place was comfortable enough and had no character at all. She had no character at all, and whatever character she wanted. Hadn't Rockmain told her she could float in and out of identities like nobody else he had ever met? He had mentioned some novel, *The Man Without Qualities*, and said she was in this mould, 'If, of course, mould is not too precise a word, Rivers!'

Probably it had grieved Rockmain that the only consistent bit of her was the bit which said she would not fuck with him, supposing he ever did actually flesh-fuck. He seemed to assume that someone who went in for holiday liaisons and would do it in aircraft lavatories must have an opening for him, too. Wouldn't you expect a big-wheel mind-doctor to spot when a woman found him unthinkable? Physician, feel thyself.

This flat could have been the home of anyone, but a cleanish anyone. Now, it *was* the home of a cleanish anyone. There were posters on the living room and kitchen walls, but posters that taken together told nothing about the occupant: a Second World War Free French General de Gaulle poster, a Sinatra poster, a bow-tied cat poster, a Humpty Dumpty humping Alice poster, a Concorde poster, a cornucopia poster. Delighted, she walked around the rooms slowly and then walked through them again, glorying in the absence of pattern. Harpur would come in at some stage to give her the final detailed briefing on entering a syndicate, and hand over the wherewithal.

The flat was on the ground floor of one of the big old decaying houses due to come down soon, when the marina reached out further with its spruce little arms and strangled another segment of the city's history. This street was only just in the Valencia, and if you wanted to evade that label you could claim to live in the Ellingham Meadows district, though there had been no meadows for at least fifty years. She liked this frontier haziness. There was a telephone but not secure and to be used only for trivia: if a firm checking her out searched the flat and heard a special tone and special operator when they lifted the receiver it could be damaging. Yes, damaging.

The costume people at Hilston had kitted her out with Laura Ashley-style stuff, not new but new enough. Seeing her off from Hilston, Rockmain had said: 'You look wholesome yet approachable. Most folk think of undercover gear as bomber jackets, black T-shirt and jeans. So, they're a giveaway – an anti-uniform which has become a uniform. I blame *Serpico*, all those decades ago. Pushers like to look respectably unnoticeable. It's supposed to reassure the customers and fool the Squad.' There was a wall mirror in the bedroom of the flat and Naomi examined her outfit there now. In her long floral skirt and amber waistcoat over a beige blouse, was she reassuring? Perhaps. She lay on the bed and found that the recollection of herself in the mirror had been shoved aside and another image had taken over. It was that Tim Roth figure in *Reservoir Dogs*. Half-way through the film you discovered he was an undercover cop, not a villain, and you watched him get himself ready in a flat quite like this to go out and infiltrate a gang. But the scene was flashback and you'd already seen him shot up and spurting blood in the first reel. Jesus. But there was no real comparison, was there? Roth included a gun as part of his preparations. She had no gun. Why the hell not, Harpur?

Someone knocked on the door. There ought to be a drill for this, and probably there would be once Harpur had called and given her some final knowledge. It might be Harpur now, though he would surely have a key: he would not want to hang about very visible on the landing, and she would not want it, either. The thing about Controllers was they had to have access. So, should she answer? Of course she should answer. She lived here. If people called you went to see who. She rolled off the bed and went to see who. The door had a judas window. It looked as if it might have been fitted very recently, perhaps by the people preparing the place for her – the people who did the poster job as well. When she put her eye to the peephole she saw a smallish black man in half-moon spectacles and wearing a first-class dark suit and dog collar. She recognized him at once and opened the door.

'May I introduce myself?' he said in a brisk Knightsbridge accent. 'I am the Reverend Bartholomew Anstruther of the

Church of the Free Gospel. I understand you have just moved in. I would like to welcome you to the district.'

'That's very kind.'

'I try to call on all newcomers as soon as possible, to make them feel at home and to tell them of our Church. I heard someone was about to take up residence here. There have been comings and goings, you know – furniture, utensils. There is a good information service in this area, oh, yes.' He chuckled. 'I might say the Church is entirely multiracial, regardless.'

'Yes, I've been there,' she said.

He smiled with grand pleasure. 'Ah? When was that?'

'Yes, I heard you preach. A while ago. The church was full.'

'Ah? Yes, it would have been full. People here are faithful to the Church of the Free Gospel. Perhaps I can be forgiven for not remembering you – one among so many faces. And are you, then, one of the Lord's?'

She wanted to ask him in but worried about the living-room poster of Humpty Dumpty giving it to Alice. 'I can remember your text.'

'Ah?'

'Appropriate. *Behold I stand at the door and knock.*'

'A lovely text, a true text, for He does stand at the door and knock.'

'Would you like to come in?' she asked.

'That would be nice. I'm sure you'd never say I molested you.'

'Well, of course not.'

'But I'm black and a minister.'

'So?'

'You know the so.'

'Come in – it's safe. Actually, I've only moved in today. Some of the decor, etcetera – I'll need to change it.'

In the living room he let his eyes pass without wavering over all the posters and sat down opposite the picture of de Gaulle. 'Here is a great yet very troublesome man,' he said. She made tea and joined him. The store cupboards seemed to have a bit of everything.

Anstruther said: 'You did not answer when I asked whether you were one of the Lord's.'

'I don't think I know what that means,' she replied.

'Ah, then you are not,' he said. 'What brought you to our Church?' He held up a hand, palm towards her. 'But please do not answer this. It was a foolish question. It was the Lord who brought you. That is His way.'

'I enjoyed it,' she said.

'I don't know your name.'

'Rivers. Angela Rivers.'

'And will you come again to our Church, now you are a resident? I hope so.'

'I'll try.'

'You're busy?'

'I might be quite busy,' she said. 'For a time.'

'Might I ask what you—?'

'Between jobs. But interviews and so on,' she said.

'Signing on?'

'For the moment.'

He put down his cup and saucer. 'This is a grand neighbourhood with lovely people, many lovely people,' he said, 'but it's best to be careful in the streets – especially at night, of course. There are some rivalries, some battles. Ordinary folk can get caught up in these outbursts by accident. It's the kind of district where the police are – well, I certainly do not say it's a no-go area for them, certainly not, but the policing is not perhaps always as obvious as it might be. They have a lot to do.'

'I'll be careful.'

'I certainly would not wish to frighten you.'

He produced a pale blue tract from the pocket of his beautiful jacket and handed it to her. This time the text was, *Believe in the Lord Jesus Christ and thou shalt be saved.* 'I'd like you to read that,' he said. Briefly he expounded the gospel message to her, sin, faith, redemption. Then he laughed and said, 'But fear not, I'm not going to preach another sermon at you, not in your own home! You've put up with me once in full flow! Please do read it, though, and then, if you have any questions, you could perhaps come and ask me at the church. It's not far. But, of course, you know.' He stood and produced a notebook: 'If you don't mind, I'll make a note of your name and address, so we may add it to our mailing list. This doesn't mean you will be deluged with junk post, please believe me. Just the occasional note about special meetings. Now and then we have wonderful campaigns in a marquee. I believe you'd like to know about these. Many, many people come, people who might not think of going to a church. Some, yes, I have to say it, quite dubious characters – even once a notorious drugs pusher. The Lord will save all those who cry out to Him. And that man did indeed cry out and went on to do His work, carrying the Word to some of our main streets, preaching in his turn.'

Naomi thought she might have heard of him through Squad reports. It would be the lad called Untidy Graham. She waited for Anstruther to say that this convert had become a backslider and was not on the Lord's work any longer, or at least not as his main career. But the minister, beginning to write, said: 'Angela Rivers, Ms, is that correct? I wouldn't say I'm a feminist, but I do approve that Ms. Why should a woman be defined by marriage or the absence of it?'

20

If Ralph Ember could manage it, a time would come when his club The Monty no longer had members like Untidy Graham.

'A word when you find a minute, Ralph?' Untidy said.

Ember, behind the bar and fiddling with some accounts, did what he usually did when Untidy tried a conversation – pretended not to hear above the jukebox and general club chatter. There was some kind of share-out going on near the pool tables, with occasional loud, angry questions about the fairness of the split. Ember would have to keep an eye on them.

'Important, Ralph,' Untidy said, 'or would I bother you? Something I spotted at the Valencia.'

Ember gave a bit of a nod. It was to signal he'd allow Untidy a little time in a minute, and to direct him towards a table while he waited. Ember poured an Armagnac and put it on the bar, then nodded again to say the drink was a gift. Untidy moved away with it in that chain-gang shuffle of his. Nobody would ever mistake The Monty for The Athenaeum while people like Untidy belonged. A lot of people like Untidy belonged.

He sat down where Ember had indicated. It was a table Ralph always favoured for discussion – a little away from the crowded parts of the club around the bar and pool area, but not so far into the shadows that folk would suspect secret plotting. Ember poured himself some Armagnac and took another glance at the party making their split by the pool tables. A couple of women were involved, egging things on, hotting up the enmities, that way some women had. Ember hated all fights on the premises, of course, but especially fights where women clawed and yelled and stacks of big denomination notes got bled over. Unthinking sods: didn't they know that now and then Harpur and Iles would look in unannounced on a terror visit? A booty fracas would really intrigue those two, and it could not help The Monty's esteem.

He went to join Untidy. As soon as Ember sat down, Graham said: 'I expect you and many others, Ralph, might like to ask whether those days I spent furthering the gospel and carrying the banner of Christ now seem strange, even regrettable to me. Maybe I should admit, Ralph, that I lack something of the tenacity of St Paul who was Saul and then became for all the rest of his life – via those grand Epistles and so on – an apostle committed to . . . Well, I wondered if you'd considered we might have some fucking undercover girl in.'

This was exactly the thing about a member like Untidy: ninety per cent rubbish, but he did get glimpses of the scene and he could come up with what might turn out insights. The woman cop in place already? Did Shale know? If so, why no notification?

'Why do you ask about undercover, Gray?'

'Why I came, Ralph.'

'It's interesting.' In a minor way, but definitely only a minor way, Ember started to have one of his panics. There was the sweat across his back and his legs felt wide and very heavy, unleglike, more akin to barrels of something weighty but not quite solid, say easy-spread cheese. Christ, he had been ordered by Barney and those women to deal with the girl before she could begin. Yet she was already around, was she? Barney could be very jumpy, very protective of his immaculateness. If he heard about the girl – and the bastard seemed to hear most things – he might organize rough ways to get Ember moving on her. Maud would certainly make Barney stop supplies to Ember, break any business link, smelly now, in her savage opinion. His firm would die, even if they let *him* live.

Untidy said: 'It's not a pleasant thing to suggest – some girl fink, I know that, Ralph – but it seemed right to put it to you as soon as I could.'

'Absolutely, if there's anything in it, Gray.' Despite his legs, Ember forced himself to stand and went back to the bar. He picked up the bottle of Kressmann Armagnac and brought it to the table. He refilled for both of them.

Untidy said: 'This is someone asking if I've seen a certain girl, twenties, around the trading streets, with description.' He put a hand on his head. 'I keep it in here. No notes.' He was obviously proud of that, the rock-bottom carefulness. 'No name.'

'Who asking?'

'Oh, a plain clothes, I'd say. Youngish chap, full of push and training.'

Ember said: 'Drugs Squad? You recognized him from the Squad?'

'Too well-dressed. This is straight CID.'

'Inquiring about a girl who might be pretend dealing as cover?' Ember asked. What you could get with someone like Untidy was that they ran into very genuine information but did not always know how to use it. Hardly ever knew how to use it. You had to get them to say what they saw and then you interpreted privately. For God's sake, no CID man or Squad officer would ask Untidy about an undercover girl – not unless they wanted her killed for one of their own little headquarters games, which was unlikely though possible, admittedly. To inquire about her fingered her. Any detective would realize that Untidy would do just what he had done and report it upwards. This lad who asked the questions was more likely to know the girl from somewhere nothing to do with policing. Perhaps from loving. He might have lost touch with her because she'd been taken out of her usual life by Harpur for this work. Possibly Alfie Ivis would have her sex life dossiered and could identify this laddy for them. Alfie was beautiful on research. Her partner would probably have a respectable job somewhere, a suit-and-good-shoes job, and this could have made Untidy think CID. 'It's quite a revelation, Gray,' Ember said.

'I asked him what's her name, but he wouldn't say. Of course he wouldn't. He'd be putting a mark on her, wouldn't he, Ralph?'

'Right.' But if this was lover-boy searching for his girl, he probably would not know her name, not her undercover name, and would certainly not offer her real one: he was already giving her enough risk. Somehow he had found out or guessed she was going undercover and wanted her back. That was natural. He worried for her skin, as an intelligent boyfriend should.

'And then there's Harpur. And then there's Iles,' Untidy said.

'Iles?' Ember replied. His panic now opened out in full, like a daisy to the sun. He knew he could not have got to his feet at this stage.

'Iles was there.'

'There? At the Valencia?'

'And Harpur. The lad went back to a car. Harpur and Iles were waiting for him. This would be to report, yes?'

'Iles in person?' Ember asked.

'In the car.'

'In person?'

'I don't know what you mean, Ralph. He was sitting there, in the car.'

The ACC must have heard that this boyfriend, or whoever, was sniffing and blundering and mouthing around the Valencia, endangering the girl. He would come down fast to look after her safety. Iles could be like that. He would take it very . . . yes, very *personally* if one of his people were menaced or hurt or killed. An undercover detective called Raymond Street was murdered a while back when on assignment. Soon afterwards, the two people who might have done it – well, who *did* do it – these two were found dead themselves after court acquittals, one shot, the other garrotted.

Appalling. The legend went that Iles brought off this little corrective on his own, grieved by Street's death, nauseated by the acquittals. No question, this would amount to exceptional behaviour for an Assistant Chief, even one like Iles, but it was what the legend said. Ember believed it totally. So did almost everyone who knew Iles. Naturally, he was never done for it. Who could do Iles successfully? And now here was the ACC getting into position again, this time to guard the girl.

'You don't look too good, Ralph,' Untidy said.

Nice insolence from a sod with Untidy's face. Ember lowered his hand to his glass and gave himself a couple of plump mouthfuls. Then he refilled the glass and poured Untidy some more. At least his hand and arm were functioning all right regardless of panic. 'Tell me it step by step, Gray.' Ember tried for decent calm in his voice, but was not sure he made it. My God, if he tried to eliminate the girl, Iles would come for *him*, personally. If he did not immediately try to eliminate the girl, Barney and those women might come to persuade him by dirty painful means to speed things – *not* personally, but they would know skilled folk.

'I'm talking to him in Dring Place and here's Harpur busying along, obviously on his way to get a briefing. Well, I disappear, Ralph.'

'Certainly.'

'They talk, then Harpur leaves. I'm watching, but out of sight. Our lad goes after Harpur. It's been planned – discretion. They don't want to be seen together for long. I follow, though unspotted, Ralph.'

'Certainly.'

'He's been told to go to Iles's car on waste ground at the corner of Elgar Street and give a full survey.'

'And Iles was personally in it?' Ember asked.

'As I say, I don't know how he could be in it if it wasn't personally, Ralph.'

'They didn't see you?'

'One glimpse of them, an audit, and I was gone, Ralph.'

'Right. Wise. But no question it was Iles?'

'A Scorpio. It *would* be Iles. He takes such an interest, doesn't he?'

'Takes an interest? In police work, you mean? Well, he would, wouldn't he, Gray? He's an Assistant Chief Constable.'

Untidy said: 'In undercover. Remember that Ray Street business?'

'Which was that?'

'Oh, you know, Ralph: Street gets killed and—'

'You don't mean the mad rumour Iles did those two in revenge – taking over from the courts, like a vigilante? Personally.'

'I don't know it's a mad rumour, Ralph.'

'This is an Assistant Chief in a British police force we're talking about, for God's sake, Gray.'

'It's Iles we're talking about.'

Yes. Ember reached that point in the progress of a panic where an old scar which ran along his jaw line seemed about to open up and weep part of his essence everywhere. It never did, but he put up a hand quickly to hold himself together. 'This is all quite fascinating info, Gray,' he said.

'What will you do, Ralph? It's grave – a fink placed like that and a big operation, with Iles, *in person*, as you say. Could fuck the lot of us.'

'Do you do any prayer these days? Did the banner get you credits with Him above?'

'Identify the girl – that's the thing, isn't it?' Untidy said.

'One priority.' For Ember this had now become the worst kind of fear because it was not just one fear, it was triple, all three major. They tore at him, and he could not tell which to run away from first. There was the dread of death from Iles. There was the dread of pain and injury done to him on Barney's say-so. And then came a third vivid dread. This was the London people – Lincoln W. Lincoln and the other two. They had shown what they would do to any competition, even a miniature slice of felony like Pilgrim. They might see Ember and his business as competition, too. Of course they would. Bigger. More serious. And if Ember destroyed the undercover girl to satisfy Barney, and to preserve his limbs and supplies, she could never help get that London team out of the way and in front of a judge. Who *could*? They were strong and talented and hard. Terrible indecision battered Ember, nearly upending his mind. Normally when he had a panic there would be one cause only. Of course, this did not make a panic manageable. The point about panics was that they were *not* manageable or they would not be panics. But a panic with a known cause had boundaries. Now, though, came this terrible all-roundness.

He wanted to test his legs again and stood carefully, half propping himself on the table and making a long-drawn out thing of collecting up their glasses and the bottle while taking support, like on a walking frame. He thought he could probably do the few steps to the bar, where he would be able to lean some more. He moved there now pretty fast and set the glasses and the bottle of Armagnac down. Then he went around behind and took a couple of twenties and a ten from the till. Untidy had also stood up and followed him. He was opposite Ember on the other side of the bar, that long slum face mottled by Armagnac and zippy with achievement. Ember set a bar mat in front of Untidy with the three notes under it. He poured another Kressmann and put this on the mat. Untidy raised the glass with his left hand and with the other sweetly palmed the mat and the money, putting the lot in his pocket.

'The Si funeral, Ralph?' Untidy said, his glass empty once more.

Ember replenished. 'I'll be there, Gray.'

'I'm Earl Marshalling,' Untidy replied. His face resumed dreariness as he switched to full mourning. 'His relations didn't want to organize it. They feel they hardly knew his life any longer. Apparently, they're right outside drugs, not even using – no idea about *The Eton* and other aspects of Si's fine professional range. Manse Shale said me to do it, because of meaningful religious connections with the Reverend Bart Anstruther, Church of the Free Gospel – entirely multi-racial although he's black. The Rev Bart will make a wholesome job of Simon – not refer to evil too much. Obviously, he *knows* of evil, but no long fucking song against coke and crack and about reaping what you sow, routine pulpit shit. The Rev is more interested in salvation and the After Life. This will be a good occasion, Ralph. Necessary.'

'Yes, it's necessary.' Probably. Ember had wondered about the wisdom of going. Funerals put you in the corpse's clique, and Si was perilous to be cliqued with. But, as long as everyone turned up, the London people could not victimize just him for displaying brotherliness. Ember had a position and would be expected. A pity it had to be the Church of the Free Gospel and not a proper religious spot, but Untidy would naturally fix it for a place he knew, and Ember definitely did not object to a black running the show. Untidy brought the bar mat sneakily from his pocket and put it back in front of Ember, only the mat. 'Pilfering I loathe,' Untidy said. 'But I'm sure you'd really like to ask about when I carried the banner.'

'No'.

'Memories of those times are still precious to me, meaningful to me. Nourishment. Just there's been . . . let's call it a shift of emphasis in my life.'

'Of course,' Ember replied. Untidy was one of those fucking insignificants fascinated by the quirks of their own lives and for ever keen to yarn about them. He had a long, bony, half-sunken face which could most likely have been edged towards saintliness if only he had stuck with salvation longer.

Over by the pool tables the share-out discussion seemed to have settled itself. People knew Ember would not tolerate violence inside The Monty. No matter how nervy he might get on general matters, his courage never faltered here. He was sole custodian. Ember had faith in the club and fine hopes. Once, The Monty had been a select club for business folk, and the mahogany panelling and brass fittings still recalled class. Ember had made sure he kept all that. But the club had begun to slide years before he bought it, and he knew real devotion would be needed to restore eminence. Searching for consolation and something to restore his sense of life's stability, he glanced at a framed blow-up photograph hanging on the wall not far from the bar. It showed club members in happy mood, about to leave for that famous outing to Paris a few years ago. On the whole, Ember considered the trip had been a credit to the club, although a French tart was abducted for nearly thirty-six hours by a couple of the outing's committee men and two pimps hospitalized when they came seeking their property. Ember urgently wanted an established overseas dimension to The Monty, and next year he might organize a visit to Madrid, with its galleries and museums and so on, or to the Vatican, which also was full of interesting sights.

21

Mansel Shale said: 'Oh, this is a death that changes every fucking thing . . . Ralph.' He almost called Ember 'Panicking', he looked so unbrilliant today, but that would not have been warm towards a dear colleague, and especially not in a graveyard.

'A fundamental development,' Alf Ivis said. 'Manse sees the way Simon went as profoundly altering our general position, Ralph.'

'Slit among marina trees like that,' Shale said. 'We got a chaos-type situation here.'

'Manse thinks we—'

'Or chaos-type situation unless we act urgent,' Shale replied. 'Pre-empt. But maybe we shouldn't discuss such matters right after a very touching funeral. Decorum I prize. Ask anyone. My house tonight for some war talk, Ralph?' Shale turned away. 'Ah, Rev,' he called, 'this was done with dignity, with feeling, start to finish and I know we're all grateful.'

They were dispersing from the hole in the ground. Shale was fond of this old-style cemetery – brave pinkish marble obelisks and the stone angels, noses mostly poxed away by weather but still pretty. Memorials tried to make the best of things. He liked that. They told the world there'd been a life even if there wasn't one now. Some of the trees around here went on for centuries and made it look like Nature had all the top cards. These memorials said *Up yours* to them, obelisks especially – they had an up yours shape. Shale hated cemeteries where nearly everything was flat so they could drive a lawn mower across easier, like the Monte Carlo Rally. So some fucking council gardener was more important than honouring those gone on?

'Who would have wished Si that cruel harm?' Ember said.

Well, Shale could have listed at least three and maybe thirty-three, but best let Panicking do his solemnities. Lately, he was getting very civic.

'Ah, tainted days, Mr Ember,' the Rev Anstruther replied. 'We cannot escape the stain. May I tell you a little story as an example, the way we preachers do? Only a day or two ago I greet a young girl, twenties, come to live alone locally, no family, no job, it seems. I speak to her of the church and our mission there, certainly, but, unfortunately, I also know it's necessary to speak a warning to such an unprotected new resident. One's always made a thing of welcoming folk into our area and telling them of the Lord, but now I have to tell them also of the perils in our streets. An unpleasant duty. This earthly body and its safety is not our sole concern, of course, nor even our *main* concern, yet it is *a* concern and one that has to be faced up to.'

'Sad, yes, and a comment on our time, certainly,' Ivis replied.

'Undoubtedly,' Ember said.

'Where?' Shale asked.

'Where what, Mr Shale?' the Rev Anstruther said.

'The street,' Shale replied. 'Just I wondered if it was one of the worst ones this girl has picked, without knowing. Perhaps she could do better. There's some still quite decent. I know that area more or less.'

'Stave Street. Fine old houses. Fine old houses, *once*,' Anstruther replied.

'Ah, *once*,' Ember said and shook his head a while. Yes, truly civic.

'Right,' Shale said. 'If you give Alfred her name we might be able to improve for her. You said alone?'

'Rivers,' Anstruther replied.

Shale said: 'Funerals – I get to a lot, Rev. A duty. This is the unfortunate way the world's going, wouldn't you say? Violence everywhere, but it can't all be on account of TV. Somehow, Rev, you knew dead right . . . I mean *just* right, how to deal with a sly bit of wreckage like Pilgrim, and all credit to you. I'm sure Si's fine old mother over there would agree. Alfie, do a word with her, in case she don't come on to the feed, and see about the money side. To a mother, even someone like Si is a loss.'

'Such a funeral is tragic, heart-rending, of course,' the Reverend Anstruther said, 'yet it brings people into my church whom I might never see, never have the chance to speak with and tell of the Lord. If I may say, Mr Shale, this would include—'

'I think Si would be delighted by that,' Shale replied. 'It's a terrible thing to have your throat cut and nothing on the plus side.'

'Did he work for you?'

This Reverend Anstruther was well known as a bright number in unparalleled dark suits but Shale could not think of getting harsh with him for his questions in a spot like this, inscriptions all around. 'Well,' he replied, 'Simon was—'

'Mr Shale and Simon had some passing business connection,' Ivis replied. 'But not "worked *for*". That's not the way of it at all. *With* now and then, perhaps, yes. Simon was into buying and selling on his own account. Part of the small unit economy, oh, yes, very much so. Very freelance. One would think of it more as a franchise arrangement.'

'And the number of the house where this girl lives?' Shale asked. 'Rivers? Can you remember? But don't worry if not. Alfie will find her. A flair with street numbers – flats, houses, regardless. He could have been a virtuoso postman.'

'Twenty-three.'

'Good. And a furnished flat but no job?'

'Seemingly,' Anstruther replied.

'Quality furniture?'

'All right. An uninhibited poster,' Anstruther replied. 'Mr Shale, a pusher like Simon would be at the sharpest end of this game, wouldn't he, even in a select spot like *The Eton*?'

Oh, such street savvy, as it was known. Revs like Anstruther loved to show they had worldly wordage like 'sharpest end'. You had to put up with it. Everyone had heard of worker priests. This was nearly pusher priests. 'How about clothes?' Shale asked.

'Clothes?'

'This girl's clothes. Something Rivers? They all right, her clothes?' Shale said.

'Oh, yes. Nice enough.'

'Just that I worry about the unemployed,' Shale said.

'Manse always has,' Ivis said. 'And badger baiting.'

'Can you go see to Mrs Pilgrim now, Alf?' Shale told him. 'She's lingering a while with Si, as we can all understand. I don't know if she looks the sort with a bank account. Can't never tell these days. People with no polish at all still got credit cards and a PIN. Ask the sort code and account number, Alfred, would you? Tell her we'll be dropping a stipend regular there Direct Debit, and let her have something immediate – cash – will you? Funerals cost.'

'Oh, you paid for this one up front, Manse,' Ivis said. 'Don't you remember?'

'I did? We gave it direct to the undertaker, I hope, not via fucking Untidy Graham? Sorry, Rev, and especially when he's a trophy of grace off and on. But I don't want no skimming in matters of a genuine funeral.' Shale looked back towards Si's mother at the graveside: 'Mrs Pilgrim had to travel here, didn't she – this is from Hull or Swansea, that kind of distance, which is a big train fare. And then that hat. That hat's bought special for today, I know it. She wanted to see Simon off right. These things mount up. Tell her everyone loved Si, Alf, even the lads who cut his throat – it wasn't personal. It could have been anyone – anyone who had *The Eton*. Explain that the woman in that spot before – Eleri ap Vaughan – she was obliterated, too. Someone's mother should not have to think he was hated for himself. Say there'll be a headstone with his full name and a built-in flower-holder for sprays which will be replenished monthly.

Would we let someone like Si get blotted out for ever by cheap London barbarians?'

They had been walking slowly towards the road but now Ivis returned to speak to Mrs Pilgrim and the other three waited near a very bonny sepulchre with dates on it going right back to the 1920s. Shale thought it had been a good turnout, not just Si's relatives but many associates. Beau Derek and his live-in, Melanie, were just ahead of them, both in proper dark gear. Untidy Graham and some other nothing dealers chatted nicely in a big group near the cemetery gates. He hoped Untidy would not relapse and start preaching at them or they'd chuck him in the fucking pit. Shale would have hated it for Pilgrim to go off unnoticed. Of course, no police had come. Even if it was true Si went to an excellent school, he was just a piece of low-life dead, that was how the police would regard it, so they did not need to turn up. You had to be super-pure as well as slaughtered to get Harpur and Iles into doing respect.

'I wonder whether you, personally, Mr Shale, have thought that in the midst of life we are in death,' Anstruther asked.

'I'm saying it to Alfred and Ralphy here all the time, Rev. You got to get pre-emptive. I forget where it comes from, that text, "Get pre-emptive", maybe the Book of Malachi, but perhaps you should have it put on the wall of your place alongside that one I noticed there at the funeral, "Boast not thyself of tomorrow". But, yes, tomorrow *is* always problematical.'

'The people cry out in their prayers to God for tranquillity and protection, Mr Shale,' Anstruther said.

'Rev, I'm doing all I fucking can.'

*

In the evening, drinking gin and peps from brilliant heavy-based glasses, Shale said: 'The timescale, Ralph. That got to be so different now.'

'Mansel and I agree totally on the new urgency, Ralph,' Ivis said, 'though not on the detail of how to deal with it.'

Shale said: 'A funeral like that and then the lovely sand-wiches and Vimto and madeira and nice comradeship afterwards at Alfie's place – all of it excellent, but now we got to ask very seriously, Ralph, where the fuck are we?'

'Manse thinks it's a matter of hitting the London people direct,' Ivis said.

'What else?' Shale replied. 'It's what I told the Rev – pre-emptive, except it can't be that in full, clearly, because they already done Gladhand Mace and Si, tragically. But us next? Of course it would be. These people are clean sweep people. That's why we got to be pre-emptive. This was the word they used back in time about hitting Russia before they had the Bomb. What's known as a concept.'

'Hit them *all*?' Ember asked.

Shale saw the bugger tremble right through. How did someone so nervy ever collect the loot for his country house, Low Pastures, and the club, even a bloody club like The Monty? 'Hit LWL only and the other two would still do their business plan,' Shale replied. 'Tommy Mill-Kaper and Digby are principals. If Lincoln W. Lincoln went, they don't care. He's just a ranker. They can spare twenty like him.'

The three were in the drawing room of Shale's house, once a genuine rectory. The Chief had an ex-rectory, too, and Shale liked this sense of comradeship. In his den room was a desk he bought with the property where rectors probably did their sermons and planned the Whitsun Treat. Shale loved this notion, also – the continuity. First, all that great church business, now him. But he had decided it should be the drawing room tonight. You showed Ralphy the best or he'd make judgements. Panicking's Low Pastures was famed for style and size and mansion-type chimneys, a paddock and exposed beams, all that. Solemn in the big red leather armchair near the curtains, Ivis said: 'But, with every respect, Manse, Ralph might have a point regarding a hit on *all* the London principals, Lincoln, Mill-Kaper and Corporeal. A lot of fire-power for us to take on in one place, you'd agree. Tommy Mill-Kaper, with this Victoria Cross grandfather – so Tom's always trying to prove the gun skills have come down to him, even if not the medal. And the question is, if I may say, Manse, the question is how do we get them into one place for a hit, anyway? They'd be so careful about that. It would *have* to be done in one spot at one time, or they're alerted.'

Well, Ivis was on the staff to help with ideas, so you had to listen to him. 'Alfie's got his own scheme, Ralph,' Shale said. 'I'd like to hear what you think of it. It brings in the undercover girl.'

'The girl?' Ember said. 'I was going to ask you about her.

I feel left out on information, Manse, a bit. I hear she's already dealing.'

'If I may say, probably *not*, Ralph,' Ivis replied. 'She's only just left Hilston. That's my understanding.'

Ember said: 'But a man's been looking for her at—'

'The Valencia?' Ivis said. 'It will be someone who knows she's going to mock-trade there eventually, but can't know when.'

Shale said: 'As a matter of fact, I'd take a bet she's in a flat with a rude poster at 23 Stave Street and called Rivers.'

'Ah,' Ivis replied. 'Ah.'

You might have thought Alfie would have got to this bit of insight on his own. Shale always enjoyed it when that meaty face of Ivis's suddenly went nearly vivid from shock and wonder at the sight of mind power. You had to ask was he worth his money, though.

'Ah,' Alf said.

Shale said: 'No job but she got furniture and fair clothes. Who supplies? She on the game? Or she provided for by Harpur? It got to be fifty-fifty this is Ms Infiltration. A dirty poster on the wall. That would be one of them crude police jokes by the people getting it ready for her. Police enjoy filth. Funny to be told by a preacher called Anstruther about a girl called Anstruther who's called Rivers.'

'Ah,' Ivis said. 'Manse, if I may say, you have *such* intuition.'

'This Rivers – if she's the one – Alfie got plans for her, Ralph.'

'Yes,' Ivis replied.

'He keeps on about it,' Shale said. 'So, tell him, Alf.'

'Certainly.' Alf put his glass on the floor for concentration and sat back, full of his bloody self despite missing that Stave Street. This was one of Alfie's strengths, he never got devastated by his dimness, he kept going, like President Reagan in the old days. 'I'd say, let her in to the firm – *seem* to let her into the firm – and put her on *The Eton* right away,' Ivis replied.

'Get it, Ralph?' Shale asked. 'Give her Si's dealership so she's an instant target. Alfie thinks the three would come for her the way they most likely arranged things for Si because they want *The Eton* above all, and we're waiting and we do them then. A sweet ambush. That's Alfred's scheme – a way to get the trio together at night in a favourable setting, the docks, and busy thinking about something else, not their security, but only doing the girl. How does it strike you?'

Shale stood and dished out more gin and peps. He thought this might soften the tension. But Ember did not answer. He would be too scared to speak right off. He wanted to see how he *ought* to speak. Shale strolled the drawing room a bit, giving Ralphy more time. On one of the walls, was an Arthur Hughes painting and a couple by Edward Prentis. Shale had a gaze close up at them again in the pause. He often told friends he was a sucker for pre-Raphaelites, those thin women with plenty of brown hair, long Oxfam frocks and frightened eyes. The hair was called tresses. He loved that word. This was something else you did not get these days, tresses, what with punks scalping theirselves.

They had a Brotherhood, the pre-Raphaelites, and Shale thought he could of had a lot of time for Brotherhoods if only they were still the thing now.

He sat down opposite Ember again. 'I don't say nothing to sway you, Ralph,' he said. 'I definitely don't regard Alfie's plan as total shit, even if I might think we got no time to fuck about being devious and fly like that. I want to hear your view without no influence whatsoever from me, Ralph.'

And he did want to hear. But before Ember answered, Ivis went very confiding, his grand voice low and deep and comforting: 'If I may say, Manse, Ralph, there'd be a first-class chance the girl would be wiped out by them during this action if we timed it nicely. An operation with, as it were, stages. Thus, she'd be gone plus the London three. This would fully restore the area to its previous pleasant useful order.'

Ember said: 'It would certainly be a great help if one of those three could take her out for me – us.'

Shale did some brain work on that. 'You been told by someone she got to be removed, have you, Ralph?' he asked. 'This would be someone influential, full of power? This is Barney boy and those lumps of old snatch down in yachting land, is it? You been ordered to do it yourself, yes, before Barney can get fingered through undercover fingering *you*? Which means you're pani— Which means you're fretful about Iles doing an aftermath. You'd dislike being garrotted and you're really worrying and looking for a way out of the situation, yes? Oh, now here comes that tearaway, Laurent.'

He chuckled a bit and shook his head a few times, pretending a bit more irritation than he felt.

Shale's son ran into the room. Actually, Shale hated it when Laurent or his sister hurtled around the place like this, regardless of the prize old furniture and ornaments and Alfie's glass on the floor. But you could not tie kids down, so he put up with it unless they got really hunnish. These were kids whose mother had disappeared with someone to have it off in Wales, for God's sake, and you had to compensate. Laurent must have heard Ivis's voice and wanted a tale or two from him. Laurent loved the way Alfie knew the whole history of the Royal Navy right back to twin screws and torching Cadiz. You mention aircraft carriers to him and he could give all the names, and about deck lifts for bringing the planes up from below. Laurent said: 'Uncle Alfie, that one about those cruisers Lion and Tiger sinking a big German ship on the Doggy Bank. All the animals.'

'Dogger Bank,' Ivis said. 'The Blucher, 1915.'

'Later, Laurent,' Shale said. 'We got a tricky little business matter to talk about.'

'I'll wait, shall I, Dad?' the boy asked.

'Yes, but not here. Wait in the other room. Alfred will come out in a minute, all salty and anchors aweigh.'

When the boy had gone, Shale said: 'As you might gather, Ralph, myself I'd go for the three of them straight, no fucking about with fucking smartarse tactics. But you think bring her into *The Eton*, do you?'

Of course he would. There was no peril for him. Get Barney's women off of his back.

'It seems a tidy little project,' Ember replied.

Shale stayed quiet for a while. He was not going to take on Lincoln W. Lincoln, Corporeal and a VC's grandson on his fucking own, was he? These two would not help, or they *would* help but without believing in it, so they'd be no good and it would not work. The three of them might finish alongside Si, which would cost Shale's estate a packet in obelisks. 'I hope Mansel Shale knows when he's outvoted,' he said. 'It's going to be even weirder if we got a Rev called Anstruther burying a girl called Anstruther that he thought was someone else. He'd know by then.'

'If I may say, Manse, it's totally in keeping with your reputation for reasonableness and balance to accept so cheerfully the views of advisers,' Ivis replied. 'I'm sure I speak for Ralph when I say I know you won't regret it.'

'Absolutely,' Ember said, the yellow jerk.

Shale thought he might take a quiet look at 23 Stave Street, all the same. Checking. It was only a guess that the girl was there, and maybe a far out guess. Shale did trust some of his guesses, though. Maybe guesses was a dim word for it. Often, they were more like what Alfie would call intuitions. The true leader's mind went so fucking fast and so right it might look like a guess or an intuition, but really it was a special kind of thought, a leader's kind – too swift for others to understand, and even for himself to understand always, only to be glad you had it from somewhere. For instance, Winston Churchill. Look at the way he just knew long before the war that Hitler was the one who had to be done. And similar was what happened when the Rev said a girl on her own in Stave Street – what you could call a thought-flash, even like inspiration.

All right, Alfie and Panicking had voted to get the girl into *The Eton* and solve everything that way. But think what these two were like. One was Alfred, a fine lad for small jobs but also someone who produced them kids he had and picked a fucking lighthouse to live in. And then came Panicking – who was panicking. Many, in fact most, were against Churchill when he called early for Hitler to be snuffed. Chamberlain. And that Edward VIII – he was around Hitler's well-known mountain eyrie sucking up to him, telling everyone the führer was misunderstood and liked dogs. Did Churchill care? A leader just *knows*, that's all.

Perhaps what Alfie and Panicking wanted would work and the girl could be taken out at *The Eton* while the London people were also done. But Shale's own thinking said something else, and he had to trust that or where was he? – he was like Alfie or Panicking, that's where he was. Shale's thinking said that if they put the girl in *The Eton* Harpur would have her protected there. Of course he bloody would. These people, Harpur and Iles, the two of them had never got over the death of that lad Street. Iles was a poisonous sod, yes, but he stayed loyal to his people, which was why the poisonous sod was so savage and dangerous. More savage and dangerous than the Chief, obviously, and maybe more loyal to his people, also. Those two, Harpur and Iles, would be on the watch more or less non-stop to make sure what happened to Street did not happen to this girl. And they would see *The Eton* was the top peril spot. If they had people watching her there and other people on call, it could mean not just the London crew would get blasted but Shale and his crew – and Panicking and his crew also, if they were all present to ambush. They had some very jolly marksmen in Harpur's lot. Panicking could not think something out like this, although he was supposed to be a leader himself. Panics bit holes in his brain, even if his brain was any good to start with. You had to use *your* mind for him.

The girl had to be knocked over, yes, or she could start observing and talking any time and fuck up everything. And Lincoln W. Lincoln and Corporeal and Tommy had to be knocked over, also, or they would get to be the twenty-first century. But these were two separate jobs. Winston Churchill would not have muddled up the Middle East part of the war and the Battle of the Atlantic. You had to do these things bit by bit, even though you was working all the time for general victory, clearly. Probably there was no easy, wrap-it-all-up-at-once way, the way Alfie and Panicking wanted. Yes, it would be worth a little vigil to make sure Rivers was who he thought Rivers was.

22

Harpur had a call from Jack Lamb to suggest a meeting. These were the sort of calls and the sort of suggestions Harpur always agreed to. Jack was perhaps the world's greatest informant and when he spoke you'd better believe it. No perhaps. He *was* the world's greatest informant and he belonged exclusively to Harpur. That exclusiveness broke all the central rules about running informants, so sod the rules. Of course, there were many rules that Harpur *did* believe in and accept, or he would not have been a police officer, probably. And he believed in the law – or, likewise, he would probably not have been a police officer. But he had decided that the rules did not quite reach Jack Lamb. And he had decided that the law now and then needed some good aid, and this might often come from Lamb. He owed Lamb. Lamb owed him. This gorgeous balance proclaimed all there was to proclaim about the relationship of a detective and his tipster: proclaimed it in secret.

'Do you watch *The Eton*, Col?' Lamb asked, when they rendezvoused.

'We watch everywhere. It's known as policing, Jack.'

'I'm heartened. Shall I tell you the situation post Si Pilgrim? But perhaps you already know it? I suppose that would be policing, too.'

Harpur said: 'Timberlake is doing good work on the Pilgrim inquiry.'

'Yes?'

'But it's not going to be a swifty.'

'No, I didn't think it would be a swifty,' Lamb replied. 'The London people will put their boy in there, obviously. Why else is Si dead?'

'In where? Which London people is that, Jack?'

Lamb did not bother to answer these questions but paced for a while. Jack frequently paced at their meetings. It gave quite a bit of weight to things. He said: 'It's already contracted with the management, Col.'

'What is?'

'*Eton* sole trading rights, for the London boys,' Lamb replied. 'What Si had. And Eleri before. Anyone attempting to compete – well, look what happened to Si. And Eleri.'

'Who told you this, Jack?' During these get-togethers, Harpur would always ask Lamb at least once about his sources. It was part of the formalities and useless.

'They won't put him in openly at once, naturally, because this might lead to an appearance of motive for Si's death and bring you down on them with your frightening notebook, Col. But dealing will continue, under the table at this stage you might say. Can they afford to leave the Eton's glossy clientèle untended for heaven's sake, even for a few days? Those elegant, moneyed nostrils might drift off to other snort venues, mightn't they, Col?'

'Can which *they* afford it, Jack?'

'*The Eton*'s proprietors, clearly, and the London trinity.

They'll have Lincoln W. Lincoln in place eventually, or even Mill-Kaper. Yes, Tommy's usually down-market, but they think *Eton* clients would like his officers' mess lineage and the hyphen.' He paced again very briefly and then spun on Harpur. 'Would I be dropping you these facts if I hadn't been fond of Si, Col – those brave little legs? Do I inform willy-nilly? I don't think so.'

Almost always Lamb found it necessary to explain his gospel of grassing. And almost always Harpur found it necessary to give attention. 'You're not a willy-nilly person, Jack.'

'Are Shale and Panicking going to put up with the loss of *The Eton*, Col, and especially Shale? Panicking believes in tactical retreats, but they'll both think they have a right to succession. They haven't. The spot's sold. I don't know what the pressures were or the money, but unquestionably sold. The local teams will try and put their own dealer in all the same. This has the makings of something very painful and untidy. What I'd be particularly unhappy to think is that you might—'

Lamb paced some more and seemed to let the sentence escape, the way Lane did occasionally. They were at one of their regular meeting spots, a Second World War concrete defence post on the foreshore. Lamb liked this place and some other old military sites they also used. He adored the distant flavour of fight-'em-on-the-beaches. Generally, he would turn up in gear that harmonized: stuff bought from army and navy surplus shops. He had on a Rommel-type grey greatcoat tonight with what might be Staff insignia, a wide-winged collar and black calf-length boots, possibly genuine jack boots. The care they took to meet in secret spots always seemed to Harpur cancelled out by Lamb's costume and size. Harpur was big enough but, standing alongside him, Lamb looked like a house against a shed. Harpur never protested to Jack about his clothes, though. The informant had all the peril, and if Jack needed battle garb for it, OK. The evening was warmish, and they had stayed outside the defence post so far. Air in there was not sweet after more than fifty years of mixed uses.

'There's been a lad around *The Eton*, Col, that's my worry. He's spending, yes, apparently, but not in a proper way – in a cover way.'

'Which lad is that, Jack?'

'What I'd be particularly unhappy to think is you might— This is a lad asking around, but not quite asking around. Do you know what I mean?'

Yes, Harpur knew. 'No, I don't, Jack, I'm afraid.'

'Asking around. Looking for someone. Trying to be so guarded. Buying as if for a habit, but no habit.'

'There's such a changing population on *The Eton*.'

'You know this lad,' Lamb stated. 'He's been busy at the Valencia, too. Same thing. You talked to him there and took him to see Mr Madness in Mr Madness's car. You wouldn't expect not to be noticed, would you, Col?'

Harpur said: 'We do pull people in down there now and then, more or less at random. For their own safety as much as anything.'

'I believe it,' Lamb replied. 'I had a little inquiry done on this lad you took in at random and for his own safety, Col, during a virtue patrol with Iles. This is Donald McWater, a section manager at Sainsbury's. He's having a relationship with one of your people. *Was*. A girl called Naomi Anstruther. *Was* called. Don seems to have lost track of her and to be concerned. The Valencia, *The Eton*, what does it look like, Col?'

'Who did that research for you, Jack? You've got talented people.'

'This McWater is a lad who sticks at it. What you'd expect from a section manager at Sainsbury's,' Lamb replied.

'These middle-class executive types love to slum at the Valencia. They think they're seeing inner city.'

'They *are*. Cities don't get more inner than the Valencia. But *The Eton*, Col? Why's he there?'

'Oh, he's read about it in the Press, connected with Pilgrim's death.'

'Of course he has,' Lamb said. 'He's looking for a frisson, you think?'

'Something like that. I've heard of frissons.'

Lamb did enter the blockhouse now and Harpur followed. It was very dark but Harpur knew where to look for him. He had often seen Jack move into this ritual. Lamb was bent down at one of the observation slits, staring out over the mudflats and receding sea. He might have been searching for an invading army, though his German kit confused the picture tonight because the enemy this blockhouse was built to spot and stop was German. He spoke over his shoulder, so as not to take his eye off danger areas out there: 'There's a buzz about that you've got someone going undercover in due course, Col. Hilston Manor former pupil. But even without that I might have wondered. This reconnoitering laddy has been cut out of his girlfriend's life because she's become someone else?'

'He's a fucking pest, Jack. I thought we'd convinced him to keep away.'

'You told him she's undercover?'

'How else do I stop the idiot? Iles warned him, but—'

'You *don't* stop him. Do you think he's afraid someone might put her into *The Eton* against Lincoln W. or Tommy?'

'Perhaps.'

'Have *you* thought about that, Col? Is this girl going to be made bait by someone? Might it be a chance for, say, Shale and Panicking to get the three London boys in a convenient stretch of the inner city's rejuvenated urban killing fields? Actually, it sounds a bit oblique and long-winded for Shale to devise, and too rough for Panicking. But Alfie Ivis? Alf gets ideas. Iles would like a battle there, wouldn't he – all of them popping off at one another so the police job is just to count bodies, not mess about with evidence and courts?'

Harpur said: 'The Assistant Chief Constable is—'

'But this girl in the centre – and on someone's list, anyway, the buzz being so strong. That makes it tricky, even for Iles.' Definitively, Lamb turned away from the observation slit. It did not look as if the hordes in landing craft would show tonight, again. He prepared to leave.

'How's art, Jack?' Harpur asked. Lamb dealt in pictures, dealt brilliantly in pictures, had bought a manor house called 'Darien' from dealing in pictures.

'Art? A treat, Col.'

'Anything really special lately?'

'Acquired or sold?' Lamb replied.

'Either.'

'Well then, Col, you'll be pleased to hear I've just acquired a Chelmonski.'

'Ah,' Harpur said.

'Perhaps it would be more true to say I am in the process of acquiring. You'll love it. Nobody does the Polish country-side with more – more Polishness, really.'

'It's a happy flair,' Harpur replied.

'And sold? Oh, sold a Tom Couture – so sensitive with women's arses, which one needs to be, as you know – and a Faed: he did more than *The Soldier's Return*, of course.'

'I'm glad,' Harpur replied. There had been a time when he would ask Jack where a painting had come from and where a painting went, just as he still asked where Lamb's information originated. He had never received answers about the art, just as he still never received answers about Jack's sources. Harpur had given up inquiring about the where from and the where to of Jack's pictures. Tonight, he did not press to know which 'processes' Lamb was going through to obtain the Polish countryside done Polishly. Jack was entitled to certain privacies in exchange for breaching the privacies of others and telling Harpur about them – though, naturally, only those privacies which fitted Jack's concept of what the honourable grass might do. Police forces laid down a wonderfully elaborate and thoughtful system for dealing with informants and for rewarding them. Harpur did approve of all this, but he did not approve enough.

On his way home, Harpur called in at headquarters to see whether Timberlake or Garland was there and had made any progress on Pilgrim's death, or even Mace's. Garland appeared but could speak of no advances. 'All the London people are super-alibied, so far,' he said. 'These hits were deftly handled.'

'Are they working *The Eton*?'

'It's possible. Tommy Mill-Kaper was there tonight, apparently taking a meal in the restaurant with a bird. Well, he *was* taking a meal with a bird. I don't know what else. He went a bit tense when I arrived, just ate and chatted the girl.'

'Yes, I expect so,' Harpur said. Garland had come up, and was still going up, via accelerated promotion. He had the style and voice that went with it, and Tommy Mill-Kaper might know enough to place Francis's booming qualities in a soaring police career. Iles used to say that if Garland was ever flung out of the service he could become a steel band.

Garland said: 'Just before you showed, sir, there was a lad at Reception asking for Naomi. They knew it might be sensitive and called me downstairs when they couldn't reach you.'

'How do they know it's sensitive?'

Garland shrugged in his fine way-of-the-world style. 'They do, sir. Custom of the service.'

'Looking for her *here*?' Harpur replied. 'What's wrong with this idiot? Does he think we're officially going to put him in touch when he's failed to find her on the street? I take it this is that fucking pestilence, her ex called McWater, yes? We'll have to lock the bugger up for obstruction.'

Garland took a Reception flimsy from his pocket and read

it: 'No, sir. Lyndon Vaughan Fitzhammon Evans. A Cardiff address. Tall, thin, fair. Twenty-six. We've asked the computer about him: two lots of taking and driving away: one bound over; one suspended sentence.'

'Cardiff? Knows Naomi? How?'

'What he calls "a most pleasant holiday friendship", sir. He said he promised to look her up but has no address or phone number.'

'Which holiday?'

'Torremolinos. That's the recent one, isn't it, the run-up break, so I don't suppose she'd tell him anything?'

'Except that she was a police officer, the idiot girl.'

'No, he wasn't sure of that. Came to the nick on spec. He said his friend Esmé – Christ, Esmé – had guessed she might be and Esmé "sees a lot, isn't it?"' Garland did a South Wales sing-song accent. 'He left. We couldn't hold him. He said he might be able to find Naomi through – well, through McWater. He knew McWater works in Sainsbury's, and McWater must have told him the town.'

'Address?'

'Only the Cardiff one, sir.'

Harpur said: 'The sod's probably here by stolen vehicle and sleeping in it. Until he finds Naomi. One or both of these cunt-struck jerks could get her finished, Francis.'

Garland said: 'I never fancied her myself. A sort of . . . well, a sort of *blurred* face. Didn't seem to know which way it was going. Highest-grade tits, though. How about you, sir?'

'No tits at all.'

23

Now and then Harpur wondered whether it was good for
Hazel and Jill that so many people connected with his job
called at the house late in the night. Although he tried to
keep the reasons for these visits confidential, they were sure
to suggest emergency and bring an atmosphere of continuing stress. This might affect his daughters permanently.
Hazel and Jill would occasionally be woken by such
intrusions and perhaps made anxious, though they certainly
never showed it, only curiosity. Perhaps the experiences
were hardening them. He would not like that. He knew some
people did find the girls businesslike for their ages. Denise
said they were all right, though, and he gave a lot of attention to what Denise thought. She knew what the young were
like, was ahead of him on some things.

Denise had not gone back to her student flat tonight but
stayed with him at Arthur Street, and Harpur was asleep
beside her in bed when she sat up suddenly and gave a little
scream, half waking him. Perhaps she had screamed twice
and he failed to hear the first: always he slept beautifully
when Denise spent the night here – what he used to call to
himself 'sleeping safe', though he would never say that
to her. Yes, she made him feel safe, but he could not tell her,
because it was absurd. How could this kid, not much older

than his own kids, make him safe? 'God, Col, wake up, will you,' she mumbled. 'Listen. It's happening *again*.'

'What?'

'Listen. This time it's not the front door, is it, like when the Lanes called?'

He put his hand under his chin and lifted his head off the pillow, to get both ears working. 'Yes,' he said. 'I hear.'

'But Keith Vine *is* dead, isn't he?'

Harpur listened again.

'Well, isn't he?' Denise said.

'Someone's tapping the kitchen window,' he said.

'I know it, know it, you dozey sex-spent sod. Keith Vine used to tap the kitchen window in the middle of the night on grassing visits. Remember?'

Still nearly asleep Harpur replied: 'Anyone can tap a window.'

The bedroom door was suddenly shoved open and Denise gasped and slid down to cover herself. Harpur switched on the bedside lamp. Jill, in pyjamas, said: 'Someone outside. Do you want me to go down and see who? It could be Des Iles. Hazel hasn't heard. She'll be really peeved.'

'No,' Harpur said. 'I'll do it.'

'I'll come down with you, in case,' Jill replied.

'In case what?' Harpur asked

'In case it's not Iles or the Lanes again. Like trouble?'

'How would it be trouble?' Harpur replied. 'Does trouble tap windows and advertise?'

'I'll come with you, anyway,' Jill said.

'No,' Harpur replied.

'Denise can't go with you. She hasn't got anything on. All chest.'

'I can *put* something on,' Denise said.

'Here's Hazel now,' Jill replied.

'Someone's tapping the kitchen window,' Hazel said. She wore a nightgown.

'You think it's Des Iles, do you?' Jill replied. 'Did he throw gravel at your window first?'

'Get knotted, rabid tunnel bat,' Hazel replied. 'Shall I come down with you, Dad?'

'In case it *is* Iles,' Jill said. 'It would be better if Hazel and I came with you, Dad. It could look bad if it's neighbours or something like that – a woman like Denise in the house so late. I mean, so young and leggy and so on, at your age.'

Harpur rolled out of bed and began to dress. 'Wait here, all of you. Or you two can go back to your rooms,' he told Hazel and Jill.

'Might it be a fink?' Jill asked.

Yes, it might, and finks would not want to meet his family, nor his girlfriend.

'Your king of finks?' Jill asked.

He had seen his king of finks only lately and Lamb rarely came to the house, anyway.

'Will you be armed?' Jill asked.

'This is Arthur Street, not Detroit.'

'To date,' Hazel replied.

When Harpur went into the kitchen he moved cagily and found he was expecting to see what he used to see when Vine called late – just a hand reaching up from below, often

wearing a mitten, and holding a fifty pence piece with which
he rapped the window. Instead, there was a man, a black
in half-moon glasses, excellent dark suit and a dog collar,
standing and peering in. Harpur had not put on the kitchen
light. He recognized the Reverend Bartholomew Anstruther.
Harpur opened the door and brought him into the kitchen.

'I may have put one of your people in terrible peril, Mr
Harpur,' he gabbled, no preacher's voice at all.

'Come inside.'

'Promise me you will act at once. She could be killed.
Will be killed.'

'Come inside and we can talk.'

'Promise me you will act at once and that you will inform
at least one other senior officer, by which I mean Mr Iles or
the Chief Constable himself.'

'I need to hear what you say. We'll go through to the
living room,' Harpur replied. 'There are no curtains here.'
He led the way.

Anstruther spoke again before he had properly sat down
on the big sofa: 'There's a woman officer of yours called
Rivers, isn't there? Or perhaps not called Rivers really, but
called Rivers for a purpose.'

'Rivers?' Harpur said.

'Angela Rivers.'

Denise and the two girls appeared in the doorway and
took seats. Denise had put on a sweater and jeans. Jill said:
'I'll make tea.'

'You can't stay here,' Harpur said. 'This is police business.'

'We get a lot of it you know,' Jill told Anstruther. 'Oh,

don't feel hurt – Dad never introduces people like you. When I say "like you" I don't mean he doesn't introduce you because you're black or the dog collar, just that people who come late usually have something to hide.'

'Shut up,' Hazel said.

'This is the Reverend Anstruther from the Church of the Free Gospel,' Harpur said. 'I met him a long while ago on a case. These are my daughters, Hazel and Jill, and this is a good friend, Denise.'

'*His* friend mainly, as you'd most likely guess,' Jill said, 'but ours, too, yes.'

'Is your place laying on of hands for healing?' Hazel asked. 'I've done you in Religious Knowledge.'

'Just the simple glorious Gospel,' Anstruther said.

'Mr Anstruther is here to tell me a woman is in danger,' Harpur said. 'Time is important. Go.'

'Is this the Angela Rivers we heard mentioned?' Jill asked.

'It's urgent,' Anstruther said.

'Who is she?' Denise asked. 'What's a minister doing here?'

'It's all right, Denise,' Jill replied at once. 'It will be genuine police business, I can tell – not some woman who's gone to a minister for help and advice in her distress because Dad's what's called foully wronged her.'

'Disappear into the kitchen and make tea,' Harpur replied. 'Perhaps you could stay there until I say it's all right.'

'All of us?' Denise asked.

Hazel said: 'If you ever really live with him, I mean every

night, Denise, you'll find there's a lot of this sort of thing – confidential crisis moments, often quite late.'

'I know it. Of course I know it,' Denise said. 'What difference does it make?'

'Could you take it?' Hazel asked.

'Well, I hope she could,' Jill replied, 'because it would be really lovely if Denise was here always – breakfast and so on.'

Harpur led them to the kitchen and shut the door. Anstruther said in a weak whisper: 'I fear I've betrayed her. It was unintentional. It was stupid.'

'You mean this woman Rivers that you spoke of?'

'Stave Street.'

'I know Stave Street,' Harpur replied.

'Shale's there now. I've seen him.'

'Mansel Shale? How?' Harpur asked.

'I told him.'

'What do you mean "there" now?' Harpur asked. 'In the—'

'In the street, watching, searching. Not in the flat yet.'

Harpur felt relieved, marginally. 'You told him how? Told him what? You don't know anything.'

Anstruther reached out with one hand, as if to touch Harpur's arm, but did not quite go the distance. It was a gesture that might be asking for help and for forgiveness, but Anstruther seemed to feel unentitled. 'This Rivers *is* one of your people, isn't she? I should have realized it at once. He was so interested. This is such a pleasant girl, with a lewd poster on the wall, which I'm sure she did not put there herself. Anyone could see it's not her own place. A duty billet.'

Harpur said: 'Told him what?'

'At the cemetery, just describing the perils of living in the Valencia for a girl, apparently alone – describing in general. Only that. An example, that was all. I gave him the wrong address.'

'But you said he's in Stave Street.'

'The wrong number. He began to ask so many questions, I felt something was not right. Yes, late on I felt something was not right. Too late on. Oh, stupid. Do you know this Shale? Frightening, in a way. I tried to backtrack – lied about the number.'

'You'll be forgiven, especially by me,' Harpur said.

'But he'll find her eventually. He'll work along the street.'

'Of course he'll find her.'

'I should have come sooner. I should have come immediately after the funeral. But I don't think it fully dawned even when I left him. I hoped I was wrong. I thought he might suspect she was a rival dealer or a tart and was interested for one of those reasons. I wanted to check whether he'd do anything. He's there, observing.'

'So far. How do you know he doesn't still think she might be a dealer or a tart?'

'I don't know how I know. But now I do.'

'Yes,' Harpur said.

Jill brought in a tray with tea things on from the kitchen. There was a fat slab of sponge cake, still in the wrapping paper. Hazel and Denise followed her.

'I have to go out at once,' Harpur said.

'Often it's like that here, Denise,' Hazel said. 'Don't get angry or jealous.'

'Why?' Denise said.

'I think you *are*,' Jill said. 'But Hazel's right for once. I don't understand what women like Denise see in Dad, do you, Mr Anstruther? That nose, and the haircut.'

'Entertain the minister,' Harpur replied.

'I must come, too,' Anstruther said. He stood up. 'I would not rest. This is a life on my conscience. And, please, you must call someone else – Mr Lane or Mr Iles.'

'I can manage,' Harpur said.

'It's necessary to call someone else,' Anstruther replied.

'Oh, I've heard of this,' Hazel said, eating a chunk of the cake that she broke off with her fingers. 'The black community.'

'What?' Harpur asked. 'Clear your mouth.'

Hazel chewed and swallowed and then said: 'You know, Dad – the black community. Don't play dumb. Obviously, they won't usually have anything to do with you – the police, I mean – Caribbeans won't have anything to do with you at all. They call the police Babylon, meaning organized evil. They sort out their own affairs. It's understandable. But if they have to, really have to, like now – this crisis whatever with the woman, Angela Rivers – if there's no way around it, and they *have* to use the police, they say always say what you have to say to two of them or more than two, so one of them can't screw you or pull you into some dirty private ploy of their own. Especially if the police are high rank. You and Iles and Lane are high rank, Dad. Like a divide and rule policy – that's how the black community works when it's to do with police. Of course, it can go wrong, because the two or more police could get together and agree what to say, and then it's worse.'

'Yes, it's my culture, Mr Harpur,' Anstruther said. 'Please, I do believe you are a good man and honest but—'

'You don't,' Jill said. 'That's not how you were brought up and no wonder. Think of your persecuted ancestors, like that book, *Roots.*' She was pouring the teas. 'The Chief or Iles? Well, definitely it's got to be Des Iles, hasn't it? Haze would say that anyway, because – well, because it's Iles. But this is another thing Haze could be right about for once. If this is truly urgent, it's got to be Iles. The Chief's like a dipped biscuit lately and needs his wife with him.' She put down the teapot. 'I'll go and phone Des, shall I? Tell him to get over here nowish. Or Hazel could ring. He'd get here really fast then.'

'Look after the guest,' Harpur replied. He went to the phone in the corner of the room and dialled Naomi Anstruther. She answered quickly, as if still up. 'I'm coming over,' he said.

'What for?'

'Don't open until you hear my voice at the door.'

'Coming at this hour? Why?'

'It will be all right. I'll have people with me.'

Jill said: 'Oh, you're not talking to Iles yet, Dad? That's the Angela Rivers, is it?'

Hazel said: 'She thinks you're coming on to her, does she, Dad?'

He rang off and called Iles. The ACC was in. Harpur gave the tale. Iles arrived six minutes later, brilliant in a hacking jacket and turquoise cord trousers. He had on one of his scarves worn draped and colourful, like an immigrant in *Godfather, Part II*.

'Dad just gave us the gunless-British-bobby crap, Des,' Jill said. 'But *you*, are you carrying something – I mean, if it's so tense, this Rivers matter?'

'Rev!' Iles replied, beaming. 'You've done all right here, as I've been told things. You drop her in it, but also want to get her out of it. This is progress.'

'Hazel would of rung herself, Des, but Big Daddy wouldn't allow,' Jill said.

'Quiet, goat shit,' Hazel replied.

'*Have* rung,' Harpur said.

*

Iles drove. Anstruther was in the back. 'There's his Escort,' he said. 'He wouldn't use the Jag for this. Thank God, he's still watching the wrong house.'

'Yes, God's not bad at times,' Iles said. He stopped the Scorpio a long way from Shale so they would not be spotted. 'We're going to pick him up. Would you prefer to disappear, Mr Anstruther?'

'Pick him up?' Harpur said. 'What grounds? I thought just get to Naomi and bring her out. The operation's finished, isn't it, sir?'

'Fuck that,' Iles replied. 'Do you want to be seen with Harpur and me, Bart? He'll know you brought us.'

'Naomi, is that her name?' Anstruther asked. 'Lovely. Biblical.'

Iles said: 'What's that verse from the Book of Ruth? "Call me not Naomi, call me Mara." They were at the alias game even then. Now it's Angela – the only difference.'

'That's over,' Harpur replied.

'Is it, hell,' Iles said. 'When we've got this far? There are cabs about, Bart. Go back to Arthur Street and pick up your car. Charge it to us.'

'Yes, I think you should fade away now,' Harpur told Anstruther. 'Then Mr Iles and I will bring Naomi out. It won't matter if Shale sees her because the whole undercover thing is finished.'

'Like fuck,' Iles replied.

Harpur said: 'But you were against it all as too risky. It *is*, sir. We've proved it. Tonight, here. We know the thing is full of leaks and perils.'

'Oh, there's a way of shaping it now,' Iles replied.

'What way?'

'I'll stay,' Anstruther said. 'If I am a Judas I will not be a slink-away Judas.'

'You're no Judas, Bart, or who does that make fucking Manse?' Iles said. 'You're Mr Public Conscience, and you're precious and scarce. Shale will appreciate that, too, should he live.'

They left the Scorpio and walked down Stave Street to the Escort. Iles pulled open the passenger door and got in quickly beside Shale. Harpur and Bart Anstruther went into the back. 'Well, now, here's a ready-made conference venue, Manse,' Iles said. 'You're a bright one, no question. You've spotted our girl.'

'Which girl, Mr Iles?' Shale said.

'Don't piss me about in the presence of a minister of the Gospel, Manse – it's a kind of blasphemy,' Iles replied. 'The three of us, that's Bart, Harpur and myself have come up with a plan for you and our girl that you're going to delight in. Plus your colleagues. I stress the involvement of the Reverend Bart, to show there can be no evil aspects, which I know you might suspect if the plan came only from Harpur.'

Shale said: 'I know you've got a job to do, Mr Iles—'

'Christ, you're wasted, Manse, a phrase-maker like you sitting around unaudienced in a little vehicle late into the night. Unaudienced until now. "A job to do" – I love it. You and the Chief went to the same spoken-word classes?'

'Undercover is one of your totally legit weapons, I recognize this, Mr Iles. I got nothing against the girl, believe me. So you'll reasonably ask, why am I outside her place? This is for the files, nothing but, Mr Iles. I got to know your gambits, yours and Mr Harpur's, haven't I? Matter of data?'

Iles leaned across and pulled a Heckler and Koch P9S automatic from Shale's shoulder holster. 'Christ, Manse, you were going to do her tonight? Really do her tonight?' He passed the gun to Anstruther. 'See what you can raise on that, Bart, for the roof fund.'

'I told you, Mr Iles, this was an archive visit. And I haven't even seen her.'

'Because you're outside the wrong fucking house,' Iles replied. 'You've run up against a Christian warrior, Manse. One of the few left.'

'I'm sold?' Shale asked.

'What's it look like?' Iles replied.

'By some fucking preacher?' Shale asked. He half turned towards Anstruther in the back.

'Poor, poor behaviour to refer to the Rev so grossly, Manse. Just wag the H and K at him, Bart,' Iles said. 'Let your charismatic finger quiver on the trigger. I keep quoting that mess in the *Pulp Fiction* car when the gun goes off by accident. Ever see it, Manse?'

'I hate that kind of degenerate movie,' Shale replied.

'Disney's cutting down output, I'm afraid,' Iles said. He slapped Shale's arm fondly: 'Here's the proposal, tripartitely formulated, as I said. You let our girl join you and put her in *The Eton*.'

'I already heard this proposal,' Shale said.

'Of course you have. Your wise friends would moot it – Alfie and Panicking. Draw the London lads. It's a gift.'

'Too dangerous,' Shale said.

'For the girl you mean? You were always tender. Leave that to me and Harpur, Manse. We'll be there with a force. London shows up, make threatening moves, we nick them, very fast. No shooting. We've got them for possession of arms, possibly attempted murder. Certainly, it could be better, stronger, but it will do. They'll go away long enough for us all to re-establish that decent scheme of life which we know is so precious to you.'

'Where will *I* be?' Shale asked.

'Where would you like to be?' Iles replied.

'They're not going to believe we'd put the girl in there without protection, not after Si,' Shale said.

'So, be there, Manse. You personally, if you like. But not more than one. And unarmed.'

'Unarmed – with that crew around and your crew?' Shale said. 'Reasonable?'

'Our crew is on your side, remember, Manse? If you were carrying anything we'd have to do you as well as London for possession, wouldn't we?'

'You'd risk your girl?' Shale asked. 'I heard you never got over that Ray Street. Now you're talking about—'

'This will be a totally planned, totally controlled incident, Manse. I don't like undercover because the officer is out of touch, out of sight, as Raymond Street was.' He paused for a moment and turned and spat from the passenger window. Then he switched back to Shale: 'This won't be like that, will it? This is orchestrated. Harpur will be about the spot himself, plus some lovely marksmen. The girl could not be safer in a castle. My kind of operation, Manse.'

Shale said: 'Well, I—'

'Manse, we've got three people here tonight who saw you outside an address you thought contained an undercover police officer while you were carrying a loaded pistol. One of those people is a minister of God, and the other two are on God's side, ultimately. We can put you away, Manse. Besides which, a court would have a giggle about you waiting at the wrong place, conned by a fucking preacher. You'd like that?'

'Don't they ever talk, this other fucking two?' Shale replied.

'They would in the box, Manse.'

Afterwards, Harpur and Iles did send Anstruther back to Arthur Street in a taxi to pick up his car. 'I like the feel of this pistol in my pocket,' the minister said. 'It's a comfort.'

'A beautiful suit, Bart,' Iles replied. 'Mind the weight doesn't make the jacket sag.'

Anstruther gazed down worriedly at the line of his clothes. 'Oh, yes, yes. I'll only carry it very occasionally.'

'Sunday School,' Iles said.

He and Harpur walked to Naomi's flat. When Harpur called she let them in. 'What's so urgent?' she asked.

'Harpur has a scheme,' Iles said.

'It takes two of you?'

'He wanted a chaperone,' Iles replied. 'His ma told him never go alone into girls' flats where Humpty was shagging Alice.'

Harpur said: 'We've had a tip that Shale wants to put you into *The Eton*. Accept.'

'Christ,' she said.

'It will be fine,' Iles replied.

'Well, yes, but I'm bound to think of Pilgrim,' she said.

'We'll be there,' Harpur told her.

'You'll have protection as soon as anything threatens,' Iles said.

Naomi said: 'This is—'

'Very close work,' Iles replied. 'Yes. Harpur's brilliant at it.'

'What about Shale?' she asked.

'Oh, he'll be there,' Iles said.

'And his people?'

'Of course,' Harpur replied.

'Also armed?'

'Of course,' Harpur replied.

Iles said: 'We've stipulated only Manse and no weapons, but he's not going to listen to that, is he? They can't trust us to make a heavy case against Lincoln W. and so on. Shale and Panicking will want something final. In any case, they'd never go helpless into the same room as those three.'

'The idea is they—'

'Destroy one another,' Iles said. 'Of course.'

'And I'm going to be—'

'This is a controlled operation,' Iles said.

'Who controls it?'

'Harpur,' Iles replied. 'That's what he is, your Control, even though Lane and Rockmain consider him shit.'

'What about you, sir?' Harpur asked.

'Do I think you're shit?' Iles replied. 'I can't answer a question like that without a lot of notice, for heaven's sake.'

'I meant, what about you, sir – are you going to be in attendance?' Harpur asked.

'I'm an Assistant Chief Constable, Harpur. Do Assistant Chief Constables go to shoot-outs?'

'What about you, sir?' Harpur replied.

'I might look in.'

'Nice,' Harpur said.

'And we'll have the Rev Bart's prayers,' Iles said. 'Harpur tells me he feels for you, Naomi.'

'Men all over the place do,' Harpur replied.

'Not Shale,' Iles said.

24

Ralph Ember had a call to go to another meeting with Shale and his people. Shale said there had been some changes. That was about all he *would* say on the telephone, except that this time the meeting would be in Alfie Ivis's place, not the rectory, and to bring Beau Derek, of course. Ember would have liked to ask what kind of changes. He wanted to know if the girl Rivers in Stave Street was the right girl and if she was dead, so he could get the bright news to Barney and the women.

There had been a couple of men in the club last evening with temporary memberships who might have come from Barney on a look around. They behaved sweetly and did not even speak to Ember direct all night, but they seemed to him a truly gifted pair: E. Latey and William Coss, both of Peterborough in the book, the one-night membership paid in cash, of course. Their signatures were very bold and deeply legible. If those two were genuinely E. Latey and William Coss, they had brilliantly genuine signatures. They did not wear boating or sporty clothes, which might have pointed to Barney and the Wharf, and would have been wrong for Peterborough. Maybe they had been coached by Barney or one of his hags. At any rate, they had on Monty-type gear – one suede jacket, one silver-buttoned navy blazer, dark middle-quality slacks for both, and plain black slip-on shoes

with smallish mock-brass buckles. Anyone could recognize
that these two had heard of style and would have done
something about it if they had the money. They did a lot of
noticing without seeming to do any noticing at all, but
Ember noticed them noticing – noticing how the club was
laid out, where Ember spent most of his time, where all the
doors were. They drank Malibu, which was right for that
kind of garmentry. If they *had* been coached it was very
thorough.

Of course, Shale could not have said on the telephone
that the girl was dead. There were two chances of a tap –
one on Shale's place, one on Ralph's. But Ember thought
Shale would have been able to work in a hint. When they
all met last time and Shale had seemed to agree to the other
plan for the girl, *The Eton* plan, Ember had not really believed
it. He noticed how Mansel kept on at the black minister
about the address of this girl new to the area, suspicions
radiantly on the go. Ember's view was that Shale did not
really give a fuck what others wanted, including what Ember
wanted. Shale especially did not give a fuck about what Alfie
Ivis wanted. Shale would call this leadership. He would trust
Alfie to wind the clock, not tell the time.

Ember had the Shale call recorded and he played it back
a couple of times, hunting nuances. Alfie came on first, a
kind of magnate ploy: 'Ralph? You're sounding very on top
of things, I must say. And why not? You work, and have
worked, damn hard and deserve all the fruits. I don't think
anyone would question this. Manse would like a word, if it's
convenient.'

A terrible mixture of feelings had churned in Ember's mind as Ivis spoke. It horrified him to think Shale might have slaughtered this girl and was going to let it be coded known now. Yet it relieved Ralph that he could get Barney to pull off those two leg-breakers and spleen wreckers from, say, Peterborough, in the glinting footwear.

Shale said: 'Ralphy, we got to have an up-date assembly. There been developments, which will require discussions. These are not matters I can decide personal, in the circumstances.'

When Ember replayed these remarks, he felt there was nothing anywhere in them to suggest that one of the 'developments' was the death of the undercover girl, if the girl called Rivers *was* the undercover girl. There would be no need for Shale to decide on anything, personal or otherwise, once the girl was dead. Why have discussions – the thing would be over? Ember thought it would be intelligent to stay away from Shale for a while if he had killed the girl, even in a street like Stave Street.

'I been in an evening meeting arranged with certain figures, Ralphy, and although this meeting did not alter the basics, I got to recognize that the emphasis been shifted, we got to adjust the emphasis.'

'Evening meeting?' Ember replied. 'Which evening, Manse?'

'A prepared meeting. These were major figures. These were figures who can get a new shape into my thinking – well, into *our* thinking, which is why talks now are required. Let's say Alfie's place this time. He's kindly offered.'

You had to wonder. Shale was the sort who would have private negotiations with other powers and only let you know afterwards when everything had been settled, and you would not get an invitation to discuss anything but to agree to it, like that Lord Cranborne. And Shale would not care much whether you agreed or not. How could he have a prepared evening meeting and nobody else know? Where? Did he mean he had been talking to London – Lincoln W. and the other two? Shale would think he could get away even with this. An agreement about who got *The Eton* franchise? He had been persuaded into that, bought into that, scared into that? Ember was not sure how he would regard this, if this is what it was. *The Eton* had been Shale's, yes – was still Shale's, maybe – but if he did a deal on it it had to mean Lincoln W. Lincoln and the others were in as partners. Where did that put Ember? Who was major? Shale had done the 'Ralphy' trick again when he rang.

The sod would know how much Ember hated to be called that – of course, he did. 'Ralphy' sounded like a retarded cousin who mostly stayed indoors and to whom kids gave old board games. This was Shale trying to bring Ember down so he would swallow any old bloody thing. Ember felt a really good rage growing as he listened to the tape. That crook in his lovely rectory was a sign of the way things had slid. That place was once a proper religious building, dating far back when religion and order had a real grip. Now it had been taken over by someone like Shale who lacked every semblance of civic dimension, and used a minister of God only to put the finger on a brave woman spy. Ember found this anger was much more comfortable than a panic, and his legs stayed as strong as trees.

At Alfie's they sat in a huge room that used to house the foghorn machinery. Now, it was Alfie's drawing room. This seemed to Ember another bad decline. The room might have saved many sailors' lives by sending out its warning calls about the rocks and shallows. Ivis had filled it with tenement furniture and carpets so thin you felt brutal walking on them, like kicking the infirm. It all made you wonder what Shale paid him. It made you wonder that Alfie stayed so loyal, if he did.

Beau said: 'Here's a fine, fine room with views unmatched across a beautiful, dangerous sea. In rough weather, this room with the tales it might tell must give you a real link with a bracing past, Alfred.'

'What it is, gents, is them fuckers Harpur and Iles,' Shale replied.

'They've come to Mansel with a proposal,' Ivis said.

'As I mentioned on the phone, we had a planned meeting, Ralph,' Shale said.

'Where was this?' Ember asked.

'And what I got to admit is in some ways this proposal is like the very one that Alfie come up with lately,' Shale replied.

'Putting the girl in at *The Eton*?' Ember asked. 'Is she all right?'

'When I say it's the same plan Alfie come up with and you agreed to, Ralph, I'm not saying, not saying in any way whatsoever, that Alfie been in touch with them two fuckers, like priming one another. I think I can say I know Alfred better than that.'

'Thank you, Manse,' Ivis replied.

'Of course, this plan from Harpur and Iles is not spot on the same as Alfie's plan, anyway, not totally. But when you sit back and think about the situation in general, really ponder it, this plan gets to look like the obvious way, I got to admit, which is why I was so glad to accept the advice of Alfie and yourself, Ralph. And Harpur and Iles – when they started thinking about it all – they was bound to come up with the same suggestions, too. But with variations, which is why we got to consult.'

'Where did this planned meeting happen to take place, Manse?' Ember asked.

'This was neutral ground, believe me, Ralph,' Shale replied. 'I hope you don't think I'd ever go into their fucking nick for talks, regardless of flattery – calling me "top banana" and "the chief of chieftains".'

'Did you get along to this meeting then, Alfred?' Beau asked.

That was not too bad as a question, although, of course, every bugger knew the answer. Ember did not mind Beau having a go now and then in discussions. You must not tell a partner to keep quiet throughout. This question made Beau look naive, or naiver. It couldn't be helped. Ivis did not reply.

Shale said: 'They insisted on what they called "princi-pals only" at this stage. In their language that meant them two and me. I said that these businesses had more than one principal, for God's sake, but they kept insisting limited numbers was better for security.'

Ember said: 'I suppose the real point of this conference here, now, is to look at the differences those two were proposing to the general plan.' On his way here with Beau in the car he had said: 'Shale's been forced to some deal, maybe by Lovely Mover and his chums, maybe by Harpur and Iles. He'll try to make out he schemed the whole thing in a beautifully organized conference. Someone cornered him on the street, I'd bet, and scared the shit out of him.'

'I think of Manse Shale as pretty strong,' Beau had replied.

'Until he meets someone stronger, like Iles, for instance.'

'Or you, Ralph.'

'Well, I know how to cope with him.'

'Absolutely,' Beau had said. 'And even with Iles.'

'I try to reason with people, that's all, Beau.'

Now, they were spread around this room in the old lighthouse, drinking the drinks Shale and Ivis seemed to think were suitable for every occasion, gin and peps. Alfie served them in children's nursery tale mugs. Ember had the old woman who lived in a shoe. The handle was missing. You might have thought it was just another try by Shale to make someone feel low. But Ember could see that the 'Tom, Tom the piper's son' mug which Shale himself was drinking from had a big chunk out of the rim. Beau would hold his Brer Rabbit mug away from him now again and chuckle at the illustrations, to show he was not fussy about what he drank from. As if anyone gave a sod whether Beau was fussy about anything.

Shale said: 'They want us to take the girl and put her into *The Eton*, like Alfie said, like you said, too, Ralphy.'

'Look, Mansel, you can call Alfie Alfie if you like and if he doesn't mind, but me, I'm Ralph or Ember. I've told you, and Beau's told you. It's just a matter of taste, obviously, and it's my taste not to be called Ralphy.'

'One thing Ralph can't stand it's that "Ralphy",' Beau said.

Shale was in a brown moquette armchair that would infect you with something if you loitered. He gazed across at Ember for a while, that imperial look he could clip on his bookie's runner face now and then. Eventually he gave an honest smile – lips, eyes, everything doing it together, an act of friendliness. 'But *they're* going to be there,' he said. 'Harpur, Iles, a regiment.'

Beau said: 'Like armed?'

'They say just them, the girl and London,' Shale replied. 'They'll pull the girl out fast and then get London for arms and anything else that could be.'

'Not us?' Beau asked.

'Me, weaponless,' Shale replied.

'Solo?' Beau asked.

'What they say,' Shale said.

Ember thought it sounded reasonable. It meant he would not have to go, nor Beau. The girl would still be alive at the end of it, but Barney would not be so upset if there was no more undercover and no more Lincoln W. Lincoln and company for a while.

'Of course, Iles knows it will be different,' Shale said.

Ivis did a worldly chuckle. 'Of course he does.'

Shale said: 'He knows we wouldn't leave something like that to the police. Some pissy little possession of firearms charges for London at the end of it.'

'But that's only if London took it all quietly,' Ember replied. 'They wouldn't, would they? They would see they were in an ambush and they would use guns. Then the police could use guns. That's how Iles thinks. I don't know about Harpur, but Iles, yes. It would be architectured.'

Shale said: 'My feeling is he wants us there, Ralph – there you are, see, I *can* do it – don't mind calling you fucking Ralph if fucking Ralphy gets your fucking bit of blood up, Ralphy. He wants us there, nicely tooled up, so we can knock these sods over for him, and no courtroom shit or evidence, anything chancy like that, just a nice corpse crop. Iles was asking us to be there but pretending to ask us *not* to be there. That's police.'

'But he'd have to hunt us afterwards,' Ember said. He knew his jaw scar was not leaking because it never leaked, and there was nothing there to leak, but he put up his hand to check and to try to stop it if it was. 'This is on *The Eton*. Witnesses everywhere. Police everywhere, observing, even if they're not shooting.'

'Well, he'd expect us to manage it better than that, wouldn't he, Ralphy?' Shale said. 'We get them three on the dockside – somewhere dark, remote – when the buggers are on their way to *The Eton*, before they're aboard. Off guard. Iles leaves us to work that out. Then, when Lovely Mover and so on are finished off, Harpur and Iles don't press too hard for revelations about who done it. Even Lane might be glad it was done and feel like blind-eyeing a bit. He been near on the sick again lately, I heard.'

'The Chief's into integrity,' Ember said.

'Fuck the Chief,' Shale replied, 'on this occasion.'

'The Chief wants peace and a discreetly run manor as much as anyone, Ralph,' Ivis said. 'He would see this as a purging operation, and one which does not put his under-cover girl at hazard. Mr Iles seeks an arrangement, doesn't he? He wants our firms to continue doing what they have been doing. He knows this trade will always continue and that it is better such trade should be tidily managed by local interests. It would scarcely make sense, Ralph, if he removed the main men of the two firms who will provide that quiet régime once London has been squashed.'

Shale stood and pulled a handkerchief from his pocket. He tied a knot in it. 'You see that, Ralph? That's to remind me permanent you don't care to be called Ralphy. Them words from Beau about you not liking to be called Ralphy have really reached me this time, Ralph, and my view is you or anyone is entitled to be called what he or she likes and, if it's Ralph, Ralph it is.'

'Thanks, Mansel,' Ember replied.

Shale stood up from his unwholesome chair, came over to where Ember was sitting and put his hand in under Ralph's jacket lapel to where the Babybarrel sat in its tiny holster. Then Shale went to Beau and did the same to him. Beau would usually have nothing to do with guns, but Ember had made him take another Baby in the car on the way here, in case Shale grew too unmanageable. Ember had even considered it possible that the London people would be here when he arrived, and there might have been a fight for position.

'At the run up to *The Eton* you'll need something bigger than those, Ralph,' Shale said. 'Work out what route they'll most likely take to the boat, will you? You're civic – you know the street layout.'

'I've taken to carrying – just something minimal – because I think Barney might have put some progress chasers into the club,' Ember replied.

'Tell him the girl don't matter either way now,' Shale said, 'if we finish London.'

'I will.' He did later that night by phone. 'All problems – the London problem and the matter of the girl – to be settled at one convenient time, Barney.'

'When?' Barney asked,

'Soon.'

'Maud's on the extension and wants a word,' Barney said.

'This just more hesitation?' she asked.

'It seemed so tidy,' Ember replied.

'Camilla wants a word.'

'Allies, confederates, accomplices – call them what you will, Ralph – am I to deduce that this "tidy" solution will, in fact, be arrived at by others on your behalf.'

'I'd prefer to say *with* others.'

'Trustworthiness of? This is always going to be a supreme consideration,' Camilla said.

'Absolute,' Ember replied.

'Law and order, Ralph. Representatives thereof, as it were. Am I to deduce that these will be among the allies before mentioned?'

'Possible,' Ember said.

'I'm not sure I like this, Ralph,' Barney replied.

'Would you happen to know an E. Latey and William Coss?' Ember replied.

'We've never even heard of them,' Barney said.

'Origins, Ralph?' Camilla asked.

'Peterborough and Next's sale.'

'Peterborough's right outside my ambit, Ralph,' Barney said.

'Whistle them off, pending developments, or they're going to be targets,' Ember replied.

'These sound very harmless people to me,' Maud said. 'Camilla wants a word.'

'Phlegmatic, indeed bovine, this is often the nature of people from those Eastern parts of England,' Camilla said. 'And very home loving. Perhaps this E. Latey and W. Coss will drift back there now, Ralph. Who knows?'

'You do,' Ember replied. 'Good.'

25

Harpur had arranged for some decent sketches to be done of *The Eton Boating Song* bar on the quiet, and even a couple of secret photographs. With these as guide, he arranged the furniture in the main Incident Room at headquarters to mock up the bar, and particularly the table where Pilgrim had always sat to trade. It was also where Eleri ap Vaughan had sat before him – with her famed glass of rum and black to indicate she was ready for business. They would try to get Naomi seated in that spot on *The Eton* soon. A week ago she had managed her contact with one of Shale's street people and was working her way into the firm. Harpur had given her some good stuff to get started with, so she could appear as a talented freelance. In her flat, talking the details, handing over the drugs, he had found his awareness of the risk she was taking on wiped out everything but the narrowest of job feelings. Rockmain's theories on sexual closeness between a Controller and girl operator seemed ludicrous.

Of course, Naomi could not be present at the Incident Room rehearsal. She must not even approach the building. On the cork wall board he fixed large photographs or drawings of Lincoln W. Lincoln, Tommy Mill-Kaper, Digby Lighthorn, Panicking Ralph Ember, Mansel Shale, Alfie Ivis and Beau Derek. Shale's showed him smoking a cigar.

Harpur's shooting party assembled for briefing. Iles and the Chief himself also came. Harpur would have eight people and himself at *The Eton*, all armed, including three women. He suspected Iles would also show but that would be as a presence only, pray God.

Of course, the part of the plan that would be unspoken here presumed the fighting would never get to *The Eton*, and Naomi should be in no peril. But things might not work like that. If it went wrong and the battle reached *The Eton*, the main plus in an operation of this sort was that it did not matter about local folk like Shale recognizing any of the officers. They expected the police party. The operation was joint. He had three long tables end to end for the bar itself, and a scatter of smaller tables placed as on *The Eton*. The briefing was going to be difficult, but difficult in a style that Harpur had often handled before, and that any senior officer had to handle. He must give them an impeccable law-and-order game plan of what would happen, knowing that this would probably not happen, and not wanting or intending it to happen. When you picked people you would work closely with, you looked for those who could listen well and repeat to any aftermath inquiry what had been said, but who also swiftly saw through what was being spoken to what was meant.

Lane addressed the group first, not sounding or looking any fitter. 'When I glance around this room I am heartened,' he said. 'I am heartened, first, of course, by the personnel I see here who will handle this difficult matter, under Mr Harpur, who has my total confidence.' He paused and

swallowed, perhaps recalling the doubts flagged by Rockmain about Harpur as Controller.

Iles said: 'Bravo, Chief. Given that face Harpur could mix
with drug wrecks anywhere and not stand out.'

Lane said: 'I am also heartened because I see people determined to help in eradicating organized crime from our patch,
and especially drugs-based organized crime, which, I regret
now means almost all organized crime. This must be an
operation of consummate delicacy and yet of utter decisive-
ness, and I am sure all present realize that and will behave
accordingly. I will mention your objective only in outline,
since Mr Harpur is going to talk about that later. There are,
as I see it, two objectives, in fact. One is to effect the arrest
of this invading London team, an offshoot of the disgustingly
powerful metropolitan syndicate led by Everton Esta Osprey
and the Right Hon., as Basil Cope idiotically likes to be
known. We do not want any of these people here. I will not
let them establish an obnoxious offshoot of their empire.'

Lane was in uniform again today, perhaps for another
function, or perhaps intending to stoke the ambush party's
morale by this formal show of status. And yet, as ever,
uniform looked bad on Lane, and he always wore it as if he
meant it to look bad. The gear was too small for him and
unpressed. He had his shoes off, as was usual for him around
the building, and wore thick khaki socks, which had slipped
forward on his feet a few inches and looked like clown's kit.
His white shirt was white enough, but his tie raddled. If Lane
were able to inspire the shooting party today it would be

because they were sorry for him, not because he gleamed leadership.

'And then we come to the second objective,' the Chief said. 'I place it second and yet it is in some ways more important than the first. I refer, of course, to the safety of Naomi Anstruther. I deliberately use her real name here, in the privacy of this gathering, and among her colleagues and friends, because it is under this name that she is valued by us all.'

'Harpur will get her out all right, sir,' Iles said. 'He's got the hots for Naomi – for Naomi and anything else under thirty without a fallen arse. He wants her returned undamaged and full of convertible gratitude.'

Lane had a smile-wince and began a rebuttal, but let it tail: 'I'm quite sure this is not true of Colin, and I—' The Chief looked confused, as though he had lost his theme. For a second, confronted by Lane's dazed face, Harpur recalled one of Iles's comments about him: that he was fundamentally stupid, with occasional flashes of half wittedness. 'I admit I have veered back and forth in my attitude to under-cover work. I was in favour, because we had nothing better. Then I came to believe it impossible to conduct safely and would have abandoned the project. But the Assistant Chief and Mr Harpur persuaded me that it could work – persuaded me, I sometimes feel, because they thought the project was essential to my well-being, my, as it were, mental well-being. If that is so, I thank Mr Iles and Mr Harpur for their consideration, but in a way I hope it is not so. I would prefer that there are sound operational reasons for proceeding with the undercover operation.'

'Certainly, sir,' Iles said. 'I'd describe the processes that led to this infiltration quite differently. Harpur and I certainly saw how important to you the scheme was, sir, and we deduced that if a mind like yours was so wholly committed then this scheme must be excellent, and perhaps the only feasible scheme. Isn't that the long and short of it, Col?'

'We are extremely lucky in having an officer available whose suitability for this kind of work was declared unequalled by an eminent psychology expert on undercover duties,' Harpur replied.

'He also thought Harpur a bag of shit, but we'll skip that,' Iles said.

The Chief was standing by the mock bar and rapped it gently with his knuckles to reclaim attention: 'Naomi has bravely volunteered as a cat's paw here,' he said, 'and it is imperative that she does not suffer for this, as did that other undercover officer we all—' The sentence dried again. Lane waited a while silent and bent to one side as from some injury – a horse kick or cosh mugging – then turned and shuffled along the bar to the door, opened it and went out. He carefully pulled the door to after himself, obviously conscious of that need for secrecy he mentioned lately, but had to reopen it briefly because the toe of one of his socks was caught and stopped the door shutting.

When he had gone, Iles announced: 'This man is a great man and deserves our best – will have our best. This man is perhaps not a platform presence, but he is a philosophizing man, a humane man. If they gave knighthoods to police officers for humaneness instead of for hatching one-way traffic schemes, Mr Lane would have been a full "sir" long ago, and not merely *our* sir. Isn't that so, Col?'

'I want Peter and Sian close to Naomi at all times, regardless of what happens elsewhere,' Harpur replied. 'That will be my own station, also. Would you two go now and take up positions at the table next to Naomi's dealing table?' The pair moved across and sat down. 'All of you will, of course, supply yourselves with drinks, chargeable to expenses, but to be paid for properly with cash, in case we are under observation by Lovely Mover or one of the others.' He nodded towards the photographs and drawings. 'I want you to be able to recognize all these people instantly.' He gave them a couple of minutes to study the pictures. Then he said: 'Our objective is more or less as the Chief outlined: we arrest the three London people on suspicion of carrying firearms with intent to commit a murder and we protect Naomi so that the murder cannot be committed.'

Iles, in shirt sleeves and dark, silk-like slacks had been standing near the cork wall and pictures but now walked around the room to check that Lane had in fact finally shut the door, then took up the position at the bar where the Chief had made his address. 'Detective Chief Superintendent Harpur and I both recognize it as a possibility that, as well as this London trio, some members of more local communities may be present.' He pointed towards the pictures of Shale, Ember, Ivis and Beau Derek. 'They have been specifically warned to stay away, or to restrict their presence to one board member only – and that one unarmed – but we both fear that this warning will, in fact, be perversely interpreted as an invitation to arrive in a team tooled-up to the eyebrows, in pursuit of the London rivals. Yes, I think that's what we both fear, isn't it, Col?'

Harpur said: 'Chief Inspector Garland with the remaining officers will take the rest of the positions in the bar or just outside, some at the other tables, some standing. Could you occupy those spots now, please? Familiarize yourselves with the layout.' Harpur sat down alone at a table on the other side of Naomi's trading spot from Peter Liss and Sian Sampson. Garland and the five officers in his group now arranged themselves as Harpur ordered. Garland had Knight, Moss, Vale, Porter and Poultney with him. Harpur said: 'I'll do the "Armed Police" shout when I judge they are about to make a move on Naomi. You draw your weapons then and not before. Of course, be prepared for resistance.'

Garland asked in that big, accusatory voice: 'How do you know, sir, that all three will come aboard? When Pilgrim was done, wasn't he forced off the boat by what seemed to be one of them and then dealt with elsewhere?'

Harpur said: 'We don't *know* the three will come. We think so.'

Iles said: 'Can't you see this is a different situation altogether from Si Pilgrim, Garland? Christ, I thought you were an accelerated promotion object.' The ACC's face muscles jumped once or twice and he said, 'If you spent less time shagging other men's wives and more exercising your supposed fucking brain, Garland, you would not come out with crap questions like that.' Iles paused and then started to shout. 'I'll tell you this, all of you, my wife can't explain now what she saw in the oaf. We have a chuckle over it together, frequently. Frequently, Garland. You've become an entertainment for us.'

'Nice to get back to the old-style self-made amusements and away from TV, sir, isn't it?' Garland replied.

Iles said: 'Si was Si and was sure to run if threatened. Naomi not so. More important, the London people will expect there to be protection aboard for the girl, won't they? Manse Shale has already lost an operative from *The Eton*. Is he going to put in another without trying to look after her? London will come knowing they can't expect a dolly target this time.'

'They expect a battle?' Moss asked.

'They expect resistance. They'll come in force,' Iles said.

'We can't keep the public out of the bar, of course, or London will know it's a set-up,' Harpur said. 'If there's shooting by us, it has to be good, thoughtful shooting.'

'What about by them?' Sian asked.

'Which them?' Iles replied.

'Yes, which them?' she said. 'London, Shale, Panicking, Ivis, Beau?'

'We've certainly got some imponderables,' Iles replied.

Garland said: 'If Shale and his people come regardless they're not going to knock Lovely Mover and so on over in a crowded bar, are they, especially if Shale knows some of the crowd is us? There'd be witnesses. Shale and his boys might get the London three, but they'd go down eternally for it. Pop goes their business. They'll try to intercept before the boat, won't they?'

'Good, good, Francis,' Iles purred. 'We think so.'

Harpur said: 'But if not, as soon as I've shouted "Armed Police", Sian, Peter and I take Naomi from the bar via the main door to the deck.' He pointed to a spot to the left of the bar. 'At that point, Chief Inspector Garland is in charge until I return. We'll get Naomi clear by car.'

Garland said: 'This whole operation seems to me about the memory of Raymond Street, not Naomi Anstruther.'

Iles said: 'If you or anyone does something, or fails to do something, that makes Anstruther come out of this in the same state as Street you're for ever finished here and everywhere else.'

26

There was a cosiness about her spot in *The Eton* bar which made Naomi almost forget why she had been put here. And, God, she hoped nothing was going to remind her – in fact, became convinced as the night progressed peacefully that nothing would. Hadn't Harpur and Iles promised her this peace?

Seated there behind the little table with the rum and black as general invitation she felt part of a heritage, the Eleri ap Vaughan heritage. It was a crooked heritage, naturally. But there was something . . . something dignified to it, also, something given stature by time. Punters entering the bar smiled to see her in place. Their smiles had gratitude and respect and trust. They knew, or thought they knew, that any trader promoted to this plum must be supremely gifted, a dealer matchless in reliability and good stuff, a dealer who could not be more devoted to their moneyed nostrils and distinguished main lines, as a good private doctor would be to their whole bodies. These were punters who had eaten and drunk satisfactorily and now meant to do the next bit satisfactorily, also. Some of the suits were silk, men's and women's. Some of the shoes looked custom-made. Some of the ties looked like Eton itself. None of the ties looked like the National Union of Mineworkers or the League Against Cruel Sports. All of the cash looked brilliant and bank-fresh and legally got, folded ready in soft, long hands or in soft, lean leather bags of distinguished muted colours, most of them Gucci, probably.

Naomi traded with flair. Rockmain was right. She loved new identities, could blank her basic self out and become . . . become whatever she was supposed to become. She was supposed to become tonight successor to dear Eleri and dear Si, but without the tragic finales, thanks. And this succession had begun to happen. Harpur and Iles were damn lucky to have her available. Suddenly, the night was enjoyable, not a terror ride. She felt disgusted by all her earlier piffling doubts.

Naomi could not see Harpur, but she saw Francis Garland and Pete Liss and Sian Sampson and most of the others. Harpur's absence was to plan. He had told her he would be close but possibly not always in view. His face was big and crude and memorable and a bit famous. He must stay concealed as much as possible. It would be mad to frighten people off after all the preparation, all the precautions. Francis Garland and the rest of the reception group looked to Naomi as relaxed as she was herself, relaxed and stupendously unpolice-like. They were in casual gear most of them, seeming to enjoy their drinks, laughing comfortably, skilfully ignoring one another, except those they had been paired off with. All the men wore jackets, to cover holsters. All the girls carried handbags, non-Gucci and bulky enough for a pistol. She gathered Iles wanted her armed, too, but that had been overruled by the Chief. Naomi was glad. Firearms did not grab her. Under some jackets and dresses, she could make out the ridges of body armour, and hoped her own was not so obvious. She prayed she would be able to shed it fairly soon. It was an inescapable reminder of her bait role here. There was no need for bait because the fish would not turn up to bite. And the armour made her sweaty.

Sweaty because of the temperature and general busyness, not nerves. What was there to be nervous about, for God's sake? But the bar had grown crowded and hot, despite an open porthole. And dishing out the nice fat little square transparent envelopes and checking the twenties and tens and even occasional fifties was hard going. A lot of these folk bought more than one package, as though they remembered that observation by Mrs Thatcher, as she was then, that every sensible housewife kept a full store cupboard. These clients had had a fright when Eleri and then Si disappeared and seemed determined now to stockpile. Or make up for missed trips while they could.

To Naomi it appeared that for once a police operation would go as it was meant to. There would be no ambush in *The Eton* bar because all the violence had taken place somewhere else. As a matter of fact, with any luck the London crew and the local crews were battling each other to mutual destruction up the road about now. The only constabulary job would be to count casualties. All this top-rate acting on *The Eton* was redundant.

And then, abruptly, she began to wonder about that. Glancing around the heaving bar she thought she caught sight for a second of someone who should have been stopped at that up the road site, a long way from here. Now she did wish she could locate Harpur to see what he made of this customer. It was Harpur only she wanted – not Garland or Peter Liss or Sian Sampson or Knight or Moss or even Iles. Harpur she had turned into a kind of talisman. He guaranteed success and safety, and he only, that big, well-known rough-house face, and that hefty body. It was all right – nothing slavish or feminine-weak. Simply, she and he had been linked as a unit for so long with this war, like veteran troops conscripted on the same day far, far back.

But Harpur was not here. She felt some fright, of course she did, though nothing catastrophic. Her priorities shifted, that's all. Her identity did one of its swings. She was total cop again, observing, scheming, ready, wishing after all that Iles *had* been able to get her gun training and a gun. She lifted her head from examining a fifty, and stared about again for Harpur. She stopped listening, half-listening, to a weighty punter of seventy-plus who would like her to take a little supper with him later.

Naomi really searched for Harpur. Although she still did not see him, she confirmed that sighting of someone else, glimpsed earlier, and recognized from the ID pictures Harpur and Iles had so often shoved before her in the run-up to this exercise. It was a man of about twenty-five in a tan-to-gold fine, loose fitting jacket which might have been specially tailored to conceal a Browning automatic. This was the lad they called Lovely Mover, Lincoln W. Lincoln, and he *SHOULD NOT FUCKING WELL BE HERE*. Nor should the man who stood with him at the bar now, where they both seemed to watch her, when the crowd allowed it, via the huge back mirror. Her memory of the mug shots told her this one was Thomas Mill-Kaper, down the pedigree line from a V.C. and still dropping. She could get sight of Lincoln and him now and then in the mirror through the shifting mob of people. Shit, but they looked untroubled, cocky, as if sure they always won and would win this time, too. Maybe.

She did not want to stare in case it was a give-away. A give-away? Give-away what? These jaunty sods knew it all. She was enraged. What had happened to the people they should be fighting – the local teams? Why weren't they annihilating one another in the roundabout cause of law and order? Were the police the only enemy they recognized? Was *she*? Naomi felt exposed. Christ, the Eleri ap Vaughan dealing point no longer seemed cosy. She realized there was a lot of her on show above the dealing table, and not all of it under body armour. The armour could no longer make her sweat. She had gone suddenly cold, hands stiff and trembling slightly, her brain icy and clear. But she did not need much brain. All she had to do was sit here and look authentic until the ructions began, and she was sure now that they would. How, how could she have believed that an operation schemed by Harpur and Desmond Iles would produce no hazards, only peace?

A woman of about sixty with a pumpkin face and in a glorious lilac dress wanted to buy. Although she flourished a sheaf of notes, Naomi could not bother with her. Instead, she glanced towards Francis Garland to find out whether *he* had noticed the arrival of Lincoln and Mill-Kaper at the bar. Garland, like all the rest of the police party, was still into amateur dramatics though, and acting like a fun night out. Impossible to tell what he had seen, or not.

Peter Liss came and stood near the lilac dress, as if queuing to buy. That was part of the game, too. A few of them had been issued money to make a purchase, as part of looking real. 'I think the cow has had a fit or something,' the woman said. 'Par-fucking-alysis, if you ask me. Is she on her own stuff, do you think, sonny boy? Wakey-wakey kiddo.' She snapped fine white fingers at Naomi.

Liss leaned forward and muttered in Naomi's ear: 'And Corporeal's at the door. He's the danger. It's coming now. Get down!'

It was wrong, a breach. Liss like all of them had orders to speak to Sian Sampson only, his companion in the Harpur–Iles party-night script. None of the group were supposed to approach Naomi, except as a pusher if they bought. Just the same, she was glad of the message.

She turned to look, saw the skinny body and the bony head of Digby Lighthorn as he entered the bar, and also saw near him two other faces familiar to her, nothing at all to do with Corporeal or with Lovely Mover or with Mill-Kaper. They were not together, this latest pair, but close in the crush of people. These two she knew from life and intimacy, actual life, real intimacy, not pictures. She must not acknowledge them. They had no place here at all. They were an utter and awful and almost dazing mystery. Had her wits gone in the stress?

Naomi heard Harpur then – Harpur bellowing 'Armed Police' twice, perhaps three times. The shooting started immediately afterwards, apparently from several parts of the bar, raw, jagged overlapping sounds that shocked her further into confusion. After a minute she felt herself pushed from the Eleri chair and dragged by her feet towards the door and *The Eton*'s deck. At least three people tugged her, Harpur one of them, Sian Sampson with perhaps Liss at the other ankle. The hem of Naomi's skirt was up to near her chin. Her behind skidded sweetly across the bar's mahogany board floor. 'You were brilliant, brilliant,' Harpur yelled. 'I'd have been paralysed.'

She could hardly hear it. She giggled, corrected that word in her bumping head to par-fucking-alysed. She hoped the lilac dress and pumpkin face had caught no bullets. But Naomi had other faces to fret about. The giggling died. Harpur howled 'Police, Police,' with something like despair in the words, she thought, and then there was more firing.

27

FOUR KILLED IN POLICE DRUGS BUST AMBUSH
by Liam Court and Melanie Wilkes

At least four people were killed last night and several injured in a gun battle after police had set up an ambush for drug gangs at the luxury *Eton Boating Song* floating restaurant in the city's marina district. This is one of the worst incidents of its kind ever to have taken place in Britain.

The police will not disclose identities of the dead and wounded at this stage, but it is believed that two prominent drug dealers may be among the casualties. Police acting on a tip off had staked out the floating restaurant. It is believed they hoped to surprise members of warring drug gangs. The *Echo* understands that an undercover woman detective was at the centre of the shoot-out. Her fate is not known.

The ambush followed a recent murder on the marina of Simon Pilgrim, believed to have been a drugs dealer with clients at *The Eton Boating Song*. Last night's battle possibly began when rival gangs tried to instal a replacement for Pilgrim.

London gangs may have sent members to colonize new provincial markets. This could have led to a 'war' between local drugs interests, intent on preserving their businesses, and the invaders. The earlier murder of the pusher 'Gladhand' Mace may have been part of this war.

Assistant Chief Constable Desmond Iles, Head of Operations, said: 'This was a tragic occurrence. Members of the public as well as police officers were put at intolerable risk by the activities of these warring drugs dealers. We hope this marks the end of a series of terrible incidents.'

Detective Chief Superintendent Colin Harpur was in command of the ambush. He said that not all details of the battle were available. It appeared that a local gang had expected to intercept the London team some way from *The Eton Boating Song*. However, the Londoners evaded them and approached by an unexpected route, so that police confronted the London group on the floating restaurant itself. DCS Harpur said about ten officers took part. One was injured. DCS Harpur said: 'The intention was only to effect arrests on suspicion of carrying weapons. The men resisted and opened fire. Police retaliated after a warning.'

Mr Jeremy Littlebann, 48, proprietor of *The Eton Boating Song* said that he was stunned by what had happened and could not praise the police enough for their intervention. 'I am also distressed to hear that drug dealing had apparently been taking place as a regular practice. Obviously, I and my staff had no idea of this and would not tolerate it for a moment if we had. *The Eton Boating Song* caters to an eminently respectable clientèle, most of whom would be aghast to know drugs might have been sold here. That will cease now. We shall be very vigilant in the future. I hope we have all learned a lesson from this tragedy.'

28

The Chief had a television set in his suite and Harpur and Iles were invited up there to see the local news. Lane watched from behind his desk. He seemed to be concentrating on sitting very erect, as if to proclaim himself unpulverized by what was screened. He wore one of his suits today. Harpur and Iles took armchairs. There were television pictures of *The Eton* and the dockside and marina. The names of casualties had still not been released but this evening bulletin contained more good speculation than the afternoon edition of *The Echo*. It gave hints of controversy in police headquarters over undercover work. The interview with Littlebann was longer than in the newspaper and his surprise at everything much fuller. They also interviewed his wife, a co-director, so that the astonishment at what had been going on at *The Eton* came double-barrelled and more theatrically heartfelt.

Lane tried to keep his voice positive as well as his body: 'Perhaps there will be benefits, regardless, Desmond,' he said.

'Oh, Mr and Mrs Littlebann will exclude drug pushing from *The Eton* for a week or two, or even a month or two, sir. But not many people go to that den for the food. Their business will drop off if there's no one at the pusher's table. And when that happens Mr and Mrs Littlebann might find themselves badly stricken by ignorance again. They're caterers to the gentry, and the gentry won't hang about waiting for their helpings of stuff.'

'Such young lives, Desmond. I feel responsible. Of course I do. This was supposed to be a limited operation, designed only to get these London people taken for possession of weapons.'

Iles said: 'They were expecting something big, I should think, sir, and they were almost right. They came to fight. They fought us instead of their competitors. There was a minor mess-up, true. These things should not have occurred on the boat, and there should have been another gang present to take care of the London louts some distance away. We could not count on that, clearly. Luckily we had an armed group around Naomi on the boat.'

'Minor mess-up?' Lane said.

Iles said: 'We come out of it with two of the London people dead, and probably the most effective ones, Mill-Kaper and Lighthorn.'

'Mill-Kaper's grandfather had a VC, I believe,' Lane replied. 'A VC for gallantry in our nations's cause. Now this from a descendant. Where, where are we going?'

Iles said: 'Oh, down, down, of course, sir, but it's a matter of controlling the pace. That fucking Lovely Mover sneaked out of it somehow. I thought I caught a glimpse, but not quite enough certainty to fire.'

'You were actually present, Desmond?' Lane asked.

'I knew you were tied up personally yourself, sir – at some seminar or Scrabble finals, a community matter, so I thought

I'd better have a little lurk, make sure Harpur didn't balls everything. He was not too bad.'

Lane watched library material about coke, crack and grass on the screen. His mind must have been moving, though. Suddenly, he said: 'But, Desmond, when you say another crew should have been present – are you telling me, that this whole situation had been, as it were, scenarioed by us? An attempt to stage a battle between these factions?'

'An expanding language, English, isn't it, sir?' Iles cried. 'Wonderful! I've never heard scenario made into a verb before, but why not, why not? Can you think of any objection to scenarioed, Harpur?'

'We have definite identifications on the two civilians,' Harpur replied. There was a picture of Pilgrim on the screen now, and then of the little urban copse where he was found. Bulletin editors thought the shoot-out worth a lot of time with full backgrounding.

'One's McWater, isn't he?' Iles replied. 'That's what it looked like to me.'

'McWater?' Lane asked.

'Naomi's ex and would-be current – would-be until last night, that is,' Iles replied.

'Oh, this is awful,' Lane moaned.

'Yes, it is, sir,' Iles said. 'The silly junior executive twat *would* keep searching for her, talking about her, advertising. It's been going on for weeks. Ignored even my threats. Last night he found her.'

Harpur said: 'The fourth dead is a lad called Lyndon Vaughan Fitzhammon Evans from Cardiff. Francis thought it might be. He's seen him before. We have confirmation now. This is another man who came looking for Naomi. He disappeared for a while and we assumed he'd given up. But he must have returned.'

'Yes, she *has* got something,' Iles said. 'But why am I telling you, Harpur? You'd sniff it through a castle wall.'

'We directed this man to Naomi?' Lane asked, in a near shriek.

'No, sir,' Harpur replied. 'But he knew where McWater worked. They were all on holiday together in Spain apparently – Naomi's pre-operation break. Lyndon Evans called on us, saw Francis and learned nothing. But he must have gone on to Sainsbury's and then gumshoed him, thinking McWater would know where she was. Eventually last night he followed him to *The Eton*, as it seems, and this time McWater had it right.'

'Did she know these men were present?' Lane asked.

'She tells me she'd noticed them on *The Eton* separately last night, yes,' Harpur said. 'But she couldn't acknowledge either – made it clear somehow that they must not approach her.'

'Oh, heartbreaking,' Lane said.

'It appears that both of them, independently of each other, tried to save Naomi when the shooting began,' Harpur said. 'Peter, Sian and I were trying to get her out, and it looks as if Lyndon Evans assumed we were the enemy. McWater wouldn't have shared that error, because he knew me. But I imagine he thought I and the police generally were incompetent and would get her killed if he didn't intervene. I saw them dashing towards us, shouted "Police" again, but Evans didn't take it in, or didn't believe it. They tried to rescue Naomi and ran into shots meant for her.'

'My God, my God, my God,' Lane said. 'So brave, such a waste.'

'I wouldn't say that, sir,' Iles replied. 'They did stop bullets intended for our girl. No Ray Street situation. We're almost sure they were not hit by police fire, aren't we, Col?'

Lane gasped, 'Only *almost* sure, Desmond? Haven't ballistics been able to—'

Harpur said: 'No, not police guns, sir. That is established. Mill-Kaper's and Corporeal's weapons.'

'Thank you, Colin,' the Chief replied. He waved a hand towards the television set, signalling that it should be switched off before worse came.

On their way back down in the lift, Harpur said to Iles: 'You knew they were not police guns. You like your little lunges against his sanity now and then, don't you, you shit, sir, even though you try to prop him up occasionally? How do you decide which to do when?'

'Col, I think of those two men dying for her. Devotion, selflessness. Do you believe there are people around who would cheerfully do that for me, too?'

'I'm not sure about cheerfully.'

29

Camilla came through on the pay phone at The Monty – that crazy gesture to security again. 'Some misgivings, some reservations, I think one has to say that, Ralph, but on the whole more or less satisfactory. This is the view here. Well, you can assume things are reasonably favourable, can't you, in that it is dear old me who is deputed to open the conversation – and glad to do it.'

'Thank you,' Ember replied.

'Barney wants a word.'

'Ralph, all right, so we miss the actual girl, but two of them down – I must say I see no continuing problem. They'll pull out. Or rather *he'll* pull out, only one left. LWL. The girl's significance is gone. Maud's on the extension.'

'They'll regroup. Esta and the Right Hon. don't chuck a chance that easily,' she said.

'It will take an age, Maud,' Barney said. 'Things should be peaceable for a while.'

'I think so,' Ember replied.

'Were you actually present?' Barney asked.

'Waiting in the wrong place.'

'Like you, you prick, if you ask me,' Maud said. 'Or did you deliberately fix it like that, to dodge the perils?'

'And how are dear E. Latey and William Coss?' Ember replied.

'Revelling in Peterborough home cooking,' Barney said.